Wildly D

The Daring Daughters Book 14

By Emma V. Leech

Published by Emma V. Leech.

Copyright (c) Emma V. Leech 2022

Editing Services Magpie Literary Services

Cover Art: Victoria Cooper

ISBN No: 978-2-492133-55-8

About Me!

I started this incredible journey way back in 2010 with The Key to Erebus but didn't summon the courage to hit publish until October 2012. For anyone who's done it, you'll know publishing your first title is a terribly scary thing! I still get butterflies on the morning a new title releases, but the terror has subsided at least. Now I just live in dread of the day my daughters are old enough to read them.

The horror! (On both sides I suspect.)

2017 marked the year that I made my first foray into Historical Romance and the world of the Regency Romance, and my word what a year! I was delighted by the response to this series and can't wait to add more titles. Paranormal Romance readers need not despair, however, as there is much more to come there too. Writing has become an addiction and as soon as one book is over I'm hugely excited to start the next so you can expect plenty more in the future.

As many of my works reflect, I am greatly influenced by the beautiful French countryside in which I live. I've been here in the South West since 1998, though I was born and raised in England. My three gorgeous girls are all bilingual and my husband Pat, myself, and our four cats consider ourselves very fortunate to have made such a lovely place our home.

KEEP READING TO DISCOVER MY OTHER BOOKS!

Other Works by Emma V. Leech

Daring Daughters

Daring Daughters Series

Girls Who Dare

Girls Who Dare Series

Rogues & Gentlemen

Rogues & Gentlemen Series

The Regency Romance Mysteries

The Regency Romance Mysteries Series

The French Vampire Legend

The French Vampire Legend Series

The French Fae Legend

The French Fae Legend Series

Stand Alone
The Book Lover (a paranormal novella)
The Girl is Not for Christmas (Regency Romance)

Audio Books

Don't have time to read but still need your romance fix? The wait is over…

By popular demand, get many of your favourite Emma V Leech Regency Romance books on audio as performed by the incomparable Philip Battley and Gerard Marzilli. Several titles available and more added each month!

Find them at your favourite audiobook retailer!

Acknowledgements

Thanks, of course, to my wonderful editor Kezia Cole with Magpie Literary Services.

To Victoria Cooper for all your hard work, amazing artwork and above all your unending patience!!! Thank you so much. You are amazing!

To my BFF, PA, personal cheerleader and bringer of chocolate, Varsi Appel, for moral support, confidence boosting and for reading my work more times than I have. I love you loads!

A huge thank you to all of Emma's Book Club members! You guys are the best!

I'm always so happy to hear from you so do email or message me :)

emmavleech@orange.fr

To my husband Pat and my family ... For always being proud of me.

Table of Contents

Family Trees

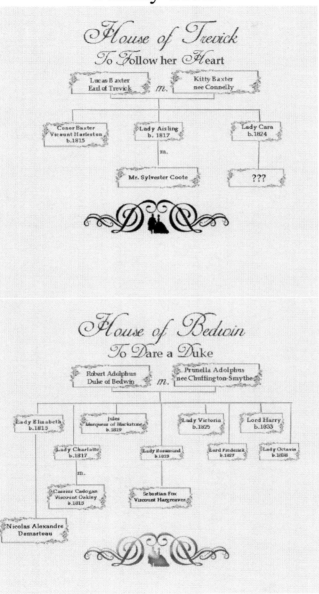

House of Trevick
To Follow her Heart

Lucas Baxter, Earl of Trevick — *m.* — Kitty Baxter, nee Connelly

- Conor Baxter, Viscount Harleston, b.1815
- Lady Aisling, b. 1817 — *m.* — Mr. Sylvester Coote
- Lady Cara, b.1824 — ???

House of Bedwin
To Dare a Duke

Robert Adolphus, Duke of Bedwin — *m.* — Prunella Adolphus, nee Chuffington-Smythe

- Lady Elizabeth, b.1815
- Jules, Marquess of Blackstone, b.1819
  - Lady Charlotte, b.1817 — *m.* — Cassius Cadogan, Viscount Oakley, b.1819
    - Nicolas Alexandre Demarteau
- Lady Victoria, b.1825
- Lord Harry, b.1833
- Lady Rosamund, b.1823 — Sebastian Fox, Viscount Hargreaves
- Lord Frederick, b.1827
- Lady Octavia, b.1838

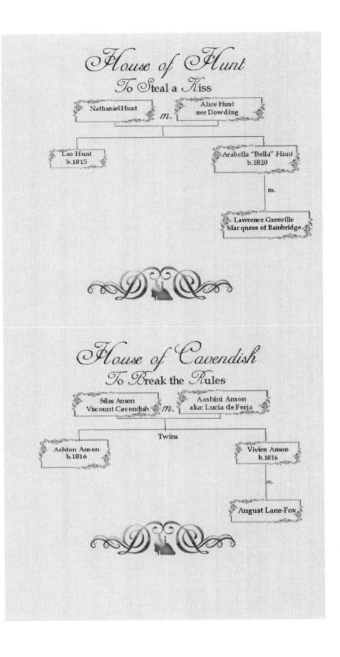

House of Hunt
To Steal a Kiss

Nathaniel Hunt *m.* Alice Hunt nee Dowding

Leo Hunt b.1815

Arabella "Bella" Hunt b.1820

m.

Lawrence Grenville Marquess of Bainbridge

House of Cavendish
To Break the Rules

Silas Anson Viscount Cavendish *m.* Aashini Anson aka: Lucia de Feria

Twins

Ashton Anson b.1816

Vivien Anson b.1816

m.

August Lane-Fox

House of St Clair
To Wager with Love

Jasper Cadogan
Earl of St Clair

m.

Harriet Cadogan
nee Stanhope

Cassius Cadogan
Viscount Oakley
b.1815

m.

Lady Charlotte Adolphus
b.1817

House of Cadogan
To Dance with a Devil

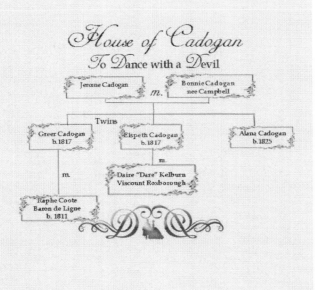

Jeronne Cadogan

m.

Bonnie Cadogan
nee Campbell

Twins

Greer Cadogan
b.1817

Elspeth Cadogan
b.1817

Alana Cadogan
b.1825

m.

Daire "Dare" Kelburn
Viscount Roxborough

m.

Raphe Coote
Baron de Ligne
b.1811

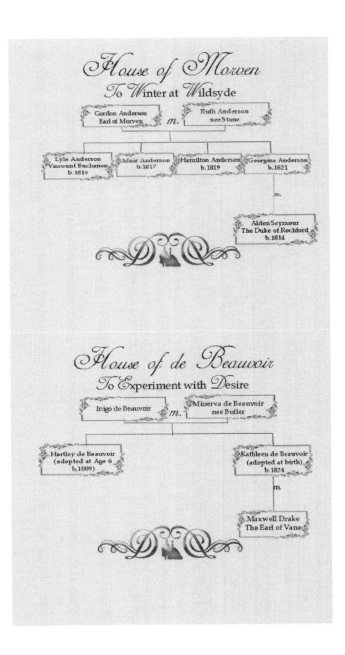

House of Morven
To Winter at Wildsyde

Gordon Anderson
Earl of Morven
m.
Ruth Anderson
nee Stone

Lyle Anderson
Viscount Buchanon
b.1816

Muir Anderson
b.1817

Hamilton Anderson
b.1819

Georgina Anderson
b.1821

m.

Alden Seymour
The Duke of Rochford
b.1814

House of de Beauvoir
To Experiment with Desire

Inigo de Beauvoir
m.
Minerva de Beauvoir
nee Butler

Hartley de Beauvoir
(adopted at Age 6
b.1809)

Kathleen de Beauvoir
(adopted at birth)
b.1824

m.

Maxwell Drake
The Earl of Vane

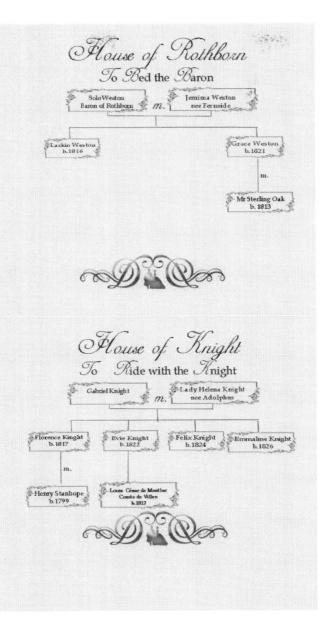

House of Rothborn
To Bed the Baron

Solo Weston
Baron of Rothborn *m.* Jemima Weston
nee Fernside

Larkin Weston
b.1816

Grace Weston
b.1821

m.

Mr Sterling Oak
b.1813

House of Knight
To Ride with the Knight

Gabriel Knight *m.* Lady Helena Knight
nee Adolphus

Florence Knight
b.1817

Evie Knight
b.1822

Felix Knight
b.1824

Emmaline Knight
b.1826

m.

Henry Stanhope
b.1799

Louis César de Montluc
Comte de Villen
b.1817

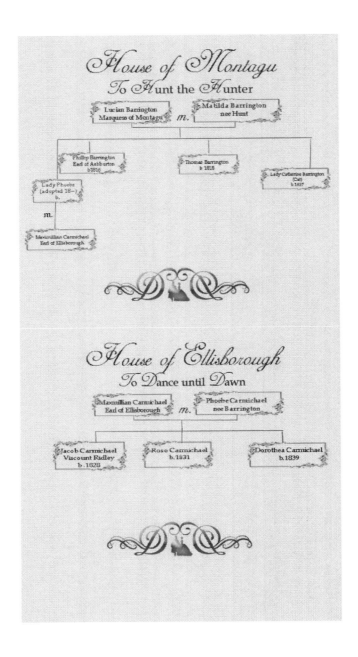

House of Montagu
To Hunt the Hunter

Lucian Barrington
Marquess of Montagu — m. — Matilda Barrington
nee Hunt

Phillip Barrington
Earl of Ashburton
b.1816

Thomas Barrington
b.1818

Lady Catherine Barrington
(Cat)
b.1827

Lady Phoebe
(adopted 18-)
b.

m.

Maximillian Carmichael
Earl of Ellisborough

House of Ellisborough
To Dance until Dawn

Maximillian Carmichael
Earl of Ellisborough — m. — Phoebe Carmichael
nee Barrington

Jacob Carmichael
Viscount Ridley
b.1828

Rose Carmichael
b.1831

Dorothea Carmichael
b.1839

Prologue

Madam,

I beg you will forgive me for writing to you out of the blue and for the haste of this note, but I fear he will discover me at any moment. Your son, the Viscount Latimer, is not dead, as many believe. He faked his demise to escape the investigation and trial for what he did at Talavera and has remade himself in Paris, earning his money in ways that I close my eyes to for fear of what I may discover. He does not let me out of his sight, nor allow me friends or correspondence. If this gets to you, it will be the greatest good fortune I ever had.

I write now so you may know you have a grandson. He is six years old and a sweeter, kinder boy you will never find. My darling Wulfric is nothing like his father and it is for this reason I fear for him. I am not a strong woman; my health is failing me, and I do not believe I will live to see him become a man. I am deathly afraid of what will happen to my son when I am gone.

Please, madam, do not allow my sweet boy to fall into his father's hands, nor pay the price for his father's sins. I beg you to come to Paris and take him back to England, for it is too late for me, but Wulfric has his life ahead of him.

Please, my lady, have pity and...

—Excerpt of a letter to Lydia De Vere, The Right Hon'ble, The Dowager Viscountess Latimer, from Lillian De Vere, The Right Hon'ble Lady Latimer.

— letter consigned to the fire by her husband.

10th November 1824, Paris, France.

"Aha! Now I have you!"

Wulfric squealed as his mother lunged and tickled him mercilessly until he was red-faced and gasping.

"Th-That's not fair, I wasn't ready," he protested, having lost another game of hide and seek. It was really not possible to play it properly in their cramped apartment, but the weather was horrid, sleet falling from a leaden sky and turning the streets into a mucky, sludgy mess.

"I win!" Mama said smugly and sat back down on the threadbare settee beside the meagre fire to catch her breath.

She seemed to need to do that a lot, and Wulfric scrambled up to sit beside her.

"Are you well, Mama?" he asked anxiously, studying her lovely face. He knew, with the certainty of all small boys who were well-loved, that his mama was the prettiest in the world. Even so, she seemed pale, and her pretty blue eyes were not as bright as they had once been.

"Of course," she assured him, giving him a warm smile. "Quite well. Now, come and finish your sums. You are very naughty, distracting me with your games when there is work to be done."

Though the words were stern, her voice was teasing and her expression soft. So Wulfric dutifully fetched his paper and pencil and did his sums while his mother looked on.

A moment later, the door flew open, and Wulfric's heart jolted as his father strode in. Wulfric dropped to the floor out of sight, huddling beside his mother's skirts, hoping the giant of a man did not notice him. He supposed his father was not truly a giant, not like the ones in the stories that ate children, but to Wulfric he was a huge, looming, angry presence that frightened his lovely mama and spoiled everything. Happily, they did not see him often, perhaps only once or twice a month. But, whenever he came, Wulfric had nightmares for days after.

Mama got to her feet, taking a step forward so Wulfric was hidden behind her skirts.

"I did not expect you, my lord," she said. "It is an unpleasant day for being out and about."

Charles De Vere, once Viscount Latimer, grunted and strode into Mama's bedroom. Wulfric wanted to tell him to stay out, for Mama did not like him in there, but he was too frightened. A moment later, his father came out again, holding a large leather box.

"My pearls," Mama said in shock. "Why have you got my pearls?"

"You forget, madam, that what is yours is mine."

Mama made an ugly sound. "How can I forget that, when you have sold everything of value that I brought to this marriage? The pearls are all I have left, they were my mother's...."

"Oh, stop your whining. I need cash and I need it quick. I'm buying a property—a house, if you must know—and I need to secure the sale."

"A house?" Mama repeated, her confusion obvious. "For us? But we can barely afford—"

"Not for us!" he snapped, irritated. "It is a business opportunity, and one that will earn us a pretty penny. Our fortunes are about to turn, mark my words. Maybe you'll wear fine dresses again and look like a lady, instead of a slattern," he added with an expression of disgust, gesturing to her worn grey gown.

"Mama *is* a lady! She's a very pretty lady!"

Wulfric regretted his outburst the moment he closed his mouth. His father's dark eyes settled on him. He huddled against his mother's side, reassured by her hand on his head, but wishing he could disappear into the furnishings.

"Cowering behind your mother's skirts again?" his father sneered. "You have ruined that boy with all your mollycoddling, Lillian. He's a snivelling little coward."

"He's nothing of the sort, and you are nothing more than a vile bully," Mama said, putting up her chin.

Wulfric held his breath and prayed as his father lifted his hand, but a second later he dropped it again with an impatient curse. "I don't have time for this," he growled, and stalked out, slamming the door.

The silence that followed fell upon them like a weight, and Wulfric tried to breathe as he heard his blood rushing in his ears.

"Come here," Mama said, sitting again and pulling Wulfric into her lap. He cuddled close, squeezing his eyes shut and holding on tight, trying hard not to cry. "Don't you listen to him. You were very brave to speak up for me like that. I'm proud of you."

Wulfric opened his eyes again, looking at her doubtfully.

"I mean it, and Mama never lies, does she?"

Wulfric shook his head, feeling a little better.

"Listen to me, my little man, there is something I need to explain to you."

"A lesson?" Wulfric asked.

Mama nodded, her expression serious. "The most important lesson I will ever teach you, so pay close attention."

"Yes, Mama," he said, sitting up a little straighter.

Mama put her hand on his chest. "In here is your heart," she said. "And you have a wonderfully big heart, Wulfric. Your heart is good and kind and full of love."

Wulfric blushed and Mama laughed, though not unkindly. Her eyes were all twinkly, like they got when he'd said something that made her happy.

"It's true, my love, but this wonderful heart of yours will get you into trouble if you do not guard it."

"How do I do that?" he asked, confused. Was he supposed to pick up a sword, or surround himself with soldiers?

"By hiding it. By pretending it isn't there."

"How?"

Mama took a breath and reached out, stroking his hair, his face. "You must learn to pretend you are like your father, hard and angry and ready to knock anyone down who says things you don't like."

Wulfric felt his mouth drop open in shock. "But, Mama…!"

"No, listen. I do not mean that you do this to people you like, to kind people, people you trust. But there are many men like your father and, until you are sure of people, you must be cautious. The world is far bigger than you realise, my sweet boy, and there are dangers, people that will see your kindness and take advantage.

You will grow to be a big man one day, bigger than your father, if I guess correctly, but until then, you need to make sure no one has the power to take anything from you. You must wear this fierce protection about you like a cloak to keep you safe. Do you understand?"

"I... I think so. But does that mean that I will be a bad man, like Papa?" he asked, not liking the sound of that at all.

Mama's face softened, and she shook her head. "No, never that, Wulfric. For beneath the cloak, you'll be just the same as you are now, but no one will know that, and so no one can hurt you. You'll be safe. Will you try, my darling, try for your mama?"

"Yes, Mama," he said, struck by the sorrow in her eyes.

He wanted to take it away, to make her happy, and so he promised.

Chapter 1

Dear Evie,

I am so jealous! Rouge et Noir sounds scandalous and exciting and the party your husband threw for you sounds so very sophisticated and romantic. I wish I could have been there and am a revolting shade of green with envy. How lucky you are to visit such places now you are married. I am not surprised everyone made such a fuss of you though, for so they should. You have quite the dashing reputation now, you know. How smug you must have felt when all those French ladies saw you were the Comtesse de Villen. Even in London, the scandal sheets reported how the female population of Paris wept at the news.

Oh, how I wish I could run away with a man who loved me like your comte loves you. It's so very romantic. This season promises to be tedious with all the same faces and how horribly spoiled I am to complain about going to parties and dancing until dawn. Except it isn't nearly as exciting as I hoped it would be. I must mind my manners and my tongue. Each year, it seems what a lady may or may not do or say becomes ever more restricted and I feel hemmed in and trapped like a bird in a cage when I want to fly.

I want an adventure, Evie. To be swept off my feet and carried away. The only person who carries me away isn't a person, but Sultan. He saw a rabbit yesterday morning and pulled on the lead so hard I fell flat on my face. I was never more mortified. I had to get up with mud on my dress and grass in my hair while all the elegant ladies muttered and sniggered behind their fans. Then the wretched beast lopes back with his tongue hanging out, looking so pleased with himself despite the rabbit getting away, and I had not the heart to be cross with him.

Perhaps I shall run away with Sultan and have an adventure. Just the two of us, far away from spiteful debutantes and men who insist on talking to my bosom. For outside of my family, Sultan is the most loyal male I have ever encountered, and I have grave doubts about ever meeting one better.

P.S. Cat is wild that you never took a dare. We have all tried to mollify her by telling her of all your daring exploits, but she would not be placated. So she took one for you. Please see enclosed.

—Excerpt of a letter to Evie de Montluc, Comtesse de Villen from Lady Cara Baxter (daughter of Luke and Kitty Baxter, Earl and Countess of Trevick)

10th October 1842, Périgueux, Dordogne, France.

Wulfric 'Wolf' De Vere, Viscount Latimer, was a conundrum and he knew it. In theory, he bore a noble title, courtesy of a father who had been an evil, violent brute… but no one in the De Vere family knew he existed. Wolf was also a criminal, and not just a minor one. In his world, he was known as *Le Loup Noir*, king of the Parisian underworld. If you wanted silks, spices, alcohol, or anything of an exotic nature, you came to Wolf. If you wanted someone to disappear, you came to Wolf. If you wanted a favour, you came to Wolf, but only if you were prepared to pay the price, and the interest was high.

Everyone knew he was not a man to be crossed, but they did not know Wolf.

People knew Wulfric De Vere was a very bad man. Though, in his opinion, everything was relative. Some would call him a criminal, which would be true. Some would call him a smuggler: also true. Some would say he lived a dangerous and violent life, and would probably end his days at the end of a rope… well, yes, that was true, but the types he dealt with wanted to stick him with knives or shoot him, which he tended to object to. In order to stop said people sticking him with knives and shooting him, he usually had to employ similar tactics. Being a smuggler, a criminal, and a pacifist was a difficult balance to achieve. Especially when every Tom, Dick, and Harry thought they'd like to take over his patch, which usually began with them trying to bury him in it.

He tried to avoid trouble, but trouble didn't avoid him. And if the wrong sort of person thought *Le Loup Noir* was not a black-hearted killer but a fellow who would just as soon sit in front of a fire with a good book and a kitten on his lap, well… they'd get ideas. The sort of ideas that would get him killed.

And so his reputation grew.

He had not chosen this life, but had it thrust upon him. It had begun when he'd tried to kill his father as a boy, to put an end to the misery the man inflicted everywhere he went, but at fifteen, he had not been strong enough. The end finally came when the vile man had tried to kidnap a young girl, to force her to work in his appalling brothel, and Wolf could not stop him. Not until his closest friend, Louis César, had appeared in his life, like a guardian angel. Louis had killed the monster that night, and the two of them had rolled the old viscount's body into the Seine and never regretted it for a moment since. Louis had reason to hate the old man as much as Wolf had.

On that night, Wolf had realised he was a criminal. An outlaw. For what had the law ever done to protect anyone from men like his father? Instead, he'd looked to Louis César as a role model for what a man could be. Yes, Louis was a thief, and did not give a snap of his fingers for the law, but he had also stepped in to protect a young woman and a boy he did not know, at risk to his own life. He was kind and generous, and he had shared his time with Wolf, something Wolf had not known since his mother had died seven years earlier. Louis even seemed to like him. It would not be stretching a point to say that Wolf idolised his friend.

Things had changed since those days. Louis had been gone for years, making a new life in England with his brother, Nic. Now both Louis and Nic were married, and Wolf was happy about that, he really was. Of all the men in the world who deserved a happy ending, Louis and Nic were at the top of the list. But that left Wolf alone in Paris once more and… he was restless.

He was a powerful man now, in all senses of the word. It had been a long time since he had needed anyone's protection or help. Nothing happened in this great, complex city that he did not know about and yet… and yet it was not enough. He was feared and respected, and alone.

He knew that a man in his position would not make old bones. There were too many ready and willing to risk everything, hurt anyone, to get to be where Wolf was. Eventually, he would make a mistake, get sloppy, forget to look over his shoulder at the right moment, and then he would be dead. The idea did not appeal. He needed to get out, to see something of the world outside Paris, and spend some of the money he had accumulated instead of cleaving to it like a dragon sleeping atop its hoard.

Though he knew it was ridiculous, his mind returned increasingly often to the world that had been lost to him, the world he would have lived in if his father hadn't been a cowardly traitor and a disgrace to his country. It was foolish to miss something he'd never had, to long for a world that would despise him on principle, and yet the sensation of loss remained, like a sore tooth he could never ignore or forget about.

He wanted to go home.

It wasn't home, he told himself severely whenever he grew maudlin, which was far more often than was comfortable. He'd never set foot in England, for his father and mother had been exiled once the truth had got out, and had settled in Paris, where Wolf had been born.

If he'd had the least bit of sense, he would gather his considerable wealth and live out the rest of his days in the South of France. It would be simple enough to find himself a lovely young French woman, settle down, and produce a litter of brats. Perhaps then he could forget the past, forget he was the Viscount Latimer, for what did that mean, anyway? So, he had a heap of mouldering property and unworked land in England. So what? Reports from his sources across the Channel had informed him some fob of a cousin had inherited but was letting the property go to wrack and ruin, frittering away what little income the estate brought in on vacuous pleasures and enjoying himself. Not that Wolf cared. Why should he? It would probably take every sou of his hard-earned fortune to put it all to rights, and for what? For the pleasure of knowing everyone would sneer at him and whisper behind his back, for no one would be fool enough to do it to his face. Wolf knew what he looked like: a large, aggressive man, willing to use his fists and brute force if the situation called for it. He stood six foot four, was built like a brick outhouse, and had obviously broken his nose more than once. A gentleman, he was not.

With a sigh, he looked out of the window of the carriage, where he waited as Louis caught up with an old friend and introduced him to Evie. Wolf had brought Louis and Evie back to the place where Louis had lived as a boy, though 'lived' was a fine expression for a boy treated as Louis had been. Survived would have been more accurate. But Wolf thought it was necessary to exorcize ghosts, and too many haunted Louis. So he had bought the house where Louis had been so unhappy and turned it into a school for boys who could never otherwise hope for an education. It had felt good to do something positive, to turn a place that had been a source of misery into a place filled with hope. It had made Wolf feel hopeful, too, that perhaps there was something better for him around the corner.

Wolf knew Evie did not want to return to England yet. She had a new and exciting world to discover here in France with her handsome husband, and Wolf could not blame her for that. But he would not return to England and face his own ghosts without Louis. He was too much of a coward to go alone but, when they were ready to return, he would go too. Then he would see what that world held for him. If there was nothing but trouble and unhappiness, which he had been warned more than once would be the case, at least he would know and stop pining for it. At least then he could turn his back on it and know there was no place for him there, without always wondering… what if?

Wolf fidgeted, trying to get comfortable, but there was never enough room for his long legs in a carriage, no matter which way he sat. Sighing, his gaze settled on the letter Evie had set down. She had said it was from a Lady Cara Baxter and had painted a picture of a beautiful, vivacious young woman who was kind and funny and clever. She'd also mentioned a magnificent bosom, or at least Wolf assumed it was magnificent, as Evie had complained about how all the men gawked at the lady's assets instead of heeding her words. Well, he was a man and not above being interested in a fine bosom, though he thought he had respect and sense enough not to gawk. Also, she had a Great Dane. A badly behaved Great Dane. Wolf was very fond of dogs and had once had a Great Dane himself, but the dear creature had been old when Wolf had come across him, and in a bad way. Wolf had nursed him through the worst and old Raggy, as he'd named him, had lived a full and happy year before dying peacefully before a warm fire on a cold winter's night.

Still, a tantalising picture of the young lady had formed in his mind, and he could not shake it free. Here was a woman who was a part of the great world Wolf was estranged from, a beautiful woman with a kind heart and love enough for an oversized clumsy hound that caused her no end of trouble.

Wolf stared at the letter. His fingers twitched.

No. No, really, it was beyond the pale to read another person's correspondence. Yes, it was true Evie had told him much of what was in the letter, but even so, it was personal, and he really ought not… Oh, what was he dithering about? He was a criminal for the love of God! He stole things. Filching a letter at this late stage in his black career was hardly going to make a difference. He was going to hell either way.

Wolf snatched it up, tucked it in his coat pocket, and hoped Evie did not notice its absence.

Having escaped the company of the lovebirds, Wolf made his way back to Paris, a long and dull journey which offered him plenty of opportunity to study the letter.

Lady Cara's handwriting pleased him. It was excessively feminine, with lots of mad loops and curly things, which did not make it any easier to read but was pretty to look at. It was also bold, which suggested to him that the lady was no shrinking violet.

Well, she owned a Dane, for heaven's sake. She could not mind drawing attention to herself, for it was hardly the kind of dog a lady would usually choose.

More than that, though, was the spirit of the creature he discovered trapped within her words. He imagined her as a beautiful bird, just like she'd written, held behind cold iron bars, staring at the sky beyond, and he longed to set her free. She wanted adventure and romance and an escape from all the rules that bound her in the world she inhabited. In his world, she could be as free as she pleased, but then she could never go back again to the place she belonged. That was the trouble with disgrace, with being an exile, and freedom for a woman like that could mean nothing else.

He laughed when he read about Sultan, and the lady's mortification, and his heart ached when he heard how the other debutantes had mocked her. Though she wrote in such an amusing way, he sensed the hurt and bewilderment behind her humorous description and wished he had been there. Just let anyone laugh or snigger at her when he was there, turning his black gaze in their direction.

By the time he returned to the imposing old chateau he called home, he could have recited the letter by heart. Now, sitting in the comfort of his study, the dratted thing called to him again.

Forget it. Forget her, he told himself. *She's not for the likes of you. She's a lady.*

You're a viscount, his brain reminded him.

He was a disgraced viscount at best, and a criminal.

She's lonely, she wants adventure, she's got a magnificent bosom and a Great Dane, his brain insisted, because really, that was all his Christmases come at once.

She's a lady, and she would faint if she even glimpsed me in passing.

Not if you wrote to her first, his brain said. *Not if you talked to her in a letter before she met you.*

His brain was an idiot.

But still….

Wolf got the letter out again and smoothed it out on the desk. There was her address, clear as day. *No.* It was too dreadful, even for him, to write to a woman who did not know him from Adam. There were rules. Or at least, he imagined there must be rules. Cara had said there were rules. *Lady* Cara. And one had to suppose receiving letters from a man one didn't know and who was known as *Le Loup Noir* would surely break one or two or several thousand of them.

No. Besides which, even if he did write, she'd never write back. Someone would intercept the letter. Or it would give her nightmares. Or she'd burn it. Or she'd tear it into little pieces. Or she'd tear it into little pieces and then burn it. She wouldn't write back. It was inconceivable. Probably.

But she might.

She wouldn't. But she *might*….

Oh, who was he trying to fool? Wolf reached for a clean sheet of paper.

Chapter 2

Paris. October 1842.

Dear Lady,

I hope that you will forgive me, a stranger, for writing to you but I happened upon your letter by chance and felt at once I had discovered a kindred spirit. I too once owned a Great Dane, and though he was a very old fellow when I got him, he was not beyond getting me into scrapes. He was a faithful and affectionate friend and I still miss his companionship. I suggest cheese. If you always have cheese about your person, and your disobedient Sultan knows this, you have a means of luring him back to you. If you often praise him and caress him for his good behaviour and slip him a piece of cheese, he will soon be putty in your hands. For the male of the species are simple creatures, no matter what form we take, and will usually roll over for a caress or a tempting morsel.

My conscience is plaguing me now and I feel I ought to point out that the above was a lie. Not the bit about the Great Dane — he was called Raggy — and the bit about the cheese and caresses was true, too. I meant the bit about happening upon your letter by chance.

I did not come across it by chance. I stole it.

Now I have shocked you, which I regret, but there it is. I am a wicked creature, and it is well that you know this at once. For clandestine letters are one thing, but I cannot abide liars. Yet I could not resist a missive which spoke about bosoms and running away with a Great Dane in the same paragraph. Really, like your unruly Sultan, I have very little in the way of self-restraint and it was simply irresistible. Perhaps you could consider your letter as a rabbit if we stretch the metaphor a little further, and you might forgive me as you forgave him.

By the by, do you not think me terribly clever for disguising my handwriting when I wrote your direction? It looks like a lady's hand, does it not? I have created an alter ego and called myself Miss Lavinia Pinkington, should anyone wish to know who you are writing to. If you address the letters thus, they will get to me. She is a rather frivolous creature with a taste for lavish hats and romantic poetry, but she has a good heart and is a devoted friend and correspondent. Any further details you must supply yourself, but that ought to get you started.

I wish I knew what you looked like. I have heard that Lady Cara Baxter is a great beauty, but I am far away in Paris and have not the chance to see you for myself. Is it true? What do you look like? What colour are your eyes?

Apologies, that was far too personal, but I feel like we might be friends in a different world, where you were not stuck in a cage and I was… well, different than I am.

Incidentally, I think I should mention at this point I am not old and toothless, in case you were fretting over such details. Which I suppose now I have written the words, that you are not doing. Such hubris, I hear you say. Well, and so it may be. Likely by now you have consigned this letter to the fire and any thoughts of the man who wrote it, too. I do not blame you, nor expect an answer, though I shall hope for one all the same. Still, you have taken shape in my imagination, a beautiful bird trapped in a cage, longing for freedom. I wish I could set you free.

I hope you find the adventure you are looking for. And don't forget to bring cheese.

Yours sincerely, a wicked stranger.

—Excerpt of a letter from a wicked stranger to Lady Cara Baxter (daughter of Luke and Kitty Baxter, Earl and Countess of Trevick).

Trevick Castle, October 1842

Sir,

Are you INSANE? Did your keeper let you out for a little bit of fresh air, only to lose track of your whereabouts? That must surely explain your address. The Fortress indeed? The mind boggles!!! Are you a dangerous madman who needs locking up in such a place, or simply a poor unfortunate who will fall down a hole or into a river if left alone? If so, I hope whoever has your welfare in their hands has found you and returned you to this secure location. If not, I sincerely fear for your wellbeing. Lunatics DO NOT prosper, left to their own devices.

Miss Lavinia Pinkington? Are you quite serious? Truly, I do not even know where to begin with that one.

*Who are you that you dare to write to a lady you have never even seen, let alone been introduced to? This is beyond anything! What do you mean you STOLE my letter? Did you steal anything else? For I must tell you if you did, you are in **grave danger**. The intended recipient of this letter was a dear friend of mine, and her husband is not to be trifled with. He will be **very angry** with you for taking something that belonged to his wife. I suggest you turn away from this life of crime before you get yourself into TERRIBLE TROUBLE!!! The only reason I am not telling my friend of your dreadful behaviour is to protect you. For I feel a man who speaks of Great Danes with such affection cannot be all bad — as mad as a march hare, without question — but probably not all bad.*

I will have your promise that you will not write to me nor to any other ladies ever again, for some might have more tender sensibilities than I and have a hysterical fit or call in the authorities. Think what trouble you might bring down upon your head!!!

I am sorry for the loss of your dear companion, though, and compassion leads me to believe that grief has disordered your mind. This I quite understand. But if you are lonely, why not get another dog to keep you company? Far better than writing to random strangers, I assure you.

I do not expect to hear from you again.

Lady Cara Baxter.

—Excerpt of a letter from Lady Cara Baxter to A Wicked Stranger.

Paris, October 1842

Dear Lady,

I was never more delighted or surprised when your letter arrived this morning. I have already read it three times and it has made an otherwise gloomy day far brighter than I have any right to deserve.

I beg then that you will forgive me for pointing out the flaw in your otherwise most excellent correspondence. (Though I did notice a great many capital letters and a surfeit of exclamation marks. I have never seen so many in one place before.) However, I digress, but I cannot promise never to write to you or other ladies again, without writing to you again in order to do so. That being the case, I like to think that this was not an error at all, but only a means of ensuring I did write back again. I do not doubt you will disabuse me of my folly.

So, for now, I shall only promise never to write to <u>another</u> random female. I should not, after all, wish to make you jealous. You are, and always will be, the only random female whom I shall importune with my peculiar ramblings.

I admit I had not considered that you might call in the "authorities" though what this might consist of, I am a little unclear. Still, I suppose I ought to let the terrifying prospect give me pause — except I'm a "wicked" stranger and such things really don't bother me overly much. You really should pay more attention to details.

I thank you for your kind words. I have often thought of having a canine companion again, but I do not know that I can bear the pain of losing another. There, not only wicked, but a coward, to boot. What a marvellous picture of myself I am painting for you. Ah well, the truth will out.

Yours sincerely, a wicked stranger.

—Excerpt of a letter from a wicked stranger to Lady Cara Baxter

Trevick Castle, November 1842

Dear Lunatic,

*You are the most PROVOKING man I have ever had the misfortune to receive strange and disturbing letters from. Of course I did not make such an error on purpose! I can only imagine my sensibilities were overwrought by the strain of receiving correspondence from a BEDLAMITE!!! Jealous indeed! Oh, yes, I'm all aflutter to be receiving letters from a deranged person who lives in a fortress and **carries cheese about his person at all times!!!** Be still, my beating heart. And just in case your poor muddled up mind cannot grasp the concept, **that was sarcasm.**

Just how wicked are you, anyway? Was stealing my letter and writing to me the height of your infamy or are you plotting to bring down the government??? Are you a libertine? A gambler? Do you lure people to their doom and make them into pork pies? I really should like to know what manner of MADMAN I am dealing with lest I feel the need to change my name and escape to Madagascar.*

Incidentally, I do not think it cowardly to be afraid of having your heart broken, but I do think it is tragic if you miss out on the fun and joy of such a loving companion because of it. They still live in our hearts, long after they are gone. I do not think Raggy would have missed out on his year with you, so why deprive another unfortunate creature of the same chance?

Lady Cara Baxter.

—Excerpt of a letter from Lady Cara Baxter to A Wicked Stranger.

Paris, November 1842

My Dear Lady,

I'm afraid I am wickeder than I am comfortable discussing with such a lady as yourself. Which must prove I am not all bad, though bad enough not to stop writing to you unless you <u>EXPRESSLY FORBID</u> *me from doing so, at which point I will trouble you no more. I do not, however, have any designs on the government so you may rest easy on that point.*

I am troubled, however, by your flights of fancy. Lure people to their doom and make them into pork pies??? I am shocked and horrified, and not a little queasy at the idea. I said I was wicked, not vile. There is a significant difference. Once again, you are failing to pay proper attention to the details. But I forgive you, for you are obviously prone to dramatic behaviour, as evidenced by the great number of capital letters, underlining and exclamation marks in your last correspondence. (Indeed, they seem to have infiltrated my own correspondence, are they catching? Like chickenpox perhaps?) How agitated you get. I wish I knew what you sounded like so I might better imagine you shouting at me in those big, bold capitals. But I still don't know what colour your eyes are, or your hair, so I have little hope of a description of your voice.

Why Madagascar?

Well, why did you go and get all sentimental and spoil an excellent scolding? I was thoroughly enjoying myself and then you ruined it by making me maudlin. I'm most put out with you. Please do better next time.

Your wicked stranger, W.

—Excerpt of a letter from W to Lady Cara Baxter.

Trevick Castle, November 1842

Dear Wicked W,

I am relieved to know you draw the line at luring people and turning them into pork pies. You have NO IDEA how this eases my mind when conversing with a fellow who is clearly BARKING MAD. Even Sultan agrees you are not to be trusted. I have read him all your letters, and he is most suspicious and believes you have nefarious intentions. Likely you mean to lure me into your confidence and then ruin me so I am forced to marry you and you may claim my fortune for yourself. At which point I shall no doubt discover you are old and toothless, after all. It is most depressing. I do not doubt you are as bad as all the other fortune hunters out to entrap me into wedlock so they may get their hands on my money, not to mention my person. I am so tired of MEN. **_You are all HORRID!!!!_**

Forgive me. That was uncalled for. I didn't even mean it. I know lots of lovely men, just no eligible ones whom I wish to marry, but I am all a-jitter this evening, having narrowly escaped such a fate just hours earlier, so you will please forgive my literary outburst. You must also excuse me if my set down is not as accomplished as either of us might wish, but the truth is, I am rather out of sorts. It's my own fault, for surely I know better than to hurry alone on receiving a note that a friend is in distress, but it looked very like their handwriting and... Oh, but there is no excuse for it. I should know better by now, but the fates were kind, and I escaped before the wretched fellow could enact his plans.

Are you truly wicked? It might be nice to know someone who could frighten away gold diggers.

Lady C.B.

P. S. My eyes are blue.

P.P.S. Madagascar was the first place that came to mind and seemed to be sufficiently far away to escape a DERANGED LETTER WRITER

—*Excerpt of a letter from Lady Cara Baxter to A Wicked Stranger.*

Paris, November 1842

My Dear Lady C,

I have not slept a wink since your letter arrived yesterday. What BLACK HEARTED DEVIL has treated you so shabbily? **I want a name and an address by return.**

I am wickeder than you can possibly imagine. Gold diggers would faint at the sight of me, and not because I am old and toothless. (I am in my prime and have all my teeth, in case you were interested.)

Your wicked W.

(I don't feel I can claim to be a stranger any longer in light of our lengthy correspondence)

P.S. What shade of blue? Please be specific. Summer sky blue or that odd purplish shade before a storm? Cornflower blue? Azure? The blue of Mary's cloak? I need DETAILS.

P.P.S. I have never said so, but please be assured that I should never treat you as anything other than a lady. I have no need of your fortune and would walk over hot coals before I saw any harm come to you. There is no need to pack for a long journey.

—**Excerpt of a letter from W to Lady Cara Baxter.**

🎩 🎩 🎩

Trevick Castle, December 1842

Dear W,

Don't be utterly RIDICULOUS! I am not about to give a ~~complete~~ virtual stranger someone else's name and address, no matter how much I may DESPISE THEM for their disgusting behaviour!!!

I am possessed of a very agile imagination I'll have you know, so do not go telling me what I can and cannot imagine. I imagined you turning people into pork pies, did I not? (Though strictly speaking it occurs to me, they ought to be more properly called people pies. Now I feel queasy.) So if I cannot possibly imagine how bad you are, that means you're worse than a people pie maker, which you expressly said you were not. DO PAY ATTENTION TO THE DETAILS!

However should I know what exact shade my eyes are? They're blue. Oh, if I must be specific, I suppose a pale blue, with a hint of green. ~~What colour are...~~

Why on earth you think I should I be interested in your age or your teeth, I simply cannot fathom.

Please do not be so foolish as to lose sleep over my wellbeing. I am usually exceedingly well chaperoned, and it was my own silly fault that I slipped away on purpose, believing I was being discreet for my friend's sake. I see now that I was gulled, and it shall not happen again. The Lady C you correspond with now is older and wiser. So stop being so silly. If you don't sleep, you'll be dreadfully grumpy, and heaven alone knows what you'll do next!!! Perhaps you'll write to the prime minister on a whim and ask him what colour his eyes are? Ridiculous creature.

I was not planning on packing for Madagascar just yet, but you must be reasonable (What am I saying??? You. Reasonable??? Ha!) If you are, in fact, an escaped LUNATIC with a penchant for writing random strangers peculiar letters, that's exactly what you would say!

Exactly how bottle headed do you think I am?

Yrs, Lady C.B.

—Excerpt of a letter from Lady Cara Baxter to A Wicked Stranger.

Paris, December 1842

My Dear Lady C,

If you will not give me the name and direction for the odious, mud dwelling lump of mouldering refuse that so callously importuned you, will you at least tell me at which event this dreadful piece of villainy was enacted? Please.

I have noticed that you have a sarcastic streak, my lady. That was not a complaint incidentally, rather an observation. I have come to look forward to each and every underlined and bold scolding you deliver to me as a boy anticipates Christmas. Speaking of which. I hope you will forgive me, for I know it must break a dozen rules of etiquette to send a lady gifts, but it is the season for such frivolity and—at this stage in our correspondence — it seems a moot point. So, my alter ego, Lavinia Pinkington, hopes you will accept the small package that has arrived with this letter with the greatest of good wishes for a merry Christmas.

I promise I shall not write to the prime minister under any circumstances.

Yrs. W.

P.S. My eyes are brown.

—Excerpt of a letter from W to Lady Cara Baxter.

Trevick Castle, December 1842

Dear W,

*Oh, you dreadful, dreadful MAN!!! You have got me into so much trouble. I have had to concoct the most ridiculous story about Lavinia Pinkington after my maid discovered your present. Really, you are the MOST **provoking** creature! Did you <u>have</u> to send me something quite so fine? I mean, I like pretty gloves as much as the next girl, but the embroidery was exquisite and so finely done.*

They must have cost a fortune. And what kind of friend sends such a gift to me when I have never introduced her to my family? Now, Mama has asked to see one of your letters!!! Lavinia's letters!!!

You must write to me at once, as Lavinia, to get me out of this ridiculous fix. I have told them we met at Lady Montagu's garden party in the summer, for there were so many people there, it seems the most likely place we could have encountered one another.

I am very sorry not to send you something of equal value and good taste for my parents are watching me most suspiciously and I dare not. Besides, it would have to be for Lavinia, and I do not believe you would appreciate the same things as she would. I have enclosed a small something, nothing really, but just a token of thanks for the lovely gloves. Even if they have caused me an endless amount of trouble!!! You must excuse the rather wonky W. Embroidery is really not my forté.

Yrs, Lady C.

P.S. If you must know, it was at the Countess St Clair's ball I was accosted, which must narrow it down to perhaps two hundred and ten possible candidates.

—Excerpt of a letter from Lady Cara Baxter to A Wicked Stranger.

. *Paris, January 1843*

My Dear Lady Cara,

I write with the hope of discovering you enjoyed a lovely Christmas and send you warmest greetings for an exceedingly Happy New Year.

Thank you kindly for the exquisitely embroidered handkerchief you sent me. The letter you have placed at the corner is not crooked, as you so critically claimed, but rather set at a rakish angle that pleases the eye. I shall keep it about my person always as a memento of a lovely afternoon at Dern Palace when I met such a kindred spirit. It saddens me we shall never again meet in person, but I shall treasure your correspondence and beg that you will continue to write to me as often as you may.

As you are such a dear companion to me, I shall confide in you that I have met someone — a man — who is quite the handsomest, cleverest, and most entertaining fellow I have ever encountered. I think you should love him if you ever had the chance to meet him in real life.

I must close now, as I am going out to shop for hats. One can never have too many.

Your dear and devoted friend and correspondent,

Miss Lavinia Pinkington

—Excerpt of a letter from W whilst purporting to be Miss Lavinia Pinkington to Lady Cara Baxter.

Trevick Castle, January 1843

Dear W,

How you can possibly believe I should be bosom bows with a ninny like Lavinia Pinkington is quite beyond me. Shopping for hats, indeed! And as for this fellow — **<u>who is quite the handsomest, cleverest, and most entertaining fellow I have ever encountered</u>** — *You conceited creature!!! Far from loving him, I think I should set Sultan upon him and leave him to his fate.*

Of course, his fate would be getting slobbered over and licked to death, or possibly knocked into a pond, as I was this very afternoon. **<u>There was slime</u>**, *I might add, but at least on this occasion no witnesses to my plight, as we were home at Trevick. I had a freezing and uncomfortable walk home, though. I think I may have a cold, which means days with a red nose and feeling wretched.*

You promised me the cheese would work, and in truth it is beginning to, but at times he is as unruly as ever. He broke three of Mama's teacups yesterday with a single swipe of his tail. We were both in disgrace for that.

We are returning to London for the season in three days, a prospect which fills me with *dismay. How spoiled and ungrateful I am when I spent so many years envious of my sister and friends who were out, and now I only want to escape another round of parties and dinners. I would rather be out walking with Sultan, even if he does knock me into disgusting ponds. It is not at all how I thought it would be, though I was warned repeatedly. And London is so dismal in January, is it the same in Paris I wonder? There are entertainments to be had, of course, but — why on earth am I telling <u>you</u> this??? It occurs to me, rather belatedly, that I still do not know who you are, or why you write me. Perhaps I am far more of a ninny than dear, misguided Lavinia, after all. For you are not respectable, are you?*

I ought not to write to you again. I shall be in London anyway, and I had better not supply you with my address, for that would be beyond foolish of me, not to mention dreadfully shocking.

I wish you all the best wicked W. Perhaps you might consider a life of less villainy and try to be a bit more respectable. At least get another dog to keep you company so you do not need to write to unsuspecting strangers.

Yrs. Lady C

—Excerpt of a letter from Lady Cara Baxter to A Wicked Stranger.

London, January 1843

Dear W,

You absolute LUNATIC!

I have just this morning been accosted by the most terrifying man I ever saw, who thrust your letter into my hand and then disappeared like smoke. I was never more vexed. You could only have received my letter a couple of days ago and how you managed to get a reply to me in such a short time and in such a manner — the mind boggles!!!

WHO ARE YOU???

Of course I am not languishing in bed and dying of pneumonia, <u>you diabolical halfwit.</u> In the first place, what manner of feeble creature do you think I am? And in the second, if I was dying of pneumonia, I would hardly be out walking for your henchmen to pass letters to. I shudder to contemplate what he might have done if I was indeed languishing in bed and not out of doors.

For your information, I am ROBUST and in excellent health, not some frail, wan waif of a girl who swoons at the slightest hint of a draught. A dunking in a disgusting pond is not my idea of a time well spent, but it is not enough to see me at death's door. How provoking you are, and yet I cannot help but be touched by your obvious concern, no matter how ridiculous. I must be losing my mind. Is lunacy catching via correspondence, I wonder?

I find it difficult to understand why my writing to you is of such importance, anyway. Do you not have friends in real life? That is, real, flesh and blood people, not the imaginary sort which I fear populate the wibbly wobbly world of your bizarre imagination — you DID create Lavinia Pinkington, so do not quarrel with me on this point. I worry you must be alone if my letters are of such importance to you. You aren't alone, are you?

I suppose I have no choice but to supply you with my address in town, for I tremble to consider what manner of device you would use to get a letter to me the next time. Perhaps you will send a tiger with your missive clamped delicately between his slathering jaws. I promise you, I shouldn't be the least bit surprised.

Speaking of slathering jaws, Sultan ate the fake cherries off a lady's reticule in the park. She was "not pleased". Yes, this is an understatement. Though really, who has fake cherries dangling from a reticule? And in January! Too frivolous for words. The strange thing is, he's never eaten a real cherry before. So why were the fake ones so tasty? I have been pondering this all morning. Happily, I discovered they were made of wax, so he can't have done himself any harm. I am going to hide my candles from now on, though, just in case.

Might you at least tell me something about yourself, if we are to continue this most peculiar and ill-advised correspondence? Your name might be a good start, as you already know mine. I warn you, if you do not provide me with one, I shall start making them up. I believe you must be English from the way you write, so why do you live in Paris? Are you a gentleman — for you mentioned not needing to trap me into marriage for my money? Or perhaps a wealthy industrialist? Or are you a clerk or a butcher? I already know you are queer in your attic, so I do not see the harm in sharing a little more.

I was forced to set this letter aside as Mama wished me to accompany her to a bookshop and I have just had the most peculiar encounter. The gentleman who so wronged me some weeks ago, the one I refused to name, was in said bookshop. On seeing me, he turned the ghastliest shade of greenish white and begun stuttering and stammering, and then fled as though the hounds of hell were nipping at his heels. I have the most peculiar feeling about this and, though I cannot believe I am asking such a thing... did you have anything to do with it?

Yrs, Lady C

—Excerpt of a letter from Lady Cara Baxter to A Wicked Stranger.

Paris, January 1843

My Dear Lady C,

I am relieved beyond measure to hear you are in ROBUST health and, as evidenced by the delightful rudeness of your letter to me, in excellent spirits.

I apologise if the fellow charged with delivering my missive disturbed you. To be fair, his job is chiefly preoccupied with the act of disturbing people, and interacting with ladies is somewhat outside of his experience. Now I have your address, however, no further measures of this nature, or any involving tigers ought to be necessary, though you never know what freakish whim of fate will make such an alarming prospect seem quite acceptable.

I thank you sincerely for confiding your forwarding address to me. I promise you, I do not underestimate the trust you have placed in me and swear to you now, upon my honour, that I mean you no harm. Far from it. Your letters are a little piece of happiness upon which I have come to look forward with more anticipation that I ought to share with you. I hope that should you ever be in need of help, you might call upon our friendship, if I dare to name it as such. I promise you, I should not let you down.

As for my name, I do not think I ought to share it with you. Name me what you will, it won't be the worst thing I've been called, I promise you. I shall do my best to match your confidence in me, however, by telling you something about myself. By blood, I am an

English gentleman, and perhaps if things had been different, someone who you might have called a friend without a qualm, but I have never set foot on English soil. I hope one day to do so, but do not fear that I would impose upon you, or embarrass you in public, for I should never do such a thing.

I am, in some respects, what you might call a tradesman, I suppose, though I confess the notion amuses me.

As to the vile excuse for a gentleman in the bookshop? Perhaps it was something he ate?

Yours, ever, W.

—Excerpt of a letter from W to Lady Cara Baxter.

Trevick, June 1843

Dear Warren, or is it Wilbur?

Summer is here at last, and the sun is shining. It is such a boost to one's morale after so many weeks of rain. I have been most envious of the lovely weather you have had in Paris and your descriptions of the spring blossom, and the lovely parks and gardens have made me long to see them for myself. But you have been holding out on me and keeping secrets, for I was so very impressed with your sketch of the fine ladies promenading in the Jardin des Tuileries. You are <u>most</u> talented!!! Whyever did you not tell me so before now? I demand you send me more. Oh, I'm being *spoiled again, aren't I? But do send me some more sketches. I was so enchanted by this one I have had it framed and it has pride of place above my dressing table where I might see it every day.*

By the way, I fell into a stream this afternoon. Mortifying as usual. And yes, I was chasing Sultan who barely got his paws wet. So unfair.

I am so glad you enjoyed The Ghosts of Castle Madruzzo! Isn't it ghastly? It's so delightfully blood curdling!!! And for once, the heroine is not a great nitwit, which is always such a relief. I cannot tell you how many times I have been tempted to throw a book across the room when the author makes the heroine do something so very idiotic I want to shake her.

I do not believe for one moment you had nightmares, so do stop trying to make me feel guilty for scaring you. You are supposed to be a WICKED STRANGER not a wet weekend. Do you mean to say all this time I have been writing to you under false pretences? I am SHOCKED and DISAPPOINTED!!!

Yrs, Lady C

—Excerpt of a letter from Lady Cara Baxter to A Wicked Stranger.

Paris, July 1843

Dear Cara,

Firstly, please forgive me for the tardiness of my reply. I did not mean to worry you and would have responded to your FIVE letters expressing concern at once, only I had a little mishap and was out of sorts for a while, but I am mended now.

Wilbur? Really? Do I seem like a Wilbur to you? I am insulted you should think so. Winston was better, and I rather liked Winter, even William, though I draw the line at Willy, but Wilbur? No.

I may have exaggerated the extent to which your bloodthirsty tale disturbed me, it is true, but you seemed so pleased by the idea of shocking me I did not wish to disappoint you. It seems I have done so anyhow so I must re-establish myself as a thoroughgoing villain, and remind you I am indeed wicked, as proven by this reply. For I ought to leave you be, my dear Cara. The past days I have had a deal too much time on my hands to think about what I have done in pressing this correspondence upon you.

I know we can never be more than this to each other, though I wish that were not so. Your friendship has become something of infinite value to me, but I wonder if I am only punishing myself by allowing this to continue, for you will meet a handsome young fellow who will steal your heart someday soon, and then you will say goodbye and I shall be bereft without your letters. I wonder what you would think of me if we met on the street, and such thinking is foolish, for I know well enough what would happen next.

Forgive me. I am not myself at present.

Yours, ever, W.

P.S. The enclosed sketch is of my study. A poor subject, but I did not like to fail you.

—Excerpt of a letter from W to Lady Cara Baxter.

Trevick, July 1843

Dearest Wallace, or Wolfgang, or Weston, or whatever your name is, I don't care!

What has happened? I have not slept a wink since your reply arrived yesterday. What little 'mishap' has befallen you that has so depressed your spirits? Where is my dreadfully wicked W and who is this dejected creature who has replaced him? I fear that matters are far graver than you let on. Are you ill? Injured? For the sketch you sent was of your office, and as beautifully wrought as it was, it suggests to me you cannot go out and about as you once did. Also, there was a fire burning in the grate and it is the middle of summer, which makes me believe you are indeed an invalid at present. Oh, do please write back to me at once, for you know how my imagination will run riot if you do not put my mind at rest.

What on earth are you talking about? What **handsome young gentleman???** *I have met no such creature I am willing to marry, I assure you. Indeed, even if such a prospect was likely, which at the present it most assuredly is not, I promise you I have no desire to hurry into matrimony.*

I should not know you if I ever met you on the street, for I have no notion of what you look like! I do not know if you are tall or short, fat or thin, handsome or plain, but surely you do not think so ill of me to believe I should reject your friendship if I were to discover you were not a perfect physical specimen? Or that I should judge you simply because others in society might decide you fail some ridiculous standard by which they measure us all?

Oh, you have put me in such lather, you VEXING creature!

Write to me at once. Yours, Cara.

—Excerpt of a letter from Lady Cara Baxter to A Wicked Stranger.

Paris, July 1843

Dearest Cara,

What the manner of devil's brew is 'Colt's foot jelly' and what do you propose I do with it? I have a parcel on my desk filled with a terrifying array of strange and disturbing preparations. You did not even give me time to write my reply!

I am NOT an invalid, you impossible girl. I am not suffering from disease, a wasting illness, consumption, TB, influenza or the bloody flux!!! The fire was lit in my office because the walls of the fortress are five feet thick and temperature averages between arctic and glacial almost year round.

If you must know, I met with a blow to the head, which laid me out for a few days. I also dislocated my shoulder and got a bit knocked about, which has meant I have not felt quite as sprightly as I usually do. A few bumps and bruises is not enough to put an end to me, I assure you, so please do not fret on my account and desist sending your noxious potions in my direction. (Brandy or Whisky, however, are most gratefully received — and medicinal too) Please rest assured I am remarkably ROBUST! Something else we have in common.

I promise you I am feeling much better and apologise most sincerely for the mawkish nature of the letter that sent you into such a pelter. The physician prescribed Laudanum to help me sleep, which always makes me maudlin. I beg you will disregard what I said as being the result of an unbalanced mind. As you have long regarded me as an amiable lunatic, I suspect this should not cause you too much difficulty.

It does not change the fact that I ought not write to you, or hold so determinedly to this unequal friendship, but so long as you wish to correspond with me, you may count on my reply.

Your affectionate friend. W

—Excerpt of a letter from W to Lady Cara Baxter.

Trevick, November 1843

Dearest Wrigley,

My amiable lunatic–no, I will not desist in calling you that when it both describes you so nicely and makes you furious.

I cannot believe Christmas is almost upon us already. We even had snow yesterday, and it's not yet December. It looks beautiful, but the roads become such a disgusting muddy, slushy mix that I have nothing but sympathy for the poor laundry maids who must try to clean the stuff off the hems of my gowns. Men are so fortunate in wearing boots and trousers. I wish I could. What a lot of work it would save.

By the way, I have discovered that Sultan fears snow. Honestly, he is the most ridiculous creature that ever lived, and I say that as his most devoted and adoring owner. He got me into the most dreadful fix today because...

—Excerpt of a letter from Lady Cara Baxter to A Wicked Stranger.

Paris, February 1844

Dearest Cara,

I am so sick of rain!!! Will this interminable winter never end? The Fortress is freezing no matter how many fires we light. I long for blue skies and am considering visiting friends who have gone south to Provence for a couple of weeks, hoping to find some milder weather. With my luck, I'll arrive just in time for the mistral.

—Excerpt of a letter from W to Lady Cara Baxter.

London, April 1844

Dearest Whittaker,

My amiable lunatic, you will never guess what happened today. I am in trouble as usual. And Sultan had been behaving so beautifully of late thanks to your advice, but you know what a devil he is for cats and…

—Excerpt of a letter from Lady Cara Baxter to A Wicked Stranger.

Paris, July 1844

Dearest Cara,

As requested, I have enclosed a sketch of the Seine at sunset. I hope you like it. And for the fiftieth and final time… No. I will not send a self-portrait. It will only frighten you to death and I'll never hear from you again.

—Excerpt of a letter from W to Lady Cara Baxter.

Chapter 3

Dearest Cara,

I am going away, so do not be anxious if you receive no letters for a little while. As soon as I am settled, I will forward my address. Do not fret. I am quite safe and well, and only going on a little voyage. An adventure, I suppose, though I am uncertain what I hope to achieve. I have questions I wish to answer and a desire to discover things about my family and my past that have always puzzled me. Perhaps it will be a new beginning, or an ending, but if I do not find out, the questions will always plague me.

Take care of yourself, dearest friend, and please don't let that wretched dog pull you into any lakes, streams, or bogs, or endanger your life in any other manner.

Your affectionate W

—Excerpt of a letter from W to Lady Cara Baxter.

10th October 1844, The Port of Folkestone, Folkestone, Kent.

Two years after Wolf's first letter…

It was raining when Wolf set foot on English soil for the first time. Not a torrential downpour, and not an apocalyptic crash of thunder followed by a lightning strike either, so there was that. Instead, a fine sprinkling of rain settled over everyone in his travelling party, as delicate as spider webs and yet still soaked everyone who stayed out in it for above five minutes.

Evie cast her husband a chagrined smile as he climbed into the carriage and cast his sodden hat aside, shaking water droplets from his dark hair. "Are you cursing me for making us leave the south and all that wonderful sunshine?"

Louis laughed and slid his arm about her, pulling her closer. "As if you think I would," he remarked, kissing her nose.

Evie squealed, pushing at his chest. "You're all wet," she protested.

"Leave the poor girl alone," Wolf replied, shaking his head. "You've been married for over two years, surely the honeymoon period is over. Can't you bicker like normal people?"

"*Non*," Louis replied, returning an unrepentant smirk. "And you wanted to come with us, might I remind you?"

"Hmph," Wolf replied, scowling. He had wanted to. He'd wanted to for a long time, but now he was here, he was wondering if he was out of his mind. Perhaps he ought to go back to the fortress. Perhaps he was being ridiculous in coming here.

"Don't look so anxious," Evie said, smiling at him. "You don't have to take society by storm. We'll do this quietly as we discussed and see how it goes. At least your solicitor has accepted your claim to the title now, so there can be no difficulty there."

Wolf snorted. "Oh, no, other than a disgruntled cousin who will no doubt wish to murder me or to hang upon my coattails."

"I suspect he'll get over it quickly enough once he meets you," Louis said, sotto voce.

"What? On account of my winning personality?" Wolf replied, raising one eyebrow.

He knew what Louis was getting at, naturally. Wolf was intimidating to look at, and he knew it. Sometimes, that was an advantage. In his line of work, it kept him alive. It would certainly help dissuade the cousin who'd laid claim to those estates that were rightfully Wolf's from making a fuss. When trying to mix with ladies and gentlemen, though, it did not put people at ease, especially when they already had reason to distrust and despise him. And, if he was ever deranged enough to consider seeking out—but no. He must not consider her. It was out of the question.

"Everyone is going to be beside themselves to see you again," Louis said, returning his attention to his wife.

Evie smiled. "Oh, it's not been so long. I think we saw nearly everyone over the summer. I hope Aggie didn't cause too much havoc for Eliza and your brother on the way home. She was so looking forward to seeing her school friends again after such a long holiday. She'll be very excited to see you again, though. Oh, but it will be good to be home. As wonderful as the past two years have been, I've missed it."

"So have I, and that dreadful girl most of all, even if it has only been a few weeks. And I cannot wait to show you our new home," Louis said.

Wolf sighed and tried to shut out the lovebirds as they spoke about the property Louis had bought for them, which Evie had never seen. Not that Wolf begrudged them their happiness. He didn't, and he had become very fond of Evie too, but it was a bit much to have their incandescent joy in each other thrust in his face constantly, when he was becoming increasingly aware he was lonely.

Money and power were cold bedfellows, and Wolf was sick of looking over his shoulder, wondering if the next attempt on his life would be successful. The attack last year had been too close for comfort and had taken him a long time to recover from. He was heartsick, longing for something he knew was out of reach, and yet… And yet. Here he was, in England, reclaiming his title and his lands, and about to create more ruffled feathers than a fox in a henhouse.

His attention returned to Evie as he heard a familiar name mentioned.

"I think Cara and her family will be there too," she said, and Wolf cursed himself for not having followed the conversation after all.

"Where?" he asked, deciding he didn't give a damn if he was being nosey or not.

Evie turned back to him. "My family are having a welcome home party," she said, and then her face fell. "Oh, I… I wish that you could come too, Wolf, truly, I do, but—"

He held up a hand. "No, if I went, the shock of my presence would overshadow their joy in your returning. We must tread carefully, as we agreed. I know that, but I thank you for your kindness."

He returned a reassuring smile as his heart kicked in his chest. He'd not expected an invitation. That would have been madness on all sides. Yet Lady Cara *was* going to the party Evie's father was throwing to welcome her home, which meant one thing.

Lady Cara was in London.

"Cara? *Cara!* Have you heard a word I've said?"

Cara jolted and turned to see Ashton Anson staring at her in exasperation. "Oh, Ash, forgive me. I was woolgathering," she said, feeling a wash of colour stain her cheeks.

That was the trouble with having red hair and pale skin: the slightest trace of emotion would have her colouring up like a tomato, a fact which delighted the less kindly debutantes with whom she shared the marriage mart. They need only whisper some spiteful comment within her earshot, and she turned the most unbecoming shade of scarlet.

"How can you be woolgathering when you have such a delightful dinner companion?" Ash replied with a tut of indignation.

Cara laughed, knowing he was only teasing her. "I beg your pardon, I have been the most appalling guest this evening," she replied, and did her best to attend the spirited conversations going on around the table.

It was wretched of her to be so distracted when her dear friend Evie was home. Everyone was so excited to see her. Not that Cara quite recognised this Evie as the one she had known before her scandalous departure from society two years earlier. The young woman she saw now was confident and self-assured in a way Cara could only dream of being. Gone was any trace of the shy wallflower who liked to hide away in corners and in her place a sophisticated woman who was not only comfortable in her own skin but glowing with happiness. Cara could not help the tiny sliver of envy that worked its way into her heart.

Somehow, though Evie had been ruined by her kidnapping—or elopement—depending on which story you listened to, with the glamorous Comte de Villen, she was still welcome in society because everyone wanted to know the dashing couple who had dominated the print-shop windows for months on end. There were rumours of murder attempts, duels, and many other fanciful stories, though no one seemed to know what had really happened. One thing was obvious, though: it was a love match. When the two of them caught each other's eye, Cara would not have been the least bit surprised if the tablecloth between them had burst into flames.

She sighed heavily, knowing it would not be long before the whole infernal season would begin in earnest, and she would have to parade about like a prize heifer for the delectation of the men of the *ton*. Really, it was too depressing for words. Worse, Cara knew she hadn't a hope of finding anyone she wanted to marry, because she'd already fallen in love with a man she'd never met. It was too ridiculous for words, and yet so typical of her to do such a nonsensical thing. She didn't even know what he looked like! They talked about so many things in their letters, much of it fun and nonsense, but other things too, serious things, and they were so well suited it made her heart ache. Yet she didn't even know his name. She knew he believed he was unsuitable, that he existed outside of society, although he was a gentleman by birth. And now the wretched fellow had become even more mysterious by disappearing. It was so depressing to know she must endure weeks, or even months, before she would receive another letter. It wasn't fair.

"Cara?"

"What? *Oh!*" Cara groaned inwardly as she realised she had once again failed to take part in the conversation. "I'm so sorry, Ash."

Ash's handsome face creased with concern as he looked at her, and he lowered his voice. "Is there anything wrong? Because I know I am a dreadfully amusing fellow, and young ladies generally fight to sit next to me. So, the only explanation is that you have something on your mind. Can I help?"

Cara sighed and shook her head. "No," she said, utterly dejected. "No one can help, but I'll get over it."

"Ah," Ash said, sympathy in his eyes. "Like that, is it? Who is the fellow? Do I need to murder anyone?"

"No, nothing like that. Just an impossible dream, that's all."

Ash nodded, studying her a little too intently. "You're sure? I'm very good at keeping secrets if you ever need a friend."

Cara smiled, touched by his offer. "You are a good friend, Ash, truly, and I appreciate it, but no. There's nothing to be done.

Now, what was it you were saying? The duke said *what* about your waistcoat?"

Two days later...

"Yes, of course, I understand, my darling girl," Mama said, taking Cara's hand and squeezing it. "The man is a disgusting satyr and in your place I should have been tempted to pour soup into his lap too, but really, Cara, you must see that the furore you caused is far worse for you than for him. He suffered a little embarrassment, but he was the Duke of Sefton's friend, and so the duke scolded you in view of the entire room."

Cara glowered, reliving that scolding with burning cheeks. Horrid, horrid man, and there had been his vile granddaughter, Lady Hyacinth, and her boon companion, the equally unpleasant Miss Crantock, both enjoying her humiliation with obvious delight.

"Oh, but Mama, it was only gazpacho, it's not like it burned him!" Cara retorted, reaching to soothe her dog, Sultan, who had raised his head and was looking at her with big, soulful eyes, worried by her agitation. "Though I admit it made a frightful mess of his waistcoat," she added with satisfaction. She tugged gently on Sultan's silky ears, making the big dog sigh with contentment.

Cara had to admit the scene last night had been rather awful— if amusing, in parts—but Cara knew her reputation was suffering. Some called her an 'original' or a 'high-spirited gel', but others were not so kind, and it was only a matter of time before she did something truly awful. She was sick of fortune hunters, though, and even sicker of those lecherous devils who thought it quite acceptable to put their hands on her without her permission. When Mr Handley—how aptly named—had grasped her upper thigh and squeezed, it had been the outside of enough and she'd reacted accordingly. Lucky for him it hadn't been minestrone.

"I know, dear, and Papa will be having words with Mr Handley, and the duke, too. I have been told not to, as we both know my temper is just as intemperate as yours. It's wretchedly unfair that they punished you when he is the one we ought to call out for his disgusting behaviour, but society always judges us women, while the men do as they please. I could throw things myself, truly, but this is hardly the only incident this year, is it, darling? Far from it, and not all of them were as understandable as yesterday's, either. If you're not careful, you will make yourself unmarriageable."

"Good," Cara said darkly, launching to her feet and stalking across the room to glare at the garden beyond. She wished they were back at Trevick where there were miles and miles of fields and woods, and she could walk Sultan for hours without upsetting some blasted coxcomb with wandering hands and more hair than wit.

"Oh, you don't mean that, my love," Mama said with a sigh. "I know it's a wretched business, but there are good men out there. There's one for you, but you must find him. Your prince will come, love."

"Yes, but there are too many slimy frogs to sort through first, that's the trouble," Cara retorted.

Mama laughed, which made Cara feel a little better. "Unfortunately that is true, which is why I chose my husband before he was old enough to fall into bad habits," she said, making Cara smile.

Mama and Papa had fallen in love as children, and found each other again despite years apart, to discover nothing had changed. It was so romantic, and so far from anything Cara had experienced to date.

"I confess, I did hope that perhaps you and Felix Knight might be compatible," Mama said wistfully, for Cara knew she had a soft spot for the boy.

Cara shook her head. "Felix is a dear friend, Mama, but that's all. That's the trouble with most of the decent men I know. I grew up with them. Think of all those summers at Holbrooke, or Beverwyck, or Trevick, when we were all together, squabbling and climbing trees and swimming in the lake. It's not like with you and Papa, because they're like brothers to me and… I just don't feel that way. I wish I did, believe me. Felix would make a splendid husband, but I want to love someone like you love Papa. I want to be swept off my feet and have a passionate romance. Is that too much to ask?" she demanded, tempted to stamp her foot in frustration.

Mama's lips twitched, but she held out her hands to Cara, who returned to sit back beside her.

"Passionate romances are not always joyous things to live through, darling. I had many, many years alone, pining for your father, never knowing if I would see him again, and you know when I found him, things were difficult for us. It might sound romantic in the retelling, but it was hard, love. Finding someone you like, someone who can be a friend and a lover too, is just as important as fireworks and grand adventures. Just bear that in mind, will you?"

"Yes, Mama," Cara said with a sigh. "I know."

"There's a good girl, and next time you feel like pouring your soup over a fellow, think again."

"Yes, Mama," Cara repeated dutifully.

Her mama stood up and looked down at her thoughtfully. "Try stabbing him with a fork under the table. It's more discreet, and you can pretend ignorance, then no one else will know the truth. Quite satisfying too," she added with a wink, before sailing out of the room.

Chapter 4

Latimer,

So, I have a grandson, do I? It might have been nice to know this some years ago, but it seems you have been too busy revelling in the gutters of Paris to pay your nearest kin any mind.

If you think society will welcome you, you're no brighter than your wicked father and I tell you now, I never liked the fellow, nor trusted him. The sort of man who beats his horses and kicks dogs is no man at all and has no business among civilised folk. I don't doubt what he treated his poor wife worse still. I've a mind to see you for myself all the same. If you're like him, it will be a brief interview and we need never bother each other again.

I'll expect to see you the morning of the 14th Oct. 10 am sharp. Do not keep me waiting.

—Excerpt of a letter from Lydia De Vere, The Right Hon'ble The Dowager Viscountess Latimer to her grandson, Wulfric De Vere, Viscount Latimer.

14th October 1844, Carlton Gardens, St James's, London.

Wolf woke with a start and sat up, alarmed to discover he wasn't at the fortress. For a split second his body surged into fight mode, expecting an attack, until he remembered. He wasn't being held hostage in vile conditions somewhere no one could ever find him. Oh, no. He was in this hell hole by choice. Flopping back against the lumpy mattress—the only one he could find in the entire bedamned house—he glowered up at the damp patch on the ceiling.

The house was a fine one, impressive even, and an address any gentlemen would be proud to call his own. Unfortunately, the place had been left to go to wrack and ruin, and his blasted cousin had stripped the place of anything that wasn't nailed down. Not a stick of furniture remained, nor a candlestick or anything else of value. Wolf had quite literally not got a pot to piss in.

He could have foisted his company on Nic, Louis' half-brother, who owed him a significant favour. It was a threat he'd held over Nic for years, and he'd almost done so, but then his conscience had kicked in, blast the thing. The rumour mill was already up and running, and whispers of just how wicked the newly discovered Viscount Latimer was were spreading like wildfire. It had taken only one meeting with Nic's wife, Lady Eliza, and the obvious realisation that she was a sweet-natured, kind young woman, to realise he could not bring such disgrace to her door. So, here he was, in the home he had longed to discover for so long—or at least, one of them—and cursing himself for an idiot. Just to make his day complete, he had received a command from his grandmother to present himself for inspection. Well, that was going to be fun.

From the information he'd gathered about the old girl, she was a cantankerous harpy who delighted in causing trouble and had somehow weathered the family disgrace by scaring half to death anyone who tried to slight her. Good God, what a family.

Still, he'd best get it over with, for as she said, she was his only kin—he refused to consider the annoying cousin. Sighing, he hauled himself off the mattress and went on the hunt for a means to heat some water to shave with.

Wolf arrived at the address on Queen Anne's Gate, Westminster, precisely at the appointed hour. He was damned if he'd give the old lady any extra reasons for finding fault with him, which was daft considering the impressive list she had to choose from. At least poor timekeeping would not be one of them.

The house was a grand one, the first on the south side of Queen Square, it rose five stories high, was of red brick and, as the street name implied, built in Queen Anne style. A snotty if diminutive butler let him in and impressed Wolf no end by simultaneously looking down his nose and up at him at the same time. Amused by this impressive feat, Wolf was still grinning as the man guided him into an overheated and over-furnished salon.

"Stop smirking, by God. You look like your devil of a father, more's the pity. I hoped never to lay eyes on that monster again," barked an imperious voice that scratched down his spine like nails upon a chalkboard.

Startled, Wolf stood a little taller as he followed the voice to an immense fireplace. Here were four wingback chairs, three of them occupied, and all surrounded by a variety of gaudily painted screens to keep away anything resembling a draught. The temperature was akin to stepping into Hades, and discovering three elderly ladies watching him with bright, intelligent eyes and expressions of avaricious interest did nothing to dissuade him from the comparison. Hell's bells, they were going to roast him alive.

"Goodness, Lydia, he's so *big*," one lady said. Her gaze lingered as she looked Wolf up and down with obvious approval. "I never saw such a big one in all my life."

The lady beside her cackled gleefully. "Well, we don't know for sure he's everywhere in proportion, though, Dorcas. Do you remember Bully Bullforth? He was a great big strapping fellow, but very disappointing where it counted."

The lady wiggled her little finger suggestively. Wolf sternly reminded himself that he could make grown men cry with little more than a look and prayed he wasn't blushing. It was merely the infernal heat in this hellish room that was making his face hot.

"Cora, hush now. That's my grandson, if you don't mind. Come and sit down, then," commanded the smallest and oldest of the three he had now mentally labelled The Viragoes. "Stop looming about. I can't abide men that loom. That's it, quick smart now."

Wolf sat down and then leapt up again as a yowl rent the air. He turned to see an overfed tortoiseshell cat glaring at him with furious amber eyes.

"Apologies, my lady," Wolf said to the cat, holding his hands out in a soothing gesture. "Entirely my fault, I ought to know better than to sit down without looking first. My only excuse is that your mistress has terrified me into stupidity."

There was a snort from beside him as his grandmother gave him a sharp look. "Terrified, my eye," she said, her shrewd, dark gaze glittering with interest. "I never saw a man more at ease with himself. Reckon nothing much frightens you."

Wolf quirked an eyebrow and looked at the assembled company. "Oh, you'd be surprised," he murmured before turning his attention back to the cat. He reached out his hand and rubbed under the cat's chin, immediately rewarded with a loud, rumbling purr. With a soft chuckle, he lifted her up and sat down, only wincing a little when the tortoiseshell arranged herself on his lap and kneaded his thighs with her delicate claws. "What's her name?" he asked.

"Regina," the old lady replied, watching him pet the cat with a sceptical expression. "How did you know it's a female?"

Wolf shrugged. "I never saw a male tortoiseshell before."

"She'll ruin your trousers, sheds everywhere," she added with apparent satisfaction.

"Nobody's perfect," Wolf replied, slanting a look at the old woman and winking.

His grandmother's lips twitched. "I suppose I had better introduce you. These two wicked ladies are my friends. Don't turn your back on them if you've an ounce of sense. Lady Dorcas Beauchamp, and her friend and companion, Mrs Cora Dankworth."

The ladies inclined their heads, their expressions intent. Wolf cleared his throat.

"Er... a pleasure, ladies."

"Oh, the pleasure is ours," crooned Mrs Dankworth.

"Yes, and there's so little pleasure to be had these days," said Lady Beauchamp with a heavy sigh. "Men don't age as well as women, and the younger ones are so disappointing. Not like when we were young, eh, Cora?"

Cora nodded, using an ornate fan to stir the overheated air. As she did, Wolf glimpsed a rather erotic painting on the fine chicken skin, which did not look at all the sort of thing a lady ought to wave about in public.

"Oh, indeed no," she said. "Men were great peacocks back then, prettier than we were, but oh, they were wicked. Such memories," she added longingly.

"Oh, hush, you two," said his grandmother, and raised a pair of lorgnettes to her eyes to study his face.

Wolf tried not to squirm, wondering what she saw.

"Hmmm," she said after a long moment of scrutiny. "You are very like your father, dark and swarthy, and those strong features. Harsh, almost. Intimidating blackguard he was, but the eyes... the eyes are different. Hmph. Well, what am I to do with you? You've left it a deal too late for a tender reunion, and I hear you've made a great muck of your reputation in Paris."

Wolf laughed at that, finding he liked this plain-spoken old harridan. "That rather depends on your point of view. My reputation in Paris is second to none."

"Pfft," she said with a disdainful sniff. "So, you're a common criminal and have made a deal of money, bully for you. What have you actually achieved with your life, hmm? Impress me, go on." She made a 'hurry up' motion with her hand.

Her question struck a nerve, echoing something he'd been asking himself of late and unsettling him further. He narrowed his eyes at her. "Why do you think I have the slightest interest in impressing you?"

"You're here, aren't you?" she said, and then gave a bark of laughter. "Oh, this is going to be deliciously fun, gels. Don't you think?"

"Oh, yes!"

"Indeed, we do," replied the other two members of the coven with relish. "Such fun!"

"What?" Wolf asked, eyeing the women with trepidation. "What do you mean? What is going to be fun?"

"You, in society. Oh, my days, they'll piss their pants when I send the invitations out."

"Invitations?" Wolf repeated, sitting up straighter and disturbing Regina, who dug her claws in to express her displeasure. "What invitations?"

"Why, to the fabulous soiree I shall hold to welcome my long-lost grandson home, of course."

Wolf stared at her, aghast. "Why on earth would you do such a thing? I assumed you'd want nothing to do with me."

"So did I," she replied baldly. "But you're rather more interesting than I thought you'd be, and I'm an old lady. I have little to entertain me these days, but you... Oh, you are going to be a delightful challenge."

"If I were a few years younger, I'd issue him a delightful challenge," Lady Beauchamp said, winking at him.

Wolf sighed.

Of course, Wolf tried to persuade himself it was mere happenstance that he found himself walking through Cavendish Square, despite the fact it took him two miles out of his way. The moment he got there, he rather wished he had not come. The square was grand and elegant, surrounded by huge mansion houses around a central, gated park. Here lived the quality, the ranks of society his father had been ejected from, and rightly so. Not that they would greet Wolf's arrival with any more enthusiasm. He wondered what his grandmother hoped to achieve with her determination to shove him in society's face. Nothing more than a scandal, and chaos, he suspected, having met the barmy old woman, but she was his only kin and, if she wanted to parade him about, he supposed he ought to let her. She'd had little enough from her family over the years from what he could gather.

Wolf paused. He studied each house until he discovered the one belonging to the Earl of Trevick, naturally one of the grandest on the square. His heart sank. What was he playing at? Cara was so far out of his reach she may as well be in Madagascar. He was only tormenting himself by coming here and... and what? Staring up at her house like a lovesick schoolboy. Good God, was this what she had reduced him to? His own damned fault. He ought never to have written to her, never to have begun....

His heart lurched as the gleaming black front door opened. A huge blue-grey Great Dane stepped out, tongue lolling, glancing back with joyful anticipation at the woman who held his lead in her small, gloved hand.

Wolf held his breath as Lady Cara Baxter stepped out of the door.

Oh God. Oh God. He should never have come. For there she was, the funny, sarcastic, intelligent woman he had written to these past years, and she was *glorious.* He had known she was beautiful from the start. Evie had told him so. It was one thing to know it, and to wonder, though. It was quite another to have the empirical evidence before him.

His heart gave an uneven thud, and he let out a ragged breath as he took her in. She was quite tall for a woman, with lush curves in all the right places, and her hair… oh, sweet Jesus. Her hair was the colour of copper and firelight, and was so tightly bound he suspected it would fall well past her waist if she were to free it of the hundreds of pins that must keep it confined. His fingers itched to touch the silky tresses, to be close to her. The need to cross the street and say, *it's me, I'm here,* so tantalising it was an ache beneath his skin as desire warred with good sense.

What if he did that? What then? Well, she would take one look at him, give a shriek of alarm, and run indoors again. He took a step back, out of sight, hidden by the overhanging branches from the park in the centre of the square. Shame for watching her in this way warred with the longing to stay, to drink in the sight of her and commit it all to memory, so he could picture her lovely face when he was reading her letters.

She stepped out onto the pavement, a footman walking several steps behind her. Wolf followed as she walked, promising himself he would let her go once she reached the edge of the square. He would let her go and not see her again. This would be enough. It must be enough.

Cara paused, turning back to the footman and allowing him to walk beside her. This must be Thomas. She had spoken of the man before, and that he accompanied her on her walks with Sultan. The fellow had a sweetheart and sometimes he met her when they were out and… yes, there.

The servant greeted a young woman and Wolf could not help but smile as he saw Cara's grin of delight at the two lovers staring shyly at one another. But then… but then the footman was leaving, going with the girl and… well, who was looking out for Cara?

Wolf made a sound of frustration, not knowing what to do for the best. He shouldn't follow her, it was an invasion of her privacy, and just plain creepy but… but she ought not be out alone in the city with just that dog for protection. Sultan was no protection at all, for despite the size of the beast, he was afraid of his own shadow, from what Cara had said.

"Damnation."

He set off after her.

Chapter 5

Dear Hester,

How fortuitous that I hear you are back in town. I have a mind to make mischief. Do come and join in the fun.

I am holding a little party. There's not a huge amount of society at this dismal time of year but I think I should scrape together a minimum of eighty decent guests, perhaps more, once they hear who the guest of honour is. You'll have heard, naturally, my grandson has appeared from nowhere, and great big thorn in society's side he'll be, too. They'll be torn between shunning him, avid curiosity, and fear of my displeasure, for I'm not dead yet.

Bring that nephew you dote on if you've a mind to. Oh, and I'm inviting Axton, so sharpen that tongue of yours too.

—Excerpt of a letter from Lydia De Vere, The Right Hon'ble The Dowager Viscountess Latimer to her old friend Hester Henley, Lady Balderston.

16ᵗʰ October 1844, Cavendish Square, Marylebone, London.

Cara hesitated on the steps of her home in Cavendish Square. Thomas had caught up with her on the corner but for the past two days she'd had the oddest feeling when she was out walking Sultan. She turned on the spot, looking out over the square, but it was the same as always, with horses and carriages passing through and people walking. Shaking her head, she went inside and let Sultan off his lead.

"Go and get a drink, then," she said cheerfully as a footman dutifully set down a large bowl of water for him.

"Cara? Oh, good. I'm glad you're back," her mother said, hurrying out into the entrance hall and waving a rectangular piece of printed card at her with obvious excitement. "It's the strangest thing! We've had a last-minute invitation from the Dowager Lady Latimer. It seems she has gained a black sheep grandson she never knew about and wishes to introduce him to society. Isn't it intriguing?"

Cara raised an eyebrow. "If he's such a black sheep, I wonder at her recognising him."

"Well, that's Lady Latimer. She delights in causing a stir," Mama said with a laugh. "She's a dreadful old woman but one can't help but like her, despite her imperious ways."

"Well, she's terrifying," Cara replied, shaking her head. "I remember when I came out, all the debutantes lived in fear of catching her eye. She often had some scathing comment that cut to the bone. I believe that was the only time I ever saw Lady Hyacinth given a proper set down. It was a wonderful moment," she said with a happy sigh.

Mama snorted, well aware that Lady Hyacinth was not one of Cara's favourite people. "We should pity the Lady Hyacinths of the world. After all, she must continue being Lady Hyacinth all day long, whereas we must only put up with her occasionally."

Cara laughed. Mama had the most wonderful way of putting things in perspective.

"Well, and when is the event to admire this black sheep?"

"Tonight," Mama replied with satisfaction.

Cara groaned. "Oh, no, Mama, you promised we could stay home tonight. I don't want to go. The season hasn't even begun yet."

"Well, I think we ought to. Oh, do come, Cara, it's bound to be interesting. I've heard the most dreadful things about the man."

"Like what?" Cara asked, dubious that even a black sheep grandson could be interesting enough to ruin a quiet evening with a good book.

"Oh, he's supposed to be a villain, a real one I mean, not just rumour and speculation. He's a smuggler of some sort, I believe, or was it a pirate?" Mama frowned. "There are so many stories flying about, it is hard to keep them all straight."

"Mama, he can't possibly be a pirate," Cara pointed out with a sigh, for Mama's imagination could take flight into the realms of fantasy if you didn't keep a tight hold of it.

"Whyever not? There *are* pirates," Mama said stubbornly. "He might be a pirate."

"Well, I suppose it's possible," Cara allowed, "But I don't think it's likely. He's a viscount, for one thing, and whoever heard of a viscount pirate? Honestly, the poor man is probably perfectly decent, and once got wrongly accused of cheating at cards or something ridiculous. So now everyone has painted him a black-hearted villain. It's monstrous unfair, if you ask me."

"Oh, and you're a spoilsport. I was so looking forward to meeting a pirate," Mama said, huffing.

Cara rolled her eyes. "I suppose he might be a smuggler," she said, feeling bad for spoiling her mother's fun.

Mama's eyes brightened. "Yes, he might indeed. Oh, how exciting. Now, come along. We must look our best if we are to meet such an interesting person."

Cara groaned as Mama towed her towards the stairs. "Not yet! It's not even midday, we've got hours yet...."

But Mama was already making plans for who would wear what colour so that they did not clash, whilst also making up wild stories about a man they knew nothing of... who might or might not be a pirate, or a smuggler, or heaven alone knew what. Cara gave in, borne along on the tide of enthusiasm that was her mama, and resigned herself to her fate.

Cara craned her neck and then put up a hand to wave at Evie as she arrived on her husband's arm. They were late, no doubt because so many people wanted to see them. Evie said they'd hardly had a moment's peace since returning to England. Evie grinned and waved back, making her way across the impressive entrance hall. Cara sighed with relief, for she had found herself in company with Lady Balderston and her nephew, Mr Godwin. Barnaby Godwin was a good-natured fellow and cheerful company usually, but he seemed rather dispirited this evening, and Cara could not get much conversation out of him. Lady Balderston, by contrast, was in high spirits and sat upon thorns to glimpse her friend's wicked grandson.

"Well, there's no shortage of guests considering the time of year and the lack of notice," said Lady Balderston with satisfaction. "Quite a triumph. Lydia must be beside herself with glee, the dreadful creature."

Barnaby frowned, looking around the throng with an anxious expression. "Do keep your voice down, Aunt. I swear the woman has the hearing of a bat, for all she tells everyone she's deaf as a post."

"You're just frightened of her," the lady said with a snort of laughter.

"I dashed well am, as would be any right-minded fellow," Barnaby retorted indignantly. "I never met a woman with such a talent for making one feel a complete clodpole."

"There, there, Barnaby, I'll protect you from the horrid old lady," his aunt said, and gave his arm a soothing pat.

Barnaby huffed and subsided into silence until Evie and the comte arrived. Lady Balderston immediately monopolised the handsome Frenchman's attention and Cara watched with amusement as the old lady flirted outrageously with him. The comte took it in his stride, teasing Lady Balderston until she blushed and laughed, shaking her head.

"Ah, comtesse, you are a lucky young woman. A good man you have there, for all his wicked ways."

Evie smiled and slid her hand through her husband's arm, gazing up at him adoringly. "I know what I have," she said softly.

Cara sighed at the way the comte looked back at Evie. *That* was what she wanted. A man who looked at her as if she was his every dream come true.

"Barnaby, it's good to see you," the comte said, once some old crony had diverted Lady Balderston's attention.

"Louis, thank God," he said with feeling. "I spent the first hour of this blasted turn out with my aunt, Lady Latimer, and her two dreadful friends. I swear I've never blushed so much in all my life."

Louis smiled at him, but his expression became one of concern. "But *mon ami*, this is not the only thing troubling you, I think? What is it? You seem out of sorts."

Barnaby shook his head and then sighed. "Oh, you may as well know, I suppose. It will be common knowledge soon enough. Lady Millicent Fortescue is engaged to be married. He's an earl, of course. I mean, I knew I didn't stand a chance, but… well, there you are," he added with a shrug.

The depth of regret in the comte's eyes surprised Cara. "Barnaby, I… I am so terribly sorry, and I promised to help you, too. I have let you down. Can you ever forgive me?"

Barnaby looked at him in surprise. "Let me down? Whatever are you on about? If not for you, I'd never have stood an earthly chance. As it was, well, I must find comfort in knowing she regrets her choice, but we all know why she made it. Can't blame her, can we? Her father put a good deal of pressure on her; she didn't actually have a choice at all."

The comte shook his head. "You are too good, Barnaby. In your position, I would not be so sanguine. I shall never forgive myself for failing you."

Barnaby gave a startled laugh. "Failing me? Don't be ridiculous. You're comparing your feelings to mine, and that's because you met the love of your life, old fellow. I was dashed fond of Millicent, and I admit *I hoped*… but it's not the same. I'm a little bruised about the edges, I admit, but not broken. I assure you. I'll live."

The comte did not look the least bit soothed by this information and so Barnaby shook his head and took his arm. "Come and get a drink and stop looking so wretched. We'll bring you champagne on our return, ladies," he added, before bearing his friend off in search of refreshments.

"Poor Barnaby, he's such a sweetheart," Evie said with a sigh. "Louis adores him."

Cara smiled. "That much is obvious."

Evie turned back to her, regarding her with interest. "I don't suppose you…?"

"Oh, no!" Cara said, holding her hands out. "Don't you dare start matchmaking now you're married."

"Spoilsport," Evie said with a sigh before waving at someone across the room. "Oh, do excuse me, Cara. I've just seen Eliza and Torie, I must speak to them."

Cara nodded and looked about the room, wondering where the guest of honour was. It was approaching midnight, and as far as she knew, there was still no sign of him.

"Lady Cara, you're looking delectable as always, I see."

Cara turned to smile at Lady Beauchamp, who greeted her warmly.

"Thank you, Lady Beauchamp."

"You remember Mrs Dankworth, of course," she added, gesturing to the lady holding her arm.

Cara nodded. "Of course I do. I'm very pleased to see you, Mrs Dankworth, and how is your great-nephew? You were worried about him the last time we spoke."

"Ah, sweet child. What a memory you have," the lady said, pleased that Cara had remembered. "He's in fine fettle, thanks be to God. His mama was in such a state and—"

"He's here!" hissed Lady Beauchamp, cutting into the conversation as a hush fell over the room. "Well, the wicked boy. He would turn up at midnight looking like the devil come to the feast."

Cara glanced at her, surprised by the delight in the woman's voice. Surely they had wanted to smooth the man's entrance into society, not create a scene? But then Mama had said the dowager Lady Latimer would make mischief, so perhaps not. She turned towards the entrance, standing on tiptoes to catch sight of the man but the crowd got in her way.

"Cara!"

Cara turned as her mother hurried over, her eyes sparkling with delight. "He *is* a pirate!" she said with undisguised glee. "Look!"

Tugging at her arm, she dragged Cara to a space in the centre of the room where they could see the man as the crowd parted before him like sheep scattering before a wolf. Cara's breath hitched.

"Oh, my," she murmured.

"See!" Mama said, squeezing her arm. *"Pirate!"*

"Pirate," Cara repeated, feeling a little dazed, for the man everyone was staring at did not look the least bit civilised.

He was the biggest man she had ever seen, saving perhaps Georgina's husband, the Duke of Rochford. This man was no duke. She doubted he was a gentleman at all, for he moved like no man she had ever seen in her life, like a predator, like he would knock down the first man who dared to tell him he was not welcome here. Her gaze travelled over him, over the thick dark hair, the intimidating slash of his eyebrows that gave him a rather sinister appearance. His nose had been broken more than once and his jaw looked to be made of granite, yet for all that, he was handsome, with a magnetic presence that drew every eye his way.

"Look at those shoulders," her mother said with obvious admiration. "And those arms. Good heavens. I bet he could pick us both up without blinking."

"Mama!" Cara protested.

"What? I'm married, not blind," her mother said with a laugh. "Your papa knows I adore him, and I'm only looking."

And Cara could not blame her. There was an odd, fluttery sensation deep in her belly, or perhaps it was lower than that, she realised with a jolt of embarrassment, but good lord, he was... was.... She could think of no adequate description other than... *what a man.*

Murmurs rippled through the crowd as his dark gaze scanned the assembly before him. In days gone by, he might have been a warrior king, but—dressed all in black, except for the snowy white of his cravat—he looked just like Mama had suggested, a pirate parading about in the guise of a gentleman. His expression was stony, a gleam in his eyes that invited them to judge him if they dared.

He stopped in the middle of the room, and suddenly Cara's heart went out to him, this man who stood all alone before society, while they all gawked at him like some captured wild thing, trapped in a cage for their entertainment. As she watched him, he turned his head, apparently looking for someone, and then....

All the air went out of Cara's lungs in a swift *whoosh* as his gaze settled on her. She swallowed, her heart skittering about behind her ribs like a frightened rabbit as his dark eyes widened a little. *Oh,* she thought, as she glimpsed something warm and gentle in the depths of that gaze. For the briefest moment, his lips twitched, and she thought that hard mouth might turn up at the corners, might smile—*at her*, but then....

"There you are, Latimer!" a crackly voice exclaimed, forcing his attention to the diminutive old lady who had planted herself in front of him. The difference in stature was comical as the big man stared down at his grandmother.

"Grandmother," he said, bowing respectfully.

A shiver ran over Cara's skin at the pleasant rumble of his voice, and she took a step closer, wanting to hear more of it.

"Well, you certainly made an entrance. I hope you're pleased with yourself, and there's me trying to persuade anyone who'll listen that you're a gentleman.

The viscount shrugged, and Cara watched his big shoulders roll with fascination. "They were expecting the devil himself from the rumours I've been hearing. I didn't want to disappoint them."

He sounded amused, bored even, but Cara felt uneasy, certain that he was not as sanguine as he made out.

"Don't sulk, boy," Lady Latimer said, as though the man towering over her was in short trousers. "What did you expect? They've heard all the stories about you. For all they know, you'll murder them in their beds if they give you an inch. Earn your place, if you want it. But if you're too afraid, you may turn around and leave the way you came. Then they'll know you for a coward, just like your father was."

Cara gasped, shocked that his grandmother should say such a thing. Her reaction must have been audible to him too, for he turned back to her again, the sharp glitter of fury in his eyes fading to something else, something sweeter... or perhaps she'd drunk too much punch for her own good.

"I thought you said I was afraid of nothing," he said, turning back to the dowager and quirking one dark eyebrow. "Make your mind up."

"You ought not be afraid of anything," the old woman said sharply. "Certainly not this crowd. You're a Latimer, by God, and before your father destroyed our name and our reputation, that meant something. Did your father never tell you our family motto?" she demanded.

Lord Latimer shook his head.

"No," she sneered, disgusted. "Of course not, for he failed on all counts. Well, for your information, it's *felis demulcta mitis.*"

"Gentle in peace, fearless in war," Cara said automatically, and then gasped as both the dowager and her grandson turned to look at her.

"Quite," Lady Latimer said with a satisfied nod. "Think you can live up to it, Latimer?"

Lord Latimer was quiet for a long moment, his heavy gaze lingering on Cara like a weight, making her skin hot and her breath come fast, but strangely, it was not in the least uncomfortable to be the focus of his attention. In fact, she was rather unsettled to realise… she liked him looking.

"I'm sure he can," she said, startling herself and her mama, whose grip tightened on her arm.

"Cara!" her mother whispered frantically.

Though she knew she ought not to have said it, she could not regret it when she saw the flare of heat and pleasure in his eyes. And then he smiled, and all Cara could think was… *Oh, Lord, what have I done now?*

"Well, what do you make of him?" Torie—Lady Victoria Adolphus—asked Cara once everyone had subsided and conversations had begun again.

Cara glanced over her shoulder, unable to shake the feeling she was being watched, though she could no longer see him through the crowd. "He's rather impressive," she murmured.

Torie nodded. "Yes, though I don't think Lord Latimer can be as bad as people make out, because Papa has met him before, and he's here, and he would never have come if the man was as dreadful as everyone says. He wouldn't let me within a hundred miles of him." She sighed.

"Your papa is rather overprotective," Cara said, smiling.

"That's what fathers are for," Mr Godwin said, as he returned from his quest for refreshments, handing them both a glass of lemonade.

"Oh, thank you," Torie said, taking her glass with relief. "And yes, I know they are, but Papa barely lets me out of his sight. Especially since Fred went gallivanting off to Paris all alone. As if I'd do that! Chance would be a fine thing," she added gloomily.

"Would you want to, then?" Mr Godwin asked in surprise.

Victoria thought about it for a moment. "No. Not alone, at least, though I should love to see Paris one day, but... Oh, I don't know, don't you ever wish something exciting would happen? Something out of the ordinary?"

Mr Godwin frowned. "Like what?"

Torie's expression lit up, her blue eyes brightening. "Like finding a treasure map and going on a quest, or... or solving a mystery, or finding a secret tunnel and following it to discover some long-lost relic."

Cara laughed at the appalled expression on Mr Godwin's face.

"Lady Victoria reads a lot of Gothic novels," she explained.

"Oh," Godwin replied, relieved. "That explains it, I suppose."

"Godwin."

Mr Godwin turned as a deep voice called his name and Cara's heart started crashing about as the sound sent shivers prickling over her.

"Lord Latimer, how do? How are you liking English society?" Mr Godwin said, as Latimer drew closer.

He made a derisive sound and opened his mouth to speak and then saw Cara. Whatever he would have said, she did not know, for he closed his mouth with a snap, his expression fixed on her. A tense silence ensued, with Mr Godwin and Torie exchanging glances as Cara felt a blush rise to her cheeks. She sent Mr Godwin a desperate look, jerking her head meaningfully.

"Oh!" he said, realising what she wanted, but then he hesitated, clearly uncomfortable introducing her to such a man.

"Get on with it," Cara whispered frantically.

Mr Godwin cleared his throat, obviously mortified, but stuck on how to get out of doing as she asked without offending her and insulting Lord Latimer, too. His lordship did not look like a man one insulted if one wanted a long and healthy life.

"Er… Lady Cara, Lady Victoria, may I introduce to you Wulfric De Vere, Viscount Latimer. Lord Latimer, Lady Victoria Adolphus and Lady Cara Baxter. She's the daughter of the Earl of Trevick," he added meaningfully, as if her father's name might protect her.

Cara and Torie curtsied, and Lord Latimer bowed politely to Lady Victoria, but took Cara's hand in his, his hold gentle as he bowed low and respectfully. Unable to tear her eyes from the image of her hand engulfed in his much larger one, Cara prayed he would not expect her to say anything, for her brain had melted.

"A pleasure," he said, that lovely rumble setting off another round of shivers as she forced her gaze from their joined hands to his eyes. Dark, his eyes were dark, rich like chocolate, velvety soft as they rested upon her. Such an intimidating, dangerous looking man he was, and yet Cara glimpsed something entirely different in those soulful eyes, something warm and gentle. Here was a man who would rescue a damsel in distress, a man she could trust. Which was patently a ridiculous thing to think, considering his reputation, but she could not shake the sensation, the feeling she knew this about him.

"Yes, pleasure," Cara murmured dazedly, barely aware of what she was saying, but needing to acknowledge that it was a pleasure for her, too.

Mr Godwin cleared his throat and, belatedly, Cara realised Lord Latimer was still holding her hand.

Godwin glared at his lordship, his expression fierce. Lord Latimer let go of her hand reluctantly, glowering a little at Mr Godwin in return.

"I think perhaps I ought to return you to the countess," Mr Godwin said, holding out his arm to Cara.

"Oh, no, Mama knows I'm fine," Cara objected, still ogling Lord Latimer in a way she did not doubt she would cringe over later, but which seemed entirely necessary at present.

She just wanted to drink in the sight of him, to revel in his presence. It felt like standing before the heat of a fire on a wintry day, though she could not understand why she reacted to him so fiercely. She had thought only of her wicked W for months now, and yet this man had stirred her up in ways she had never experienced before or believed possible.

"All the same," Mr Godwin protested, sounding increasingly anxious.

"Settle your feathers, Barnaby," Latimer said, though not unkindly. "I won't eat the lady. Too many witnesses," he added, a devilish glint in his eyes.

Cara snorted and then clapped a hand over her mouth in appalled shock. Honestly, he'd think she was a little nitwit if she kept gaping at him and making such unladylike noises for heaven's sake. He'd reduced her to acting like a silly child. Yet she seemed quite unable to stop herself, like there was something magnetic about him reeling her in.

"How was the journey from Paris, my lord?" Mr Godwin demanded, his voice remarkably fierce, forcing Lord Latimer to tear his gaze from Cara.

"Long," he replied, turning his attention back to Cara.

"Paris?" Cara queried, something flickering in the back of her mind. "You've come from Paris?"

All at once, the shutters came down, the warmth of his gaze vanished like a fire screen placed before the hearth. "Indeed," he said, his tone bored. "And my grandmother is making rude gestures at me, suggesting she wishes for my attention. If you would excuse me."

He was gone before Cara had even got used to the idea of him being there at all. If one *could* get used to such an overwhelming presence standing so close. She wasn't entirely sure it was possible.

Mr Godwin let out a breath of relief and rubbed a hand over his face. "Your father is going to murder me," he said, sounding wretched.

"Oh, poor Mr Godwin," Torie said sympathetically. "You really had no choice. Not with Cara glaring at you so furiously and him being the guest of honour, we are here to see him after all. Besides which, Lord Latimer is rather fierce."

Mr Godwin stiffened, obviously wounded by the implication he had been afraid to stand his ground.

"Oh!" Torie said, looking horrified. "I did not mean to suggest he frightened you. Not in the least, but you are always such a gentleman, and I know you would dislike making a scene at such an elegant event. And we do not really know Lord Latimer yet, or how he might react if you had slighted him by refusing the introduction."

Torie's cheeks blazed, her expression one of such distress that Cara's heart went out to her.

"I'm sure Mr Godwin thought nothing else," she said soothingly.

Torie did not look soothed. Instead, she turned a beseeching expression on him, laying her hand on his arm. "Did you, Mr Godwin?" she asked. "I truly meant no offence. Were you offended, though?"

Mr Godwin stared at the arm on his sleeve as if he'd never seen such a thing as a lady's hand or his sleeve in the same place before, and then he stared at Lady Victoria. "Of course not," he said, and then seemed to shake himself, as if waking from a dream. "I... I think I had better... I've just remembered... please excuse me, ladies."

Cara and Torie watched him go, bemused.

"Oh, and now he hates me," Torie moaned, burying her face in her hand.

"Nonsense. You just overwhelmed him a little, dearest. You are a duke's daughter, you know. Some men find that a little intimidating."

"No, I just put my foot in my mouth and rambled on about treasure maps and secret tunnels, and *oh,* why didn't you stop me!" she wailed.

Cara looked at her in surprise. "Torie?" she said, studying her friend's flushed face with interest. "Do you have a tendre for Mr Godwin?"

"No!" Torie replied at once, far too quickly. "Of course not."

Cara's lips twitched into a sympathetic smile. "Oh, love."

Torie set her empty lemonade glass down on the nearest surface before turning back to Cara and putting her chin up. "Please excuse me, Cara. I'm going to find the nearest lake and throw myself in it."

"As you like, dear," Cara said, her voice trembling with suppressed laughter. Well, at least she wasn't the only one acting like a besotted nitwit this evening. Sighing, she made her way through the crowd in search of her mother.

It was not until much later, as she finally collapsed into bed when the sky was growing lighter and dawn stole the night away, that she realised what the niggling feeling was that had so unsettled her.

Paris.

Lord Latimer had come from Paris.

But, no…. It was simply a coincidence. Tens of thousands of people lived in Paris, many of them must be Englishmen too, just because her wicked W — Cara's heart skipped.

His name was *Wulfric.* Wulfric De Vere, Viscount Latimer. The black sheep of the Latimer family.

She sat up in bed with a start, staring into the darkness.

Her wicked correspondent was an English gentleman. A disgraced English gentleman, living in Paris, and he had just gone away and....

Cara leapt out of bed, fumbling for her tinder box, and coaxed a flame so she could light a candle. The moment it was lit, she knelt beside her bed, tugging out a large box where she kept all her treasures, including the hundreds of letters from W. With shaking hands, she snatched up the last one she had received and unfolded it, scanning the page until she got to the bit she wanted.

> *Do not fret. I am quite safe and well, and only going on a little voyage. An adventure, I suppose, though I am uncertain what I hope to achieve. I have questions I wish to answer and a desire to discover things about my family and my past that have always puzzled me. Perhaps it will be a new beginning, or an ending, but if I do not find out, the questions will always plague me.*

"Oh, my," she said, gasping as she stared at the letter, wondering if she was being ridiculous, but... but then she remembered the look in his eyes when he had seen her tonight. He had looked so fierce, so proud and alone and... and *devilish,* until he had looked at her. At that moment, everything had changed. Then there had been warmth in his eyes, affection and... recognition.

"Oh my," she said again, giving a startled laugh and hugging the letter close to her, happiness and excitement expanding her heart until it overflowed, filling her chest with joy.

He was here. Her wicked W was here, in London. He was not Warren or Wilbur, Winter or Winston, he was Wulfric! Wulfric De Vere, Viscount Latimer.

"Wulfric," she said aloud, understanding now why she had been drawn to him so forcibly, why her heart had thundered, and her body had reacted so tangibly to his nearness.

It was *him*, her amiable lunatic, her wicked W, the man she had fallen in love with one letter at a time, and she was not about to let him get away.

Chapter 6

Dear Mr Godwin,

*Please forgive me for writing to you like this.
Of course, I am aware that is not at all the
done thing for an unmarried lady to write to a
gentleman, and I pray you will not think too
badly of me. It is only I was so mortified by
the idea I might have insulted you I did not
sleep a wink last night. I heard from Papa that
you are going to stay at Heart's Folly for a
while with the Comte and Comtesse de Villen
and I knew I would not have another chance
to speak to you for some time. I could not
leave things as they were. I simply had to let
you know I hold you in the highest esteem.*

*I know we have not spent a great deal of time
in each other's company, but I think you are
the kindest and most honourable gentleman I
have ever met. I was so touched when I heard
you had gone to France to help your friend,
the comte, and then to hear how you looked
after Miss Smith too, proves to me what kind
of man you are.*

*Well, now I don't doubt I have said too much,
and I shall dither for the next hour whether to*

put this letter in the post but, no. I must be brave and ensure that you do not believe I think of you with anything less than admiration.

—Excerpt of a letter from Lady Victoria 'Torie' Adolphus (daughter of Prunella and Robert Adolphus, Their Graces, The Duke and Duchess of Bedwin) to Mr Barnaby Godwin.

19th October 1844, Heart's Folly, Sussex.

Barnaby sat at the breakfast table at Heart's Folly, a letter of the kind he never in his wildest dreams expected to receive held in his hand. Unsurprisingly, he was the only person awake, though it was past ten o'clock. Louis was not an early bird, and since he was so obviously enamoured of his wife, Barnaby could hardly blame him for enjoying a leisurely morning.

He stared at the letter in consternation and sighed.

"By Jove," he muttered, not for the first time that morning, shaking his head. "By Jupiter."

"Good morning, Barnaby." A cheery voice cut through his jumbled thoughts as Miss Agatha blew into the room like a friendly zephyr, all bouncing dark curls and bright blue eyes.

"Good morning, Agatha," Barnaby replied, still distracted by the letter, his gaze falling to the words *kindest and most honourable* as colour rose to his cheeks.

"It's Aggie," Agatha said with a sigh as she piled her plate high with kedgeree. "Not Agatha. I keep telling you and I wish you would…. Whatever are you looking like that for? Did the kippers disagree with you?"

"Huh?" Barnaby said, having already lost the thread of the conversation.

"Oh, is it a love letter?" Agatha said, correctly interpreting the reason for his distraction. She ran to sit next to him, peering over his shoulder. "Do tell! Who is it from?"

"Mind your own beeswax, impertinent chit," Barnaby said, blushing harder and folding the letter back up.

"Aggie, are you tormenting poor Barnaby again? What have I told you, *mon enfant*?"

They both looked up to see Louis in the doorway wearing a thick silk robe. He smothered a yawn, looking rumpled and sleepy, and far more relaxed than Barnaby had ever seen him. Married life suited his friend very well, Barnaby noted with satisfaction.

"But he's got a love letter, Papa," Aggie said with a mischievous grin.

Louis' expression brightened with interest, and he walked into the room, dropped a kiss to Agatha's dark curls, and turned his dazzling blue eyes on Barnaby, who groaned inwardly. Now he was for it. It was dashed hard to keep anything from Louis.

"Is this true, *mon ami*? Have you an admirer?"

"Well, if I have, it's news to me," Barnaby said gruffly, reaching for his coffee. "It wasn't a love letter, if you must know. The lady was just clearing up a misunderstanding, that's all."

Louis poured a cup of coffee for himself and sat down, eyeing Barnaby with interest. "Agatha, what makes you think it was a love letter?"

"Because he was all pink-cheeked and couldn't take his eyes off it, like he couldn't believe it was real," she said, snorting with amusement as Barnaby sent her a reproachful glare.

"Such a tattletale," he grumbled.

"Agatha knows it is important to tell the truth, Barnaby," Louis said with a paternal air of approval. "It is something we have both learned, have we not, child?"

"*Oui,* Papa," Agatha said cheerfully, giving Barnaby a significant look of encouragement.

Louis' lips twitched as he too turned back to Barnaby and raised one dark eyebrow. Barnaby groaned and fished the letter back out of his pocket. Agatha brightened and Barnaby wagged a finger at her. "Not for your eyes, wicked girl. Here, if you must see it, but keep it to yourself. It's private," Barnaby said, handing it to Louis.

Louis tutted at him. "As if I would do anything else!"

"Oh, so you won't tell Evie?" Barnaby said dryly.

Blue eyes met his. "A fair point," Louis allowed. "I shall keep it to myself, word of honour."

Barnaby watched as Louis unfolded the letter and read, his smile becoming wider as he got to the end. "My, my, Barnaby, Agatha is quite correct. A love letter indeed."

"Oh, it isn't," Barnaby protested, even though the sentiments expressed were rather warmer than they needed to be if the lady was just ensuring he had not been offended.

Louis rolled his eyes. "Don't be a twit, Barnaby. You know the lady is expressing an interest in no uncertain terms. In fact, I would say that was an invitation to court her."

Barnaby shook his head. "No," he said firmly.

"No?" Louis looked at him in surprise. "The lady does not please you? She's very beautiful, and a sweet creature. I think you would suit very well."

"No." Barnaby repeated, glaring at his friend to ensure the point went home.

"But why?" Louis demanded in consternation. "I mean, I am not suggesting you rush out and marry her, but surely you ought to get to know her, spend a little time…"

"No!" Barnaby said again, rather too forcefully this time.

Louis sat back, surprised by the outburst. His gaze flicked to Agatha, who had devoured her plate of kedgeree and was watching the exchange with obvious interest.

"Ma puce, as you have inhaled your breakfast with such unbecoming zeal, would you mind taking a cup of chocolate up to Evie, *s'il te plaît?"*

Aggie huffed and got to her feet. "You just want me out of the way so you can talk," she grumbled.

"As ever, you are most perspicacious. Away with you," her papa said, watching as she dutifully poured the chocolate and left the room, rolling her eyes on the way. "Dreadful creature," Louis said fondly before turning his attention back to Barnaby.

"Explain yourself," Louis said once the door had closed behind her. "Why will you not even consider the lady?"

"Must I spell it out?" Barnaby said irritably. "Lady Millicent was out of my reach, and I knew it, but did I stay away? No. I expended a great deal of energy only to be rejected because I'm a younger son. I've no fancy title, nor any chance of inheriting one unless there's an apocalypse, and though I'm comfortable enough, I'm no duke or earl and that is what Milly needed. Her pa was set on her marrying up, and he was only a viscount. Lady Victoria is a duke's daughter, and so far above me I'd get vertigo even considering it."

Louis considered this for a long moment. "I understand your hesitation, and Bedwin is a formidable bridge to cross, however, I believe this differs from the situation with Lady Millicent."

Barnaby snorted and folded his arms. "How so?"

"Well, you were in pursuit of Lady Millicent."

"Oh, ho, me and every eligible bachelor in London," Barnaby retorted.

"Oui, exactly so. Her father is also a snob, from what I understand, and his daughter's happiness appeared to be of minor consideration. I have heard much of this man she is marrying, and he is thirty years her senior. The poor girl can hardly find much to celebrate there."

Barnaby's face darkened. "And so? I feel wretched that she's marrying some doddering old so and so, but he's an earl and rich as Croesus. What's that got to do with Lady Victoria?"

"Everything," Louis said simply. "I know Bedwin. He is unusual, certainly, especially for a duke, and his children's happiness is paramount. More to the point, his duchess would never allow their children to marry for position alone. No, Bedwin won't marry her to some old man when you're there, handsome and young, steady and good-hearted. Not if you are her choice."

Barnaby snorted, shaking his head at this description.

"I'm only twenty-six, I'll grant you, but steady and good-hearted don't count for much in a contest of this nature. You must take my word on this, Louis. *Nice* is not an attribute that wins fair maidens."

Louis tutted. "I beg to differ, especially if the lady has an ounce of sense, which I believe she does or she would not have written such lovely sentiments to you. Perhaps you would not be Bedwin's first choice, but you might remember Eliza is married to my brother. My *half*-brother."

Barnaby considered this for a moment and then shook his head. "No. It's no good. Once bitten, twice shy. Rich noblemen besiege Lady Victoria wherever she goes. I'm not about to make a cake of myself vying for another heiress. I'll get a reputation as a fortune hunter, and that I ain't and won't ever be."

"Well, of course not," Louis said, clearly exasperated now. "But the young woman has put her pride, not to mention her reputation, on the line by writing to you, and such an intimate letter. You cannot ignore that, for I think she more than admires you, Barnaby. I should say she's smitten."

"Who's smitten?"

Both men looked around as Evie came into the room, her gaze curious. She looked radiant, dressed in a beautiful gown of deep green that brought out the colour of her eyes. Louis' expression softened when he saw her and he held out his hand to her, drawing her close. "Barnaby has sworn me to secrecy, *mon amour*, but I believe he might permit me to tell you, he is admired."

"Well, I should think he is, any young lady ought to count her lucky stars to marry such a man," Evie said, with apparent sincerity, startling Barnaby so much he did not know which way to look.

"Well, I… I say, that's… dashed nice of you to say so, Madame…."

"Oh, no, don't be formal, Barnaby, we're friends. Evie is fine, and I'm not being nice, I'm being honest. Whoever she is, I should say she's a very sensible young woman."

"There, you see, my lady has spoken, and she is never wrong," Louis said, tugging Evie so she fell into his lap with a squeal.

"Louis!" she protested. "You're embarrassing Barnaby."

"Oh, no," Barnaby said, getting to his feet and feeling very much *de trop* in the circumstances. "I was going to pop out, anyway. Stretch my legs. What time is Lord Latimer arriving?"

"He'll be here for dinner," Louis said, smiling at Barnaby with amusement. "And I insist that the two of you make friends. I cannot have two of the people I love best in the world growling at each other."

"I do not growl," Barnaby protested. "He's the one doing all the growling. I've tried to be amicable, I assure you."

"We know," Evie said hastily, elbowing Louis and giving him a look. "It's Wolf, we both know it."

Louis sighed. "I suppose so, but he is truly not as he appears."

"Well, good, because he looks like he wants to bite my head off whenever I open my mouth," Barnaby said, huffing.

"He's just a bit jealous," Evie soothed. "I think he's missed Louis these past years, and then to discover he has made such a dear friend in his absence... well, it's rather put his nose out of joint. I believe he's been very lonely. We really need to find him a wife," she added, turning back to Louis, who nodded.

"Oui certainement," he said, his expression thoughtful. "We must find them *both* wives."

"Oh, no," Barnaby wagged a warning finger at Louis, narrowing his eyes. "No, you don't. I congratulate you both on being so happily settled, but I will thank you for keeping your meddling confined to Lord Latimer's affairs. You can matchmake him to your heart's content, just leave me out of it."

"Such ingratitude," Louis called after him as Barnaby hurried out, closing the door behind him.

Wolf locked up the house in Carlton Gardens, reflecting that he didn't know why he bothered. It wasn't like there was anything to steal. He really needed to get the place put to rights, but until he knew whether there was any point in staying, he did not know how to go about it.

Picking up the small suitcase he'd packed, Wolf strode off, heading for London Bridge Station. It was a fair walk, a good forty minutes, but he wanted to stretch his legs and sitting in a cramped carriage did not appeal.

Louis had invited him to Heart's Folly for a few days and Wolf was looking forward to a decent bed, a hot bath, and a bit of civilisation. He was still smarting a little after the party his grandmother had thrown for him. Whilst he understood he must earn his place in society, if they'd even allow him to try, her blunt speech had shocked him. Foolish of him, to consider the old woman might have any affection for him, knowing how she had hated his father, but still, he admitted to being a little disappointed. Though he supposed he *had* been sulking rather, turning up at midnight like he had and glowering at everyone. But he'd heard all the rumours flying about him and they'd sounded like they expected Satan and his imps to come barrelling through the door and start sacrificing virgins. It had irritated him into behaving badly, and he'd had every intention of giving them the spectacle they'd come for. He'd been all set to create chaos and head back to France on the next boat, and then he'd seen *her*.

Or rather, she'd seen him.

He had expected her to turn away once their eyes met. He had expected her to gasp and hide behind her mama. But why? Why had he expected that, when the woman who wrote those funny, prickly, wonderfully entertaining letters was so bold and alive? Perhaps because so many people looked at him and judged who he was before he even opened his mouth. They expected a brute and a devil, and he rarely had the chance to show them otherwise. But Cara… Cara had *seen* him. He was sure of it, and he had longed to tell her there and then, wanted so badly to tell her who he was, but… but he ought not think of her at all, let alone drag her into his life when he would only dirty her reputation. He must keep away from her, at least until he could find his place among these judgemental snobs, assuming that was even possible. After his performance at the party, he had not made the best first impression. Still, he had behaved himself after his dramatic entrance and, whilst people had not fallen over themselves to speak to him, he had not been given the cut direct. Yet. So perhaps there was hope for him.

An odd prickling sensation crackled up the back of his neck and Wolf slowed for a moment, turning to look behind him, but the streets were busy this morning and, if anyone was following him, there were plenty of opportunities for staying hidden. Still, he'd not lived this long by ignoring his instincts and he carried on walking, his nerves all on alert.

Cara wondered if she had lost her mind, but she hurried on, Sultan's lead clutched in one hand, the dare she had taken from the infamous hat held tightly in the other. She kept glancing at it, hoping it would give her courage. Her mother and her friends had all taken dares, and they'd all married happily, so... Her heart skipped again, and she raised the crumpled bit of paper once more, staring at the writing.

Dare to chase the wildest of dreams.

Sultan whined, turning back to look at her, and Cara realised she'd stopped in her tracks in the middle of the bustling street.

"Don't go giving me those big puppy dog eyes," she said as Sultan sent her a mournful gaze. "I'm no doubt in enough trouble, and you just cost me a fortune. I mean, I know you like cheese, but really, did you have to swipe such an enormous chunk off that market stall, you wretched creature?"

"Woof!" Sultan replied softly, his head down, aware he was in disgrace.

"Oh!" she exclaimed, looking up to see Lord Latimer had turned the corner ahead of them and disappeared out of sight. "Oh, drat it. Now we've lost sight of my lovely lunatic, and he's got a suitcase! What if he's going away and I never get another chance to speak to him?" she demanded of the dog, who wagged his tail sheepishly.

"Woof!" he said, tail wagging with excitement as Cara picked up her skirts and ran after her wicked W.

"Well, let's hope you're right but, if he's heading for the train station, I won't have long and… and oh, I've so much to say to him! Oh, come along, we must hurry. He's getting away from us."

Cara decided her dare had been very specific about *chasing* her dreams, and so ignored every rule of propriety and ran full tilt in pursuit of the man she had dreamed of for so long. Sultan bounded happily at her side as she prayed no one recognised her. A young lady did *not* run, but most especially not a young lady in mourning.

In fact, a young lady in mourning for her grandmother ought to be sitting at home with no entertainment at all, going quietly out of her mind. Well, to the devil with that. Especially when the person she was supposed to be mourning was a wicked old woman who had made her darling papa utterly miserable. Cara was certain the nasty creature had died the night of the party expressly to ruin her life. It was the sort of thing she *would* do, for she'd conspired with the old earl to keep her mama and papa apart, though she knew they loved each other dearly, and now, the moment Cara set eyes on the love of her life, the horrid woman went and died! It was just too much to be borne. Thankfully, Cara had got out of the house on the pretext of walking Sultan, and Thomas was meeting his sweetheart and so… she had come directly to the address she'd discovered belonged to Viscount Latimer, only to discover the house had been closed up. She had turned around in despair, just in time to see him striding away, suitcase in hand. What else was she to do but follow him?

Oh, but she was going to be in trouble for disappearing for hours. Never mind that. She would just have to blame poor Sultan and say he slipped his lead, and she had to chase him all over London. It wouldn't be the first time.

By the time they got to London Bridge Station, Cara was hot and flustered and very out of breath and… and she'd lost him.

"Oh, no!" she cried, turning in a circle, scanning the crowds, but there was no sign of... "Oh!" she shrieked, as the man himself appeared before her as if he'd stepped out of a puff of smoke.

"What the devil are you playing at?" he demanded, looking so cross and fierce that for a moment her courage failed her

She took a step back in fright, but then she remembered just who this was, and threw herself into his arms.

"It's you!" she cried, staring up at him, clutching at his lapels, uncaring that they were standing in a busy public place. This was destiny. This was true love. This was... well quite probably very ill advised, but she didn't care. "Don't deny it. I know it is. I just know it. You're my wicked W, my amiable lunatic. It *is* you, isn't it?" she demanded desperately.

The fierce expression disappeared, and that soft look came into his eyes that made her brain melt and her knees turn to blancmange. "You'd best hope so, you addled creature, or you've just made a rather terrible mistake," he said wryly.

"It is you!" she squealed, jumping up and down with delight.

"Hush, Cara, for heaven's sake, you'll ruin yourself if anyone sees," he said, glancing around them before taking hold of her hand and towing her along behind him, out of sight. He drew her behind a trolley piled high with baggage and then stared down at her, as though he could hardly believe she was real. His dark brows tugged together as he noted her attire.

"Why are you all in black? What's happened?" he asked, such concern in his expression her heart did a giddy little leap behind her ribs.

"Oh, for my grandmother," she said impatiently, not wanting to waste their limited time talking about her. "She was a mean old witch, please disregard it. It's the merest lip service, I assure you. We're all delighted."

He gave a startled laugh at her appalling frankness but, unlike most gentlemen who encountered Cara's particular brand of honesty, he looked amused rather than shocked. But then his eyes grew serious, and he shook his head.

"What on earth do you think you're doing, following me about?" he asked her, his voice gentle now.

"What did you expect me to do?" she demanded. "I worked it out the night of the party. I knew… I just knew there was something, I felt it. Didn't *you*?" she added desperately, suddenly panicked, wondering if this feeling was one-sided, if perhaps she had imagined the way he'd looked at her.

But there it was again, that look in his eyes that made her want to throw caution to the wind and follow him anywhere he wanted to go. Tentatively, he reached out a hand and touched her cheek, such reverence in his expression that her breath caught.

"Cara," he said, his voice heavy with regret. "Cara, I…."

"Oh!" Cara yelped as her arm gave a sudden jolt and the lead she'd wrapped about her wrist dragged over her hand and jerked free. With a joyous bark of delight, Sultan took off in hot pursuit of a large ginger cat.

"Oh, Sultan!" Cara yelled in frustration. "Sultan, get back here this instant!"

Sultan ignored her.

"Good Lord, haven't you trained that wretched beast yet? Wait here," Wulfric told her and ran after Sultan.

Cara, who was not about to let either of them out of her sight ever again, followed.

Chapter 7

Dear Agatha,

I am going to have an adventure of my own. So there. And if you tell anyone — especially Fred — I shall never speak to you again.

I am going to go to the Egyptian Museum in Piccadilly. There's an exhibition of a talking machine which I simply must see! But it closes on Friday, and I am "in disgrace" again.

Papa is very cross with me because I told the Misses Leominster that they were lying toads. Which is grossly unfair because they are liars and very toad-like too — do not tell me you don't agree. But they would insist that Lord Kilbane was an occultist and quite mad, which is ridiculous. His brother, the one that died, was mad by all accounts but Kilbane is as sane as you or I. But they were telling these whopping great lies and vile stories about him, just to entertain their stupid friends who were all squealing with delight, naturally. Honestly, I was so cross I was tempted to throw my lemonade in their faces. But I did not. I resisted temptation and only said what was perfectly true. So why is it I am in disgrace when they were the ones in the wrong? It is most unfair, and now I shall miss the talking machine which I was longing to see. But I am determined that those horrid girls will not spoil it for me. I shall go anyway. You just see if I don't.

—Excerpt of a letter from Lady Catherine 'Cat' Barrington (daughter of Lucian and Matilda Barrington, The Most Hon'ble Marquess and Marchioness of Montagu) to Miss Agatha de Montluc (adopted daughter of Louis César and Evie de Montluc, Comte et Comtesse de Villen).

19th October 1844, London Bridge Station, London.

The blasted dog could move that was for sure. Wolf tucked his suitcase under his arm and hurtled after him. Sultan left the public areas in hot pursuit of the cat, and Wolf cursed as the dog headed for the far platform, where a goods train was being loaded. The conductor was walking up and down the platform and looked as if he was almost ready to wave the train off, which naturally meant the wretched dog chased the cat directly into one of the carriages. Well, at least he had the ridiculous creature cornered now.

The car was loaded with boxes and crates and what looked like wrapped bolts of fabric, with only a narrow aisle running down the centre. Furious barking came from the far end of the carriage.

"Oh, Sultan! You wicked boy!"

Wolf turned, exasperated to see Cara had followed despite his instruction to stay put, and was squeezing down the aisle after him… a difficult feat considering the width of her skirts and petticoats.

"Stay there," Wolf commanded her as he set down his suitcase and put his hat atop it before moving slowly towards the dog.

"Oh, but you'll frighten him," she said, shaking her head, inching forward anyway. "He can be funny with men."

"I'll manage. Do you have a treat for him?"

"Yes, cheese, like you suggested," she replied with a smile, tugging a small bundle from her pocket and unwrapping a handkerchief to reveal some cubes of hard cheese. "Here. Though he snaffled an enormous piece of cheese from a stall on the way here, so he might not be as delirious about accepting it as he usually is."

Wolf muttered under his breath about badly behaved dogs and edged closer. Sultan had cornered the cat who was wedged in a narrow space between two crates and was yowling and hissing unhappily.

"Sultan," Wolf said, his voice firm but kindly. "Here, boy."

He held the cheese out. The dog glanced over his shoulder at him suspiciously, growled, and turned his attention back to the cat.

"Sultan. Come here, boy," Wolf said, trying to sound encouraging.

Sultan growled again.

"You see! Oh, do let me," Cara said, trying to push past him in the confined space.

Wolf gasped, shocked to his bones as her hands went to his waist to steady herself while she eased through the narrow gap, her body too close to his, and then everything happened at once. The cat hissed and swiped at Sultan, who yelped and backed up hastily into Wolf, pushing him off balance. The cat exploded from between the crates and shot from the carriage like a bullet, with Sultan leaping up and scrambling over the boxes in pursuit before flying out of the door after the cat. Wolf had greater problems, though, as he tried to find his equilibrium, but Cara was clinging to him, pushing him farther off balance. He went down with a crash and Cara followed with a squeal and a flurry of petticoats.

For a taut moment, Wolf could not breathe, could not move. His brain had frozen, his body rigid with shock, stunned into immobility at the feel of the woman he had dreamed of for the past two years plastered against him. Cara's lithe body covered his, touching in all the most interesting places as her warmth seeped through his clothes. Their eyes met and for that fraction of a second, time stood still. Wolf wanted it to stay that way, too.

Before either of them could say a word, there was a shrill whistle from outside, and the door to the train car slid shut with a loud bang.

"Oh, no," Cara exclaimed, scrambling up and inadvertently kneeing Wolf in the bollocks.

He sucked in a sharp breath and held back a curse of pain as she ran to the door and tried to tug it open. When that didn't work, she pounded on the door with her fist.

"Help, *help*! We're in here, let us… *oh!"* she cried, stumbling and sitting hard on her backside as the train jerked into motion. She turned to stare at Wolf, who groaned. "Oh, dear," she murmured.

"Now it all becomes clear," he muttered, his voice strained, once he could speak again without squeaking.

"What becomes clear?" she demanded, sounding rather indignant.

"How you are always falling into streams or lakes or getting yourself into trouble."

"Well, it's not my fault," she retorted, folding her arms.

"It is, for you've not trained that dog to behave as he ought."

A flash of irritation glittered in her blue eyes, visible even in the dim light of the carriage. "Well, I've done my best," she said with a huff, tugging irritably at the ribbons of her bonnet and casting it aside as if it had offended her. "And recently he's been a perfect gentleman, but when he sees a cat, it all goes out the window."

Wolf sighed and got to his feet, brushing the dust off his clothes. "He's young yet," he allowed. "Does he know enough to make his way home?" he asked, knowing how devastated she'd be if the dog got lost.

Cara nodded. "He's run off in the past and made it back, but all the same," she gave a dejected sigh. "Oh, it will frighten the poor darling when he discovers he's all alone, and if he does go home without me, Mama and Papa will be in a dreadful tizzy... Oh, drat and bother. I shall be in such trouble. *Again,*" she added mournfully.

Wolf's heart went out to her. She looked so dejected. He moved towards her and reached down, taking hold of her arms to help her up, startled when he discovered she was lighter than he expected, and he had pulled too hard. She stumbled towards him and clutched at his lapels to steady herself.

"This is where we began," she said, gazing up at him with an endearingly crooked smile.

"So it is," he replied, too aware of her closeness, of the delicate perfume that teased his senses, making him want to get closer, to press his face to the soft skin of her neck and inhale.

"Where do you think the train is going?" she asked, sounding a little breathless, never taking her eyes from his.

"I don't have a clue."

He didn't much care, either. Cara was in his arms, *his* Cara, and she was looking at him as if he'd hung the moon. No one had ever looked at him that way before. He almost laughed. Well, they wouldn't, would they? Not when he was the villain. The reminder was a timely one.

"Cara," he said, his tone regretful, but he had no chance to say what he needed to say, to tell her they could not be friends, let alone anything more, because just as he had steeled himself to say the words he did not want to speak aloud, she stood on tiptoe and pressed her mouth to his.

It only lasted a moment and then she drew back, her eyes wide and startled, as though she could not believe she'd just done such a reckless thing. Well, she was in good company there.

Wolf's breathing hitched, desire slamming into him with the force of a runaway train.

"You ought not," he began, but she silenced him again, pressing her mouth to his, a little more forcefully this time, and for longer.

Her eyes were still closed as she pulled away and her tongue darted out, wetting her lips as if seeking the taste of him. The sight sent a bolt of lust arrowing directly to his groin, and he bit back a groan.

"Cara," he said desperately. "You've really got to stop doi—"

But she didn't stop, she kissed him again. God knew Wolf was no angel, and there was only so much temptation a man could bear. He slid his arms around her, pulling her close, and kissed her back. He kissed her as he'd dreamt of kissing her, teasing her mouth open until he could slide his tongue inside and taste her.

She made a startled sound of surprise but, rather than pull back, she pressed closer, following his lead eagerly and demanding more. He was only too happy to oblige, his hands gliding up and down her back, circling her narrow waist. Wolf was just getting started when she pulled away, gasping, a hand to her chest.

"Oh. Oh, my, I… I can't breathe," she said, sitting down heavily.

Thankfully, there was a box directly behind her or Wolf suspected she'd have hit the ground with a thud. Her poor bottom would be black and blue if she kept that up, and then he decided it would be better for his sanity if he avoided thinking about her bottom.

"My word, you really are good at that," she said, staring up at him in wonder.

Wolf tried not to preen, reminding himself sternly that she was an innocent, and he... well, he most certainly was not.

"I just need to catch my breath for a moment," she said, fanning herself with her hand. "Then we can try again. There must be a way of breathing and kissing at once. I just need to learn the knack of it," she added thoughtfully.

"Oh, good Christ, stop!" he exclaimed as his heart gave an overexcited thud behind his ribs.

"What?" she said, gazing at him, the picture of innocence.

"You must not say such things, nor go around kissing men you don't know. Especially men like me. You only met me five minutes ago!" he said, raking a hand through his hair in frustration.

"No, I didn't," she objected.

He cursed and rolled his eyes. "Very well, a few days ago, but that hardly counts, we barely spoke and—"

"We met two years ago," she interrupted. She did that a lot, he realised, either with kisses or words. "When you sent me that ridiculous letter. Whatever possessed you to do such a thing, anyway?"

She was staring at him now, and Wolf could not help but gaze back. He shrugged, a little embarrassed now that he'd done such a thing as steal Evie's letter, even though he'd confessed to it so long ago.

"I don't know. Evie was talking about you, and I liked the way she spoke of you, and the fact you had a Great Dane. I thought... I thought you might be someone I'd like to know."

"I'm glad you did, you great lunatic," she added, and with such affection that a strange melancholy ache began in his chest. It wasn't quite pain, but more… longing.

He shook his head, and she drew in a sharp breath.

"You regret it?"

"No!" he said at once. "No, of course not. At least, not on my part, but good grief, Cara, can you not see how much trouble you are in? We've no idea where this train will stop or if we will even get you back home before nightfall. Not only that, but you're with *me*. If anyone saw us together, you're ruined. If anyone sees us together wherever we end up, you're ruined. And if, God forbid, we can't get you home before morning—"

"Yes, yes, I'm as ruined as ruined can be," she said, rolling her eyes at him. "There aren't degrees of ruination, you know, you daft creature. It's all or nothing."

Wolf rubbed a hand over his face and sighed. He sat down on the crate beside her. "I don't want to mess your life up," he said softly, slanting a sideway look at her.

She leaned into him and rested her head on his shoulder. "You couldn't. You haven't. You're the most wonderful thing that ever happened to me."

He snorted at that, incredulous that this glorious, gorgeous girl could possibly say such a thing about him.

"And you think I'm a lunatic?" he demanded. "You're soft in the head, you are."

"No, I'm not. I'm perfectly sane and reasonable. It's everyone else that's daft. I mean, who could resist falling in love with a pirate?"

Wolf jolted, staring at her. "Wait. What? What did you say?"

Cara laughed. "Well, Mama insisted you were a pirate, and I must admit when you strode into your grandmother's house glaring at everyone and all in black, I did think—"

"Not that bit!" he protested, turning towards her, his heart beating so fast he felt giddy.

"Then what... Oh," she said, and the colour rose to her cheeks in a dramatic rush, startling against her pale skin. "I didn't mean to say that," she admitted, giving a nervous laugh.

Wolf told himself to calm down. Obviously, it was a mistake. Of course it was a mistake, a slip of the tongue. She hadn't meant to say that because she didn't mean it. She couldn't possibly mean it.

"No," he said, his voice too gruff. "No, of course not. I shan't regard it. I knew you didn't mean it that way, of course, I—"

"What? Oh, I meant it," she grasped his arm, interrupting him again. "Of course I meant it."

Wolf stared at her, astonished. "You did?"

His voice sounded odd to his own ears, uncertain and disbelieving.

She nodded, struggling to hold his gaze, looking down and then up again from under thick amber lashes. "Yes, I... I just didn't mean to tell you yet. In case I frightened you away."

Too many thoughts tumbled through his mind, emotions rising inside him in a great tangled web he hadn't a hope of sorting through. All he knew was he wanted her, but he did not want to hurt her, to damage her, and being with him would likely estrange her from the world she knew. They would cast her out, like they had cast out his mother, and he could not bear that for her.

"There, see? I have frightened you," she said, her voice sad as she studied his face.

Wolf shook his head. "Cara, I can't. I don't know if I can find a place for myself here, but the chances are I'll never be welcome in society. There's no future for us, you must see that. You'd be lowering yourself, getting involved with a known criminal, you don't understand what—"

"I understand you," she said, not letting him finish as usual, and pressed her mouth to his.

Wolf closed his eyes, enchanted by her, beguiled by her words, by her nearness and the touch of her lips. Nothing had ever tasted so sweetly innocent, so devastatingly pure as her kiss, as the precious words she had given so earnestly, and it wrecked him, breaking apart the walls that he'd surrounded himself with for so long, shattering every defence and leaving him exposed and vulnerable.

A deep woof from the carriage ahead of theirs had Cara pulling back, her eyes widening with delight.

"Sultan!" she exclaimed happily, completely oblivious to what she'd done to the man before her. "He's on the train!"

Chapter 8

Dear Lady Victoria,

Thank you for your letter which I received this morning. I am honoured to be the recipient of such generous praise, if an undeserving one.

I beg that you will not give the matter another thought. I am not the least bit offended.

I send you and yours the heartiest of best wishes.

Yr obt svt.

B Godwin.

—Excerpt of a letter from Mr Barnaby Godwin to Lady Victoria Adolphus (daughter of Robert and Prunella Adolphus, Their Graces, The Duke and Duchess of Bedwin).

19th October 1844, on a goods train. Somewhere.

Cara regarded Wulfric cautiously as the train rumbled on to an unknown destination. He was staring into the distance, his head braced on one hand. He'd been awfully quiet for some time now. When Sultan was quiet, it usually meant he was up to no good, like chewing one of her slippers or making a bed out of her second-best cloak. She could not help but think this was a little the same, except her lovely lunatic was destroying his peace of mind.

"Stop that," she said, aware she sounded imperious and not caring.

He jumped a little, turning on the crate he was sitting on to look at her. "I wasn't doing anything," he said, looking indignant.

"Yes, you were. I know you. You were sitting there reproaching yourself for writing letters to me; for getting me mixed up with a notorious, black-hearted villain; for the fact we're sitting on this train on the way to heaven knows where."

His scowl deepened, and he sat up straighter. "I was not."

"Pfft. However have you survived this long as a criminal? You're a terrible liar," she said, shaking her head.

He snorted, folding his muscular arms so the material of his coat strained across his biceps in the most fascinating way. "Shows what you know, because I'm an excellent liar. Second to none, actually. If there were awards for lying, I'd a have a cabinet full of gleaming trophies. Those big, heavy silver ones with two handles and inscriptions with the date on."

"You are the most ridiculous man," she said fondly.

"Now, you stop *that!*" he said sternly, pointing a finger at her.

"What?"

He wagged the finger a bit more. "That… That tone. You know the one."

Cara gazed at him blankly. "I promise you, I do not."

He huffed. "It's your affectionately teasing tone. I bet you use it on Sultan all the time."

She considered this. "Yes, you're right, of course. I do. Don't you like it?"

Wulfric crossed his arms tighter. Really, he must be putting a tremendous strain on his seams. She hoped his tailor was a good one.

"Of course, I like it," he grumbled. "Which is why you must stop it. It's too… intimate. It'll come to no good."

"See, I *knew* you were wallowing in guilt!" she said triumphantly. "And I can only think that your definition of 'no good' and mine are vastly different."

He sighed. "I just know I am going to regret this, but… in what way are they different?"

She held her arms out, gesturing to their surroundings. "Just look where we are."

One dark eyebrow quirked. "Stuck in a train carriage en route to god knows where. You're probably ruined, and the dog we were trying to recapture is in the next carriage. Yes, that definitely sums up 'no good' to me," he said dryly.

She threw up her hands, exasperated by his lack of imagination. "That's because you are looking at this all wrong. I admit the circumstances might be a little… *trying,"* she said, ignoring his snort of outrage. "But we're having an adventure, and I say we should make the most of it and have some fun."

"Fun?" he repeated, looking so bewildered by the idea she laughed.

"Yes, fun! And it will be fun because you're with me. I usually have adventures with Sultan—inadvertently, to be sure— but they can be rather difficult because I must get out of trouble all by myself. But I feel safe with you, Wulfric, and I'm so glad you're here."

"You are a very long way from safe, Cara, and it strikes me you have far too many adventures. I live in constant terror of discovering you've fallen into something you can't get out of."

Cara frowned as he continued to stare at her, something in his eyes she couldn't read.

"What?"

He looked away, picking a stray dog hair from his trousers. "You called me Wulfric."

Oh. "Don't you like it?"

He shrugged. "Everyone calls me Wolf."

A slow smile curved over her lips. He glanced back at her and then his gaze held, his eyes warming at her reaction.

"Wolf," she repeated softly. "Oh, I like that. My wicked Wolf, who's really rather a lamb."

She laughed as he made a sound of disgust, glowering at the floor of the carriage.

"It's true," she insisted, daring to shift a little closer to him so that their arms and legs touched. She leaned into him, one hand braced on his shoulder as she whispered in his ear. "You're a lamb in wolf's clothing."

He turned his face towards her, and they were so close, his breath fluttered over her skin, making her shiver with the desire to close the distance.

"I'm no lamb, Cara," he warned, his eyes growing dark. "And I don't want to hurt you, but you'll get hurt, love. If you get mixed up with me, you'll—"

Too impatient to let him speak any further nonsense, she pressed her mouth to his. His breath hitched as she dared to touch his lips with her tongue. One arm slid around her waist, pulling her closer as his hand came up to cup her face, his touch gentle as he stroked her cheek. His kisses were soft, teasing, endlessly patient as he taught her how this was supposed to be, the slide and parry of their tongues. This time, she did not forget to breathe, though how she was supposed to think of anything so mundane when she was this close to him was beyond her. He was so solid and warm, and she wanted to snuggle into him and bury her face against all that... that wonderful *maleness*. Desperate to get nearer, she shifted onto her knees on the crate. Oh, that was better, like this she could look down at him. She stroked his thick hair back from his face as he stared up at her, his big hands circling her waist.

"You have the most beautiful eyes," she said, getting lost in their velvet darkness.

"They're just brown," he said with a huff, as if that was as ordinary as eyes could get.

She tsked. "No, they're not. At least, not *just* brown. They're flecked with gold and amber and bronze. Beautiful," she whispered, and then leaned down and kissed his nose, which had clearly been broken a time or two. It gave his face strength and character. "You're beautiful."

"You're barmy," he said, but there was a strange note to his voice, and such wanting in his eyes, her heart ached. Had no one ever said such things to him before?

"I'm perfectly sane," she said with a sniff, putting up her chin. *"You're* the lunatic."

"I hear the capital letters when you speak, did you know that? And the underlining and the explosions of punctuation."

"And how about a dramatic pause...?" she asked, her lips hovering over his.

"Those are pure torture," he groaned, sliding a hand behind her neck and pulling her mouth to his.

Cara wrapped her arms about his neck, kissing him frantically, plundering like she was the pirate and he her captive, and she liked the idea so much she gave a little moan. Wolf echoed the sound a moment later, his hands dropping to her bottom, cupping her through too many layers of petticoats and skirts, oh, and she wanted more. She broke the kiss, wanting to demand he give her what she wanted, but she did not know how to ask. Instead, she moved, clumsily trying to straddle his thick thighs.

"Christ! Cara… No! No," he said firmly, picking her up and putting her back down on the crate. He walked away from her, leaning back on the farthest wall of the carriage, breathing hard, his face set in hard lines.

"What's wrong? What did I do? Did I do something wrong?" she demanded anxiously, bewildered and hurt that he had set her aside.

His fierce expression melted into something tender and frustrated and he shook his head. "No, of course not. You couldn't, but… this is not what you want, love."

Cara pulled a face, rather infuriated by that answer. Arrogant devil. "How can you know what I want better than I do? And I assure you, I was very much getting what I wanted, and I was about to get a bit more, until you put me aside like a half-eaten sandwich."

"A half-eaten sandwich?" he repeated in disgust, wrinkling his nose.

"Yes, the kind with fish paste that nobody likes," she grumbled, folding her arms.

"Fish paste? Whatever—" He shook his head, holding up one hand to stop her from explaining further. "Don't be daft, woman! Good grief, you are the most exasperating—"

"You put me aside!" she insisted. "Why? You liked kissing me too! Didn't you?" she added, suddenly uncertain, because what did she know about men? She'd been kissed precisely two times. Neither experience had been the least bit like kissing Wolf and, if he kissed like that, it was because he knew a good deal about kissing and… *other things,* and….

"Stop being a little nitwit!" he said, throwing his hands up. "If you'd actually let me finish a sentence, I might—"

"I am not a nitwit!" she retorted, stung.

Wolf turned his back on her and leaned his head against the wall of the carriage with a tortured groan.

"Save me," he murmured., which was apparently an appeal to God, or whatever pagan deity a man called Wolf might worship instead.

Either way, it was not terribly flattering.

Cara waited, simmering impatiently but doing her best to look calm and unruffled, despite having been thoroughly ruffled. She desperately wanted to persuade him to ruffle her a good deal more, but she sat stoically, arms folded, back straight as he hauled in a deep breath and turned around.

"You're everything I could possibly dream of, Cara," he said, his voice soft, and she abandoned her stiff pose at once in favour of gazing at him adoringly. She must look like Sultan eyeing the Sunday roast. "You're every birthday and Christmas and sunny day rolled into one glorious package. I've wanted nothing like I want you in all my life. But you deserve to be loved by a man who won't bring you and your family shame, a man who can marry you and give you everything that you want at the *appropriate* time—on your wedding night, for instance—not in a train carriage, for heaven's sake, and that's not me."

"Oh," she said, all the air leaving her lungs in a rush as the beauty of his words sank into her heart. "Oh, Wolf. What a lovely thing to say, only—and forgive me for pointing it out at such a moment—but there's one teeny tiny thing you got wrong."

He gave a snort and rubbed a weary hand over his face. "You astonish me. Go on, then."

"You are quite right I deserve to be loved, but neither society, nor my family, should have the deciding vote. If people look at you and think I should be ashamed, they're simply wrong-headed idiots with cheese for brains, and I want nothing to do with them. I wish to be loved by the man of *my* choosing, and I choose you. That is… if you want me too," she added magnanimously, for he sounded as if he wanted her very much, but one ought not take things for granted.

"You don't know what you're saying," he said, his voice gruff, though that longing look was back in his eyes.

Cara got to her feet and walked towards him. "I do. I know very well."

"No, Cara, stay over there," he said, making desperate shooing motions. "I can't think when you're near me. You make me insane. I'll do something I ought not, and—"

"I can't wait," she said, smoothing her hands up over his chest, sliding her arms about his neck, and tugging his head down.

He groaned and kissed her again, his arms banding around her, pulling her flush against him, so close she could feel the shape of his arousal, hard and demanding against her softness, making her impatient to discover more of this magnificent man. She pressed her hips closer, and he made a harsh sound that seemed to tug at her core, her insides turning hot and liquid as she took his kisses and asked for another and another, and *oh, yes, please don't stop.*

She was dazed, overwhelmed and hungry for more, for him and for this intoxicating feeling. He smelled so good: clean male skin, leather, and something tart and citrus. His mouth left hers and began a burning path down her neck as his hand cupped her breast and squeezed gently. Cara gasped, burying her face against his chest and inhaling deeper that maddening scent as she covered his hand with her own, holding him against her breast.

"Yes," she whispered.

"Cara," he said, his eyes dark and heavy with lust, and then the carriage jerked to a halt.

Wolf held her to him to stop her falling, his breathing harsh as he raised his head, looking as dazed as she felt, like he'd just emerged from a dream.

"We've stopped," he said, his voice deeper and huskier than before.

"I don't want to stop," Cara protested. She wanted never to stop, never to get out of this carriage where the outside world would intrude and spoil everything.

He smiled and touched her cheek with the back of his hand, but let her go. She wanted to protest, to demand he finish what he'd begun, but he was already moving to the door of the goods cart and peering out through the gaps in the wood.

"Hell!" he muttered.

"What? What is it?"

"There goes Sultan," he cursed before yelling and pounding on the door. "Hey! Hey! *You!* Let us out of here. *Oi!* Yes, you! Hurry up!"

He walked back to pick up his suitcase and hat and her discarded bonnet. He put the hat on.

"Stay out of sight for a moment," he counselled her, dropping the bonnet onto her head as he went.

Cara nodded, fumbling with the ribbons and finding herself quite unable to make a bow. Her brain and her fingers seemed to have been disconnected. She was still reeling from his kisses, that was the trouble, from the feel of his wonderfully warm hands on her, and she was rather indignant that he wasn't suffering the same sense of disorientation. He seemed to have returned to reality with no ill effects and it was business as usual, whereas she… she… *Good heavens.*

What was she supposed to do if she could not persuade him they belonged together? Kisses like that did not happen along every day. Admittedly, she did not have extensive experience in the field of kissing. Was kissing a field, or did that only apply to medicine? She had a sudden vision of thousands of people in a field in the countryside, kissing. Cara shook her head to clear it.

Still not herself yet, then. What had she been saying again? Oh, yes, not much experience kissing. No, indeed, but she was not so addlepated as to think she'd ever find anyone else who made her feel like *that*.

Finally, the door slid open, and Cara hung back whilst Wolf jumped down and exchanged a few terse words with the conductor, who seemed less than pleased that he'd picked up a stowaway.

"Come on, whilst no one is looking," Wolf ordered, holding out his hand.

Cara took it, staring down at the ground, which was a long way off as only the front of the carriage had drawn into the station with a platform.

"Here, come along," Wolf said, holding out his arms to her.

Cara set her hands on his shoulders and jumped, only to find he had caught her, setting her carefully down like she was made of spun sugar. She stared up at him and sighed.

"Stop that," he ordered her. "I can't be expected to think when you sigh over me."

"I can't help it," she said with another heavier sigh. "I'm smitten."

"You are not smitten, you're... temporarily addled," he corrected, apparently quite serious. Taking her hand, he towed her behind him. "I think Sultan went this way. He was following a cart. Do you think the cat was on it?"

"I don't have the slightest idea. Never mind the cat. What do you mean I'm temporarily addled? Are you always this dense?" she asked, almost running to keep up with his long strides. "Or is it a recent development?"

He glanced back at her and shook his head, apparently not deigning to answer, instead steering her around the back of a large shed and out of sight of the platform, where dozens of passengers were awaiting the next train. The goods train they had travelled on gave a shrill whistle and pulled out of the station whilst the five carts, which had been swiftly loaded from the contents of one of the railcars, rumbled towards the road Wolf had been heading for.

"Ouch!" Cara stumbled on the uneven ground and almost fell to her knees as pain lanced through her ankle.

"Cara!" Wolf said, catching her in his arms. "What is it? Are you hurt?"

"My ankle," she said, wincing. "I turned it."

Wolf crouched down before her, still holding one hand to steady her, and gently massaged her ankle. "Does that hurt?" Cara shook her head, and he stood up again.

"Can you walk on it?" he asked, concern in his eyes.

Cara took an experimental step and whimpered. "N-No," she said miserably. "No, I'm sorry."

He let out a harsh breath. "You've nothing to be sorry for. It's my fault, I ought not to have rushed you—"

"Oh, don't start that," she said crossly. "I should have been looking where I was going instead of gazing at you, but like I said, I'm smitten, besotted, and generally in a very bad way."

Wolf stared at her and sighed. "And you say I'm the lunatic," he muttered, before lifting her up like she weighed no more than a sack of duck down, and she knew *that* wasn't true.

"Oh," she said, and kissed his cheek.

"Someone will see, you ought not…." Wolf began and then shook his head, clearly deciding to save his breath. He picked up his suitcase and carried on, staring down the lane where in the far distance they could see a cart disappear over the brow of the hill, with Sultan trotting merrily behind it.

"Drat the naughty creature," Cara said with feeling. "Now, what do we do?"

She looked at Wolf, whose face had set with determination. He turned back towards the platform they'd just come from and started walking. "Now, I put you on the next train back to London. I'll go after Sultan and—"

"No!" she said furiously. "No, you won't!"

"Just for once, would you let me finish?" he demanded, stopping in his tracks in order to glare at her.

"Not when you insist on talking nonsense. I don't have the time or the patience for nonsense."

"Nonsense?" he said in outrage. "This, from the most nonsensical girl in the entire world!"

"I am not."

"You are."

"Am not."

"You…." He snapped his mouth shut and Cara grinned at him. He gave a helpless laugh. "Oh, love. Come on. Be sensible."

"But I don't want to be sensible," she said, tightening her hold on his neck. "I want to be wild and daring and just a bit wicked. I want to chase my dreams."

"Cara, this isn't a game. It's your life," he said, as if trying to coax a petulant child. "I don't know where the devil we are, but if there is a train station, it's a busy place. What if someone sees us together? There will be consequences."

"Stuff the consequences. It's *my* life. And I am going to win at it," she said triumphantly.

"I literally just said—" he began, and she silenced him the best way she knew how, by pressing her mouth to his.

He closed his eyes, the taut lines of his mouth softening beneath hers, the tension leaving his broad shoulders as she stroked his neck and his face. When she pulled back and saw the dazed look in his eyes, she knew she had won.

"How can I keep fighting you when I don't want to fight you at all?" he said with a groan.

"Excellent. Then stop doing it and enjoy the adventure with me," she said with satisfaction.

"I'm going straight to hell," he grumbled, and turned back towards the path Sultan had taken. He stopped in his tracks.

"Oh, don't change your mind already!" she protested. "Do I need to kiss you again?"

"No," he said thoughtfully, before flashing her a devilish grin. "Well, not right now, anyway, but you did say wild and daring, didn't you?"

"Yes!" she said, perking up.

"And what about... a little bit unlawful?"

"Ooooh," she said. "In what way?"

He snorted. "The way your eyes light up ought to be illegal," he said, shaking his head, and then hurried along the path to where one of the carts they'd noticed earlier was parked beside the road by a copse of trees, the horse nonchalantly cropping grass.

Wolf set Cara gently down on the driver's bench, slid his suitcase under the seat, and climbed in.

"Where's the driver?" Cara whispered, her eyes wide with delight and excitement.

Wolf wanted to laugh and hug her at the same time.

"Call of nature," he whispered back, gesturing to the trees before geeing the horse into motion.

They'd only gone a few yards before Cara's expression became pensive. "Wolf, what if the poor man loses his job? And the person whose goods these are? I know I said I wanted to be a bit wicked but…."

He smiled at her and leaned over to kiss her nose. "Don't fret, kitten."

"Oi!" bellowed a furious voice from behind them.

They turned back to see a short and very rotund driver trying to run after them. He managed about ten steps before he stopped, gasping and red-faced.

"That's my cart!" he shouted, puffing hard.

Wolf fished in his pocket and drew out a handful of coins, tossing them to the side of the road. "We'll leave it at the first coaching inn we come to," he yelled back. "What's your name?"

The fellow gaped at him. "Roberts," he said, looking incredulous. "Bill Roberts."

"Sorry to inconvenience you, Mr Roberts, but needs must," Wolf called back cheerfully. "It will be waiting when you get there."

He turned back around and gave his attention back to the road before slanting an amused look at Cara. "Just a *little* bit wicked," he said with a wink.

Cara beamed at him and planted a kiss on his cheek.

Chapter 9

Dear Emmeline,

Papa says I might invite you to come and stay with us for a few weeks if you are able to before we leave town for Christmas. Do please say that you will. I am thoroughly blue devilled, having made a complete fool of myself over a gentleman. I think I've just been very gently brushed off. Do come so I might share all the mortifying details. I need cheering up.

We are all so looking forward to joining you and your family at Heart's Folly for Christmas. Are you horribly envious your big sister has married such a beautiful man? I suppose not. You're far too nice for that, aren't you? I hear Evie is planning a lavish celebration, as it is their first in England since she married. Though your Christmas in France with them last year sounded splendid too, even if I did miss you.

Of course, Aggie is beside herself and is already counting down the days even though it's only October, though I can't help but suspect it is as much because Fred is coming as because she'll be celebrating Christmas with all of us.

I can't wait for your come out. At least you and Alana will make the marriage mart seem a deal more bearable.

—Excerpt of a letter from Lady Victoria Adolphus (daughter of Robert and Prunella Adolphus, Their Graces, The Duke and Duchess of Bedwin) to Miss Emmeline Knight (daughter of Lady Helena and Mr. Gabriel Knight).

19th October 1844, Between Colchester North Train Station and Colchester.

Cara looked about them with interest as the streets got busier, the roads becoming lined with small shops and people bustling to and fro, going about their business.

"I know where we are," she said, grinning at Wolf. "This is Colchester."

Wolf gave her an anxious glance. "You know people here? Is there someone I can take you to while I—"

"No." She narrowed her eyes at him and shook her head. "No, there isn't."

Wolf sighed. This was madness. He knew this was madness, but he couldn't seem to make himself stop. But what man could stop when Cara was there, urging him on? He stole another glance at her, hardly able to believe she was real. The sun glinted on her glorious hair, shimmering copper and gold, as if she'd trapped firelight in each silken strand. There was a scattering of freckles across her nose that made his chest ache with tenderness, though he did not know why. Freckles had held no fascination for him before. Now he had the desire to stare at them for hours, and an even fiercer desire to seek the places she'd hidden the rest, for surely there were more? But it was worse even than that, for when he looked into her eyes, he could not help but get lost, to forget good sense and his best intentions, his desire to keep her safe, to act with honour. When he gazed into her eyes, he became utterly helpless to resist her, no matter how mad her schemes were. He opened his mouth to say, 'no Cara, that is a terrible idea and will end in calamity,' and all that came out was gibberish. He blushed to consider how far gone he was. And wasn't that the most ridiculous thing of all? Him… *blushing!* It was a sorry state of affairs when *Le Loup Noir* had been tied up in knots by a slip of a girl, but there it was. Good God, Louis would laugh himself sick if ever found out.

"You're doing it again."

Wolf turned to find those dangerous blue eyes fixed upon him.

"Doing what?"

"Fretting."

"I am not fretting."

"Yes, you are. You're worrying that you're getting me into trouble, and you ought to make me see sense and you can't understand why you keep falling in with my plans."

Wolf glared at her. "Will you stop *doing* that! Are you a witch? It's like you crawl into my brain and listen to my thoughts. It's very disconcerting."

She snorted, a most unladylike sound that he found charming all the same. Devil take it, he was in a bad way.

"Don't be ridiculous," she said tartly. "The trouble is that we are fated to be together. Like Romeo and Juliet, but without the poison and the dying, or at least, I hope so. The point is, it's inevitable, like two magnets we were drawn together, and even an ocean couldn't keep us apart."

He returned a sceptical expression. "It was only the English Channel, love. I was in Paris, remember, not Madagascar."

She huffed at him. "Don't be so unromantic, I was making a valid point."

"My apologies." Wolf held his tongue.

"You can't resist me because you don't want to, just as you admitted yourself. So you may as well get used to the idea and *please* stop fretting. It won't change anything, because each time you get an attack of conscience, I'm just going to talk you into doing what we were going to do in the first place. All it means is that I must spend a deal of time and energy reminding you that I'm fabulous and you can't live without me."

She flashed him a dazzling smile and Wolf did not know whether to laugh or cry, because he was very afraid she was right.

They stopped at the Red Lion in Colchester and Wolf arranged for Mr Roberts' horse, cart and goods to be stored safely for him. Next, he spent a good half hour haggling over a dog cart and pony, which he knew damned well were worth two-thirds of the price he ended up paying for them. He did not have time to do better though, too aware that Mr Roberts' would be close behind them and well within his rights to call for a magistrate. They needed to be away from here as fast as possible. The least he could do was get Cara through this ridiculous affair without causing a scandal. Though how was beyond him. Dressed in mourning black with that shock of brilliant red hair, she was striking and unforgettable. Someone would realise who she was eventually, and then those consequences she'd spoken of so blithely would come crashing down on their heads. She'd regret this mad adventure then. She'd regret him, and the truth of that made his heart hurt.

Once the sale had completed to both parties' satisfaction, Wolf interrogated anyone he came across about Sultan. Happily, a dog of that remarkable size and colour was unusual, and it was not too long before one of the stable lads told him he'd seen the dog following a cart as it travelled through the town and exited onto the Ipswich road. The same story was repeated by one of the ostlers, and so Wolf felt reassured the information was accurate enough to risk setting out in the same direction.

When he returned to Cara, it was to discover she too had been busy. He had settled her in a private parlour with her damaged ankle set upon a cushioned stool, and had refreshments sent to her. He returned to discover her sipping tea and eating sugar biscuits, a loaded picnic basket and blanket set beside her.

The way her face lit up when she saw him made all his worries and concerns fly away like so much thistledown as her smile drove everything sensible from his mind. Happiness surged through his veins, foolish and intoxicating, and quite irresistible.

"I sent a note home to my parents, explaining I'd got myself into a bit of a fix," she said, smiling up at him. She handed him a biscuit and carried on. "But I assured them I was quite well and would be home safely before they knew it."

Wolf could not imagine her parents would be greatly soothed by such a note, considering Cara had written it, but he kept that thought to himself and ate the biscuit in one bite.

"I hope you don't mind," she added, gesturing to the enormous basket. "But you've not eaten, to my knowledge, and I thought a picnic would be a splendid idea, as the weather is being kind to us."

Wolf smiled his approval. "Certainly. I'll go and settle up."

"Oh, no. It's all paid for," she said airily.

Wolf scowled. "Cara...."

She rolled her eyes at him. "Oh, don't look so put out. You might remember I'm disgustingly wealthy, and I always keep emergency funds on me in case of... well, emergencies," she added cheerfully.

He sighed and shook his head. "I'm not put out, I'm only trying to take care of you, and I really wish you would have fewer emergencies. It's very stressful, worrying about you all the time."

"I know. It's lovely that you do, and that you are trying to keep me out of trouble. It's a thankless task, I know. I shall kiss you later to make up for it," she added, merrily unaware of the devastating affect her words had on his equilibrium.

Shaking his head, Wolf called for a servant to take the basket out to the dogcart, and lifted Cara into his arms.

She sighed happily, reaching out to squeeze his biceps. "So strong," she said, her admiration so blatant Wolf's cheeks felt hot.

She noticed at once, obviously.

"You are too adorable," she said in a choked voice, struggling not to laugh.

"I'm not the least bit adorable," he grumbled, glowering at her as he carried her outside. "I'm big and scary, and I'd thank you not to forget it."

He ignored the way she studied his face, though her brazen approval seemed to wrap around him like a wool blanket on a wintry day, warming him when he'd not even been aware of the chill. Wolf set her carefully on the seat of the dogcart and climbed in beside her.

"It's cosy," he said apologetically, for he took up rather a large amount of space.

"I like it," she said, blue eyes glinting.

Wolf laughed and got the pony walking out.

They travelled the first half an hour in companionable silence as Colchester was busy with carts and carriages, horses and stray dogs, and all manner of hazards. Cara didn't chatter but looked about her with interest and let him concentrate as he navigated the throng, though it was a deal easier with the little dogcart and pony than with a carriage and horses. Once they were free of the town and on a quieter stretch, she turned back to him, studying his face.

"Tell me about your life, Wolf. You once said you were the son of a disgraced nobleman. Lord Latimer was labelled a coward and traitor, I believe. Is that right?"

Wolf stiffened, not wanting to discuss it, but her hand settled on his arm, gentle and reassuring.

"Your father might have been those things, Wolf, but you are not him. I know that, and I should never blame you for the things he did."

He let out a slow breath, keeping his eyes on the road ahead. "It's common knowledge, so you could ask most anyone, but my father was a lieutenant colonel and first liaison with General Cuesta of Spain after the battle of Talavera. His job was to ensure the proper care regarding the treatment of those wounded during the battle, close to one and a half thousand men. Wellington didn't trust Cuesta to ensure their safety, and with good reason. But my father did not want to hang around waiting for the French to arrive any more than Cuesta did. They abandoned the men to the French. My father tried to blame Cuesta, and came up with some cock-and-bull story, but the truth came out in the end."

Cara was silent and Wolf did not want to look at her, to see disgust and embarrassment in her eyes, but he told himself if it was there, he'd best see it and get it over with. But when he turned to look at her, her blue eyes were shining with tears.

"What? What's wrong?" he asked, unsettled by the compassion in her eyes.

She swallowed and shook her head. "I am just wondering what kind of father such a man would be," she said, her voice uneven.

Wolf felt his throat tighten. He shrugged, striving for nonchalance. "About what you'd expect, I imagine."

Cara reached out and covered his hand with both of hers. She was not wearing gloves and the sensuous touch of her soft skin warming his rough hands made his heart skip.

"I'm so sorry."

"He died a long time ago," Wolf said, with a satisfied edge to his voice he could not hide.

Not that it had been his doing. Louis had killed the monster, felled him when Wolf had not been strong enough to do it himself. He owed Louis his life, and so much more.

"What of your mother?"

Wolf smiled then and turned back to Cara.

"She was wonderful," he said simply. "She died when I was quite young, but I was so lucky to have her as long as I did. When I was with her, I knew I was the most important boy in the entire world, because someone as beautiful and lovely as her could not possibly love someone unless they were very special. She made me feel like I was the centre of the universe. She would have liked you," he added, meaning it.

Cara's cheeks turned pink with pleasure.

"I'm glad," she whispered. "I'm glad you had someone wonderful who loved you. I think you must be very like her."

Wolf's expression darkened, and he shook his head. "I'm like my father."

"You're not. Not a bit!" she retorted, so fierce Wolf could not resist leaning over and kissing her.

Oh, lord, but he ought to stop this. She was the Earl of Trevick's daughter and, when the man found out who she was with... Christ, he'd want Wolf strung up by his balls. Wolf wouldn't blame him.

"I meant I look like him," he amended. "It's hard sometimes, looking in the mirror and seeing his face there. He terrified me when I was a boy, and… and sometimes I'm afraid I'll turn into him."

"That could never happen," she said staunchly.

Wolf shook his head. "You don't know me, Cara. Not entirely. I have a temper, and when I lose it…."

He let out a breath, uncomfortable with this conversation, though it was better that she knew the truth, rather than putting him on some pedestal he was so far from deserving.

"Have you ever hit a woman?" she demanded, her expression cool.

"Christ! No!" he exclaimed, horrified by the idea.

"A child, then, or someone who was smaller than you?"

"No!" he stared at her, hurt and offended, but she carried on regardless.

"Have you taken advantage of someone poor, or forced your attentions on a woman who didn't want them?"

Wolf stared at her, his guts in a knot. Too appalled to answer, he just shook his head. Then Cara took his face between her hands and kissed him hard.

"Foolish man," she whispered. "I suspect I know what makes you angry, and I imagine I would be angry as well. Perhaps if I were a man, I'd use my size and my power to do something about it too, but I know you'd never hurt me. You'd hurt no one who did not deserve it."

"You don't *know* that," he insisted, though he was unsure why he argued with her when he hoped that much was true. His life had been a violent one, and the knowledge disgusted him, and yet he could not regret the things he'd done, not when others would have suffered if he'd stood back and done nothing.

"I do," she insisted. "I know you."

She held his gaze until Wolf could bear it no longer, feeling unequal and undeserving of the admiration in her eyes. But she slipped her arm through his and leaned into him, her head resting against his shoulder, and Wolf could not remember ever being so happy.

"Cara?" he asked sometime later.

"Yes?" she murmured sleepily, and he glanced down to see she'd closed her eyes.

"I'm sorry, were you asleep?"

"No, just resting my eyelids," she said, smothering a yawn. She stretched and Wolf hastily averted his eyes, afraid he might ogle the way her breasts moved as she lifted her arms and pushed out her chest. "What were you going to say?"

"It was a question, actually. You said you know me and so I wanted to ask... do you know who I am? *What* I am?"

She frowned, clearly not understanding what it was he was getting at. "What you are?" she repeated, looking a little impatient. "I know you are the son of a disgraced nobleman, and that you have been involved in... criminal activity, in Paris," she said carefully.

"Is that all you know?"

Cara shrugged. "Oh, I heard a lot of nonsense spouted about you, but I try not to listen to gossip. You're not really a pirate, are you?" she asked, her expression lighting up with interest.

Wolf rolled his eyes. "Certainly not."

"Oh," she sighed. "Mama will be so disappointed."

"You mean she'd be pleased if you'd run off with a pirate?" he exclaimed, outraged.

"Well, perhaps not pleased," she allowed. "But whatever you are, she'll understand the attraction. She thought you were magnificent, so I don't see how she could blame me for losing my head over you. Mama is very romantic and has the most vivid imagination. She was forever getting my poor father into trouble."

"This explains a good deal," he said gruffly.

Cara only laughed. "Yes, it does."

Wolf shook his head. "Did you never wonder how I knew Evie?"

Cara shrugged. "I've not had time to think about it, but I assumed you met her in Paris. When the comte ran off to France with her, all kinds of stories came out about him. It was an open secret he was involved with his brother's club, Rouge et Noir, but then there were other stories, criminal activity on a grand scale. People gossiped about how he was involved with the Parisian underworld, smuggling rings—even murder, for heaven's sake—though that was so far-fetched no one paid it any heed."

Wolf said nothing and Cara looked up at him, her gaze questioning.

"Louis César is my closest friend. More like a brother, actually. When he took Evie to France, he came to me," he said, knowing he ought to have told her this from the start. She would have heard rumours about him, but no one would have given an innocent girl the unvarnished truth. Yet, Louis' scandal had dominated the print shops and gossip sheets for weeks and months. She could not have missed it.

Cara's mouth fell open as she correctly added up the information she must have heard when the scandal broke about Louis and Evie and what she knew about Wolf.

"Wolf," she said softly. *"Le Loup Noir!* I never even thought and yet… it's obvious. How did I not see it?"

"Because you don't know me as well as you think you do," he said quietly. "Because you're too good-natured to think ill of anyone, even when they deserve it."

"Well, that's not the least bit true," she said flatly. "I promise you, I've thought terrible things about Lady Hyacinth and Miss Crantock. I pray daily for them to get boils, or for their maids to singe their hair, or to get a mighty set down from Lord Montagu. I once spent a whole afternoon walking around Vauxhall Gardens fervently wishing Lady Hyacinth would fall face first into a muddy puddle before the entire *ton*. Oh, I'm quite vile, I assure you," she said with an airy smile.

Wolf stared at her, uncertain if she was joking or not, but she seemed quite serious.

She looked exceedingly smug, the dreadful creature. "Well, I may not be a pirate, but if you will insist on regarding me as some innocent little angel, I'm afraid you will get a shock. I'm really not. Not even close. Just because I'm a virgin doesn't mean I'm sweet, you know."

Wolf choked, torn between laughter and outrage and Cara only watched him with satisfaction, a wicked glint in her eyes.

"You mean to say I've been duped?" he said, slanting her a look. "You're not half so nice as you've made yourself out to be."

"Oh, not even a quarter," she said gravely. "I harbour all sorts of wicked thoughts and I'm not the least bit sorry, either. Really, *Le Loup Noir* ought to watch his step associating with such a ghastly young woman. I might corrupt him."

Wolf gave a snort of laughter, staring at her. He knew his heart was in his eyes and there wasn't a damn thing he could do about it. "I should say it's a deal too late for that."

They stopped for a picnic near a pretty little village called Bamford, finding a sheltered spot by the river, away from prying eyes. They'd last had a sighting of Sultan about a mile back, which suggested they were still on the right track.

Wolf knew they ought simply to press on, but he could hear Cara's stomach rumbling. Then he'd remembered what she'd said about having an adventure, and just giving in and enjoying it, and he wanted to give in so badly. He wanted to relish every second in her company, even though he knew he'd be a fool to pin his hopes on her. They'd have their adventure, find her ridiculous dog, and then her parents would discover what she'd done. With luck, they could keep it quiet and there'd be no scandal, and they'd explain to Cara that she would marry Wolf over their cold, dead bodies. He might be a criminal, but cold-blooded murder was not his thing, and he didn't think Cara would like it much if it was. So that would be that.

He started as she thrust a pork pie in his face.

"You're doing it again," she said crossly. "Now eat that. You're getting gloomy because you're hungry. Everything looks better with a full belly, especially as we have cake, and cake solves everything."

"Cake does not solve everything," he said, unable to let that one go.

"Everything," she said firmly.

"You're addled, you are."

"And you're a lunatic. So what? Oh, and if it's...." She peered into the basket. "Oooh, fruitcake! Well, now, fruitcake solves everything in double quick time, you'll see."

Wolf devoured the pork pie in an astonishingly short space of time and accepted a bottle of ale. "You're a blessed fruitcake. Were you this daft when you wrote to me? I can't believe I've been writing letters all this time to someone so entirely deranged."

Cara helped herself to a large slice of cake and shrugged. She popped a piece into her mouth and chewed happily.

Wolf frowned. "You can't have cake yet, you've not eaten anything else. Cake is for after."

"I like cake best, though."

"That's not the point," he protested.

"It is entirely the point."

"There's ham," he said, inspecting the basket. "And cheese, some good bread... oh, and a chicken pie. Have some pie."

"When I've finished my cake," she said, before adding. "I'll have some cheese, though."

"After the cake?"

"No, with the cake? What is *wrong* with you?"

"Wrong with *me*? No one eats cheese and cake."

"Of course they do. All the best people eat cheese and cake," she said airily.

"Like who?" he demanded.

"Well, me, obviously."

Wolf stared at her for a moment, and then silently passed her a thick slice of cheese.

Cara took a bite of the cheese and sighed happily. "You don't know what you're missing," she taunted him.

"Challenge accepted," he said, cutting a piece of cake and a piece of cheese and eating both in one go.

"I didn't mean at the same time!" she said, laughing. She sat up on her knees, watching his face intently. "Well?"

Wolf chewed, refusing to give her any clue what he thought of the peculiar mix. He swallowed and licked his lips, very aware of the way her gaze fell to his mouth and lingered.

"That," he said.

"Yes?"

"Was...."

"Yes?" she said impatiently.

"Delicious," he said, and dived for the cake. Cara squealed and pushed him away.

"No! It's mine! You didn't even like cheese and cake; you scoffed at me!"

"I never scoffed," he said, laughing now, holding her off him by grabbing her wrists.

"You did, you scoffed, and now... now you know I was correct, you want to scoff my cake! Oh, you are a villain!" she protested, though her eyes were alight with laughter and mischief.

Wolf knew he ought not get caught up in the delight in those blue eyes. He ought not to forget consequences and ruination, and her parents, and the fact he was so far from suitable that it made him feel sick every time he thought about it. But he did. He got caught in that blue gaze, and her silliness, and the joy she made him feel when life had become so joyless of late. And so he did something reckless and stupid and wonderful, and tumbled her back onto the picnic blanket. He held her wrists above her head, his knees on either side of her thighs, and just looked his fill for a moment. Her beautiful copper curls tumbled all around her where they'd escaped her pins, and her breasts strained against the confines of her gown as she stared up at him, breathing hard after their tussle. Wolf drank in the sight of her, that alabaster skin and the scattering of freckles like stars in a night sky. Her cheeks had flushed a delicate pink, and the look in her eyes was all too easy to read.

"Yes," she whispered, just in case he was having any trouble deciphering the fire blazing there.

Wolf lowered his mouth to hers, brushing his lips gently back and forth, laughing softly when she tried to take more and lifting his head away.

"So impatient," he scolded.

"I am, yes," she admitted as he laced their fingers together. "I hate waiting for anything."

"Oh, dear," he said sadly.

"Please," she said, her breath fluttering over his skin.

Smiling, he kissed her again, a soft press of his lips that ended when she tried to take more. She grumbled and shifted beneath him, trying to get closer but he held his body away from hers.

"Wolf, please, I want to touch you. Stop teasing, I... I'll go mad...."

Bad idea, bad idea, bad idea, his brain told him. Wolf ignored it.

He kissed her again, as she'd wanted him to kiss her, devouring kisses that did not sate the hunger gnawing at him but only made it worse, made him want more and more. Wolf released one hand, deftly undoing the long line of tiny buttons that marched down the bodice of her gown, and smoothed his hand over a delicately embroidered corset. He regarded the metal closures, aware he ought to undo the ties at the back, but far too impatient. He flicked them undone, and she gasped as the busk released and the corset fell loose. Beneath was only the thin cotton of her shift. Wolf's heart ratcheted up a notch, and Cara made a startled sound as his hand closed over her full breast. She pushed up into his touch, wanting more.

Wolf groaned as he felt her nipple tighten under his palm. He gently squeezed and caressed before rubbing his thumb over the hard little bud.

Before he could play anymore, she put her hand to the back of his neck and tugged so hard he overbalanced, almost crushing the life out of her as he fell half on, half off her.

"Cara, are you—" he began, afraid he must have hurt her, but she had her own plans as usual.

"Shut up and kiss me, you lunatic," she commanded, pressing her mouth to his.

She shifted beneath him, and they fought her skirts and petticoats until he lay between her thighs. Her breath caught, and she stared up at him, clearly shocked by the intimate position. Wolf lifted himself away at once.

"Sorry," he began.

"Where do you think you're going?" she demanded, catching hold of his waistcoat and tugging him back down.

He laughed, kissing her again, lost in the pleasure of it, hardly aware of what her busy hands were about until he felt her palms skim over his sides and up his back beneath the shirt.

"You feel so good," she whispered. "So big and hot, oh, how I want you. I feel like I've wanted you forever."

Any sensible part of his brain dissolved on hearing that. All he wanted was to please her, to hear more about how much she wanted him, to touch her how she wanted and make her feel good.

"Want you, want you...." she whispered as he kissed a path down her neck to her breast. Cara cried out as he suckled her, stroking his hair. "Oh, that's so good. You're so good, so good."

The words struck something inside him, pleasure shivering over his skin as he paused to look down at her. She stared at him and smiled as if she'd learned a secret, stroking his cheek.

"So lovely," she murmured.

The blush might have been mortifying if she hadn't looked so very pleased with herself as understanding lit her eyes.

"Show me how good you are," she whispered.

Wolf's breath hitched. "Cara," he said, his voice hoarse. "We ought not...."

"Yes," she said. "I said yes. Touch me."

He let out a ragged breath and sat back, reaching for the layers of heavy black silk and the froth of petticoats beneath. Wolf pulled them back, exposing her ankles, dragging the material higher until he revealed her calves. She wore black silk stockings, so fine he feared his rough hands might snag the delicate fabric.

Wolf stilled. Another inch and he'd see her garters, the silken skin of her thighs, and then… He didn't think he could do this. His cock was throbbing within the confines of his trousers, and he didn't think he'd ever been so hard before in his life. But, if he touched her like this, he would not be able to let her go. It would be impossible. He would condemn her to a life with him, with all the scandal and disgust that went with his name.

"Wolf."

The way she said his name was so tender, so filled with understanding as she watched him.

"Look at me," she whispered.

How could he not? He looked, his heart hammering in his chest as she took hold of the bunched-up mass of skirts and petticoats and raised it higher. She teased him, moving slowly, so slowly, revealing herself by tiny increments so that by the time he saw her garters, the ribbons bold as brass against the black stockings, he was beside himself.

"Red," he rasped, laughing and groaning at the same time. "Wicked girl."

"So bad," she said, devilry glinting in her eyes. "What are you going to do about it?"

Wolf could not say, could not speak, though the things he wanted crowded his mind, jostling for him to tell her, but now he could see her milky white thighs and, oh God, the glint of copper curls.

"Cara," he whispered, his chest heaving with longing.

She let out a breath of laughter, clearly amused by his dazed expression and he could hardly blame her, but everything she offered him was overwhelming, everything he had believed he could never have when he had wanted it so very badly.

"Well, are you going to touch me or not?" she asked, breathless laughter in her voice.

"Christ, yes," he said.

"Get on with it then!" she exclaimed, sending him a look of fond exasperation.

He flashed her a grin and dared to put his hand on her ankle, so fine and delicate beneath his large hand. Carefully, he slid his palm higher, revelling in the warmth beneath the silk stocking, desperate to put his hand on her skin but making himself wait. By the time he got to her garter, his mouth was dry, and he had to bite back a moan as he trailed the backs of his fingers over her satiny inner thigh.

"Yes," she whispered. "Like that. Oh, your hands, so warm and strong. I love the feel of them on my skin."

Wolf dragged his gaze from the glorious sight before him to meet her eyes, dumbfounded by her. She was so bold, so utterly unafraid, and completely herself. He had met no one like her in all his life and he might as well give up fighting it because he was hers to do with as she pleased. Somehow, he thought he'd been hers from the moment Evie had described her so casually, intriguing him enough to steal her letter.

"Tell me what you want," he managed. "I'll do anything."

Cara sat up on her elbows, watching him keenly, then she reached out one hand to touch his mouth. Wolf held still as she traced the curve of his lip.

"My friend Greer told me something wicked," she said.

"Oh?" he replied, striving for nonchalance when his heart was kicking like a mule behind his ribs. "What did she tell you?"

144

"She said… that the closest thing to bliss was when her husband used his mouth on her."

Wolf closed his eyes, wondering if he'd spend before or after he made her come, because he did not think he could take much more.

"Where?" he demanded, almost growling the words in his desperation to hear her say it, though of course he knew damn well where she wanted him.

He heard the rustle of fabric and opened his eyes to see her drag her skirts higher with one hand, whilst the slender fingers of the other trailed through the copper curls between her thighs.

"Put your mouth here."

She tipped her head back, laughing as he practically dived between her legs, but then her laughter died, her breath hitching as he sifted through the fiery curls, parting her delicate flesh and licking. The taste of her made him lightheaded, and he moaned against her skin, seeking more while she writhed beneath him, bucking and twisting about so much he had to hold her still.

Wolf could not remember ever being more aroused as she praised him, telling him *yes*, and *more*, and how good it felt, how good he was, how lovely he made her feel. He was every bit as intoxicated as she was, overwhelmed by the delight he took in bringing her pleasure, and she was so close. He wanted to make her come, but never wanted to let it end either. But she was practically sobbing now, begging him, and so he slid a finger inside her as he gently sucked and she shattered beneath him, her climax shuddering through her, filling his senses with the taste of her.

Two indignant crows lifted from the trees behind them, cawing furiously as her cries disturbed the peace of their surroundings. Finally, it was quiet once more, the only sound Cara's breathing as she gasped and laughed delightedly, because this was Cara, and of course she would laugh.

Wolf collapsed, resting his head on her thigh, intoxicated by her, thrumming with unspent lust. He hardly dared move, for the slightest friction against his cock was going to have inevitable results.

"Oh, that was… lovely," she said with a voluptuous sigh of contentment. Wolf felt her fingers stroking his hair. "You are lovely. Such a sweet, darling man. So good. You made me feel splendid."

Wolf closed his eyes, letting her words fill him, warming him from the inside. When had anyone said such a thing to him? He'd always enjoyed pleasing his bed partners, quite unable to find his own pleasure if the woman he was with had not. Not being an idiot, he knew too that he was sought after, that women liked the way he looked, liked that he seemed rough and dangerous and wicked. They wanted him that way, too, wanted him to be that person, hard and aggressive, to take instead of giving. A bit of rough, he supposed. He'd always obliged, because… why wouldn't he, if it was what pleased them? It pleased him too, sometimes, but… but Cara saw something else, and he could remember no one else ever letting him be gentle… letting him be himself.

He nuzzled the tender skin at the apex of her thigh and pressed a kiss there. She sighed again.

"You have been so very good, I think you must have a reward," she said, a teasing note to her voice that made his heart skip and his cock leap.

He raised his head, and she sat up, grinning at him.

"Would you like that?" she asked, one delicate red eyebrow arching in enquiry.

"Yes," he said at once. "Please," he added, and earned himself a delighted smile.

He moved so that she could kneel beside him, and he gazed up at her in wonder. She was all undone, her hair cascading around her shoulders, the red glinting brighter than ever against the dull black silk of her gown. The dress gaped open, her full breasts spilling out, spangled with freckles. Her mouth, swollen from his kisses, was the same deep pink as her nipples. Acres of black silk and frothy petticoats cascaded around her, and Wolf thought he had seen nothing so dazzling, so heart-stoppingly glorious in his life.

"You are the most beautiful thing I have ever seen," he said, reaching out to touch her hair.

"There's a coincidence," she said, her blue eyes warm and full of happiness as she looked him over, and then slid a hand over the straining placket of his trousers.

Wolf made a deep, guttural sound and held his breath, squeezing his eyes shut. *Don't come, don't come, don't come,* he begged internally, not wanting this to be over, but knowing it would not take much. More rustling made him look down at himself to see Cara bending over him, pressing her mouth against the rigid shape beneath the fabric of his trousers.

"Oh, good Christ!" he exclaimed, and the moment she sat back, he tore at the buttons on his falls, freeing his aching cock and wrapping a hand around himself. Two strokes was all it took, and he was coming, harder than he could ever remember doing before. Cara's voice drifted over him like a caress, her words of praise sending him higher, that approving look in her eyes as she watched him, only making it go on and on until he was shaking and utterly spent.

He collapsed with one arm flung over his eyes.

"You are going to kill me," he gasped, laughing helplessly.

"Well," she said with a considering tone, "just imagine what would happen if I'd actually put my mouth on you."

Wolf groaned and resigned himself to dying young. "What a way to go," he whispered as she snorted and collapsed beside him with a flurry of petticoats.

Her hand found his, and she laced their fingers together.

"You're not going anywhere without me, though," she said tartly.

And Wolf could do nothing but grin.

Chapter 10

Dearest Mama and Papa and Conor,

I'm so sorry. I know you must be frantic by now and it's all my fault, but Sultan has got me into a bit of a fix. Yes, again. I know. I can hear your remonstrations from here, but please don't fret. The truth is, I'm having the most marvellous time and I'm quite safe and well, so do try not to worry. Don't bother with a search party, I shall be home in one piece before you know it with my naughty hound in tow. Much love to you all.

—Excerpt of a letter from Lady Cara Baxter to her parents (Luke and Kitty Baxter, The Earl and Countess of Trevick) and her brother (Conor Baxter, Viscount Harleston).

19th October 1844, On the Ipswich Road, Suffolk.

It took them a long while to tidy themselves up, mostly because kissing was too delicious and one kiss led to another and, before they knew what was happening, they had undone all their doing up.

In the end, Cara had scolded him, even though she had been the ringleader, unsurprisingly, and told him they must hurry and find Sultan. So off they set again, asking along the way and reassured by the amount of people who had taken note of the horse and cart with the huge grey dog trotting along behind it.

Cara chattered while Wolf drove and he delighted in her stories, as mad and rife with exclamations and capitals and underlining as her letters had been. He heard about her parents, and her madcap mother, her sister Aisling, who had married a lovely man *who had no title*—underlined—and was *ecstatically happy,* in capital letters. He also heard about her brother, Conor, Viscount Harleston. It was obvious Cara admired and loved her older brother, and also that he was the protective sort who would want Wolf's blood if he knew what they'd been up to.

Just as he was about to worry himself into a knot, Cara leaned over and kissed him.

"Noo-ooo," she said, giving him a stern look and wagging a finger at him.

Despite himself, Wolf snorted and coaxed the pony into a trot.

Dusk was upon them by the time they got to Diss in Norfolk. Even if they retrieved Sultan, the moment they arrived in the village, Cara would not be home before nightfall. As there was no sign of the aggravating dog, Wolf resigned himself to the fact that they must find a place to spend the night. How he was going to survive without giving in to Cara's demands to deflower her—and he had no illusions on that point—he hadn't the faintest idea. The idea made him simultaneously hot with lust and cold with horror at the idea of taking her virginity when her parents would be horrified when they discovered who he was and what they'd done. It would be no surprise if her father took him to a secluded spot and shot him. Wolf wouldn't blame him one bit.

The thing was, *if* they were going to be together—and that was such a fanciful idea he could hardly bring himself to believe it was even possible—they *must* marry, and they could not marry until he was respectable. That was all there was to it. He must go back to his grandmother, cap in hand, and beg her and her bawdy friends to do everything in their power to help him succeed. So, until then, he must stand firm and not give in to Cara when she tried to seduce him.

Ha!

Bloody buggering hell, he was doomed to failure. No. No, he must not think like that. Cara was worth treating with respect and doing things properly, as they ought to be done, so... so... he would just do what needed to be done. Or rather, not do what he was desperately in need of doing. He wondered if it was possible to die from balked lust, because he had no doubts about just how much temptation was going to be laid before him. Hell, she only needed to give him that look, the considering one from under her lashes that told him she was thinking dangerous thoughts, and it felt as if he had a crowbar stuffed down his trousers.

"Whatever is the matter now?" Cara asked, wrinkling her nose in consternation. "You look like you're standing on the steps of the scaffolding, awaiting your turn at the noose."

Wolf huffed. "Don't be daft. I'm just wondering if that dog of yours is here or not."

"Well, even if he's quite determined to get that poor cat, they can't travel indefinitely. The driver will want to stop overnight, and the pony will need resting, so we had best do the same. Is that what you're fretting about? We'll just pretend to be husband and wife, that's all. No one will know."

Wolf made a pained sound, even though he'd been expecting it. "And what if someone recognises you?"

Cara shrugged. "Mama and Papa have been sat upon thorns since I came out, waiting for the scandal to break."

"What scandal?" he asked at once, wondering what she hadn't told him.

She turned to frown at him. "Any scandal. We all knew it was inevitable. It's a wonder I've escaped this long, to tell the truth, though there have been a few... incidents."

"What incidents?"

"Well, last week I tipped a bowl of soup into Mr Handley's lap."

Wolf shrugged. "Accidents happen."

"Oh, it wasn't an accident," she said, darting him a swift smile. "I did it on purpose."

Wolf went still, a sudden and familiar swell of rage filling him. "What did he do?"

Cara turned to give him her full attention. "My," she said softly. "No wonder people are frightened of you. How fierce you are when you look like that."

Wolf waved this away, impatient. "What did the devil do that you felt the need to pour soup into his lap?"

"He put his hand on my thigh, very high up too, and then he squeezed."

She shuddered, and Wolf wanted to break something with his bare hands.

"Here," she said, gently easing his stiff fingers off the reins and taking them herself. "You'll spook the pony, holding them like that."

"I'll kill him," he growled, too furious to protest.

"No," she said with a sigh. "You won't, for that would only make matters worse, I'm afraid. But I thank you for the thought. He is a vile creature. I learned later that all the young ladies fear sitting next to him and his wandering hands. I had been lucky to escape him for so long, it appears."

"Lucky indeed. The idea that you must all endure this man, that to sit next to him is simply bad luck…. A pox on the fellow. He ought to be horsewhipped. I hope the soup was boiling," he said savagely.

"No, sadly. Gazpacho, but it made the most frightful mess on his cream silk waistcoat," she said with undisguised glee. "So, there's that, and Mama was only a little cross, and then only because the Duke of Sefton scolded me in front of everyone and she was afraid for my reputation. She said next time I should stab him with my fork under the table. More discreet. Isn't she marvellous?"

She turned to him with a delighted smile.

"And your father?" Wolf demanded.

"Oh, he's going to have words with Mr Handley and the duke. I suspect I shan't have any trouble from that quarter again, but of course Mr Handley will stay away from me—he's quite eligible, you know—and so others will follow suit. Not that I care, but it's all quite ghastly and I detest it. I thought coming out would give me more freedom, but I'm beset by rules on all sides. I rather hate it," she said.

"Cara," he said, frustrated beyond bearing. "I wish—"

"I know," she said, leaning over to kiss his cheek, although they were in full view of the street. "And I adore you for it."

Wolf sighed.

"Now," she said, as if getting down to business at last. "We need to decide who we are. I think Mr and Mrs Jenkins. We met when you got caught in a storm and my father let you shelter in our stables. We corresponded secretly for years—always better to stick roughly to the truth—and you finally declared yourself six months ago. We are newlyweds off to visit relations. There, that should suffice. What do you think?"

Wolf gaped at her.

She blinked at him, the picture of innocence. "What? If we're to be husband and wife, it needs to be believable. What if they ask us how we met?"

"Why on earth would anyone ask?" he demanded.

Cara wrinkled her nose. "Why on earth wouldn't they?" she replied, looking completely bewildered.

Wolf snorted and let her have her own way.

They stopped at The Ram, a pretty coaching inn along the Ipswich road with high gables and a cosy aspect on an evening that was becoming chilly now the sun was almost set. The pony needed resting and there was no escaping the fact they would need to stay somewhere. The inn was not a large establishment, and busy enough at this hour in the countryside, when people became intent on their dinner.

Wolf settled Cara in a private parlour and left her to order their meal whilst he made arrangements for the pony and booked their accommodation. He did this mostly in the vain hope that he could arrange two rooms, to which he knew she would strongly object. Fate was not kind, however, and the only room remaining was their best one.

"A fine big double bed," the innkeeper said with pride. "Big enough even for a strapping fellow like you, sir, if you don't mind me remarking it."

Wolf laughed and shook his head. "Not in the least."

"Sleep like a babe, you will," the man predicted, but then the fellow hadn't yet clapped eyes on Cara.

Wolf returned to the parlour to discover the meal being brought in.

"Just in time," Cara observed happily, and ladled out a huge serving of lamb stew, studded with pearl barley and jewel-bright chunks of carrot.

It was served with creamy mashed potatoes and Wolf devoured two servings, only now realising how hungry he'd been. Dessert was a treacle tart that Cara went into ecstasies over, eating more of it than Wolf, who had never had much of a sweet tooth. He watched her with delight, wanting more nights like this, wanting all her nights, forever. The desire to keep her close to him was so intense that, when he considered all the obstacles before him, a pain struck at his heart with such force he felt winded by it.

Cara drained the last drop of wine in her glass and gave a contented sigh.

"That was divine, but now I must inspect their very best bedchamber. Take me to bed, husband," she said, such a twinkle in her eyes that Wolf's skin ached with wanting.

Wolf went to her and lifted her into his arms, aware her ankle was still sore.

"Oh, it's lovely," Cara exclaimed as he pushed the door open with his foot and entered the room, ducking under the low lintel.

He had already manoeuvred his way up the cramped, creaking staircase and narrowly escaped doing himself an injury on a low beam on the landing. Now he was relieved to discover he could stand upright. A large four-poster bed dominated the room and Cara laughed with delight when she saw the half dozen mattresses.

"I shall need a ladder," she said, shaking her head.

"No, you won't," Wolf said, carrying her over and putting her down on it with care.

Cara sighed and kept her arms linked around his neck, not letting him go. "It's comfy," she whispered, pulling him down for a kiss.

Wolf obliged her and then straightened, shaking his head.

"No, Cara."

She blinked up at him, as though he were speaking a foreign language.

"No?" she repeated. "But why not?"

Wolf let out a shaky breath and took a step back, and this time she let him go. He felt her blue eyes follow him, aware of the confusion there.

"Because we're not married, no matter what it says on the register. I'm not returning you to your parents having…." He waved a hand to illustrate the point. "They'll have little enough reason to think well of me; I'm not about to make matters worse. Not when they're quite bad enough."

"Bad enough?" she repeated, a flash of hurt in her eyes.

"Cara, no," he said at once, horrified that he had been clumsy enough to insult her. "I didn't mean it that way. Christ, surely you know every moment in your company is a joy to me? I never want to let you go, but… but I want to do things properly."

She quirked an eyebrow at him, and he laughed.

"Well, as properly as I can in the circumstances. When we've retrieved Sultan, I'm going to go to my grandmother and ask her to help me. To see if she can make me respectable, or at least not so very scandalous that I would alienate all your friends."

Her lips twitched into a smile. "You've not met my friends yet. I think they'll like you just as you are."

Wolf shook his head, unable to believe that. "I'll do everything I can to make myself a better prospect for you, love. That is… I mean… if you want me to," he added hastily, wondering if that had been too presumptuous.

She snorted at that. "If I want you to? You really are remarkably foolish sometimes. Have I not made my feelings clear yet?"

Wolf returned a rueful smile. "I know you like kissing me, but kisses aren't a life, Cara, and passion fades. You might come to regret—"

"The only thing I regret is that you are all the way over there," she said tartly, and then sighed at the warning look in his eyes. "Very well. I will behave. Word of honour."

Wolf gave her a sceptical glance, and she sighed impatiently. "You wish to do things properly. I understand this and will not tease you with my advances. What? Did you think I would set out to seduce you?"

"Yes, actually," Wolf admitted.

Cara huffed. "And if I were a man, what would you think of me for that? For not taking no for an answer. How lowering that you believe I am not to be trusted."

"I never said—"

"No, you didn't need to, but no matter. The point is, I shall be good. But I do have a request."

Wolf frowned. "What request?"

"Please don't sleep on the floor, or the chair, or something equally noble. I would like to sleep in your arms at least. Just sleep. I promise."

She looked so very earnest that Wolf smiled, the idea too tantalising to deny even though he would endure a night of utter torture. "All right, then."

Wolf went out again to give Cara time to get ready for bed, and returned an hour later to discover her sleeping, her red hair already escaping the haphazard plait she'd put it in. Wolf stared down at her, too many feelings tangling in his chest. Desire and want were there, but tenderness too, and the need to protect this extraordinary girl, this vibrant creature who made him see the world in an altogether different way.

It was as if he'd forgotten how to see colour and, the longer he spent with her, the brighter the world became. She lived with such joy, with such anticipation for what would come next that sometimes he forgot to breathe, caught up in the adventure with her. He was spellbound, entirely captivated, and no matter what he had to do, he would make her his own.

Carefully, Wolf climbed into the bed, still wearing his shirt for modesty. The mattresses dipped alarmingly as he lay down and Cara rolled towards the depression he'd created.

"At last." She sighed happily as she snuggled against him with a little shiver.

She wore only her shift and Wolf could feel the plush softness of her breasts press against him, the warmth of her palm as it settled upon his chest.

"You're so hot. Far better than any warming pan," she murmured, wriggling closer still before subsiding and falling back to sleep.

That little shiver had gone directly to Wolf's cock, which was immediately standing at attention, ready for action. Groaning inwardly, he wondered if being honourable was perhaps overrated, and resigned himself to a very long night.

He rose at dawn, too aware of the lush, warm body at his side to stay another moment, though leaving the bed was one of the hardest things he'd ever done. For a long moment he stood, staring down at Cara. Her hair had escaped the confines of her plait entirely now and spilled over the white pillow, the fiery colour startling even in the dim light of dawn. Tenderness filled his chest at the sight, and the desire to climb back in and take everything she offered was only matched by his desire to treat her with respect. She deserved a husband she could be proud of; the very least he could do was try to repair his damaged reputation enough to cause her no shame. They must hurry and get Sultan back so he could take her home, and pray they caused no scandal in the meantime.

Wolf arranged for a maid to help Cara dress, then ordered her breakfast, paid their bill, and went out to check on the pony. Passing by the kitchen, he stopped in his tracks to smell the delicious odours coming from the open door. Breakfast had been an especially delicious plate of sausages, bacon, fried potatoes, and eggs. Feeling very much in charity with the cook, he peeked in at the doorway to see a sturdy-looking woman of middling years, up to her elbows in flour. She was giving two young maids orders whilst rolling out a large slab of pastry. Seeing Wolf, she paused.

"Forgive the interruption, madame. I just wanted to thank you for a delicious breakfast. The best I've had in years," he said.

"Oh, aye," she said suspiciously, though her cheeks pinkened at his words. "Nothing special, I reckon."

"I beg to differ. I have lived all my life abroad and, whilst I have never been disappointed in breakfast, I did not know I was missing such a treat. I thank you for that."

"Oh, well, then. You're welcome. Not from round here, are you?" she said, looking him up and down with interest.

"No," Wolf said, grinning at the maids, who giggled and flushed. "Just passing through. I don't suppose you'd consider letting me buy some of that lovely looking bread there?"

He gestured to the half dozen golden loaves cooling on a tray.

"Reckon I might," the cook said, giving him an indulgent smile. "Want some ham to go with it and a bit o' butter?"

"You're an angel," Wolf said, pleased with himself.

"And you're a devil, I reckon," the lady said, but with the air of someone who liked a bit of a devil.

She made him up a parcel to take, and Wolf stowed the food in the basket on the dogcart. He hitched the pony, paying one of the stable lads to keep an eye on things whilst he went to fetch Cara, and hoped she'd be up and ready by now. He knew society folk rarely rose before midday, but assumed she was as eager to find Sultan as he was. He wanted to get back to London and speak to his grandmother as soon as possible.

Wolf was perhaps not as surprised as he ought to be to discover her breakfasting in the private parlour he'd paid for. The place was thronged with people, all of them talking at once.

He stared at Cara over the crowd, and she caught his eye, putting down her teacup and beaming at him.

"They've come to tell me about Sultan. I requested the landlady to ask around and this is the result. Everyone has been so helpful," she said, bestowing that dazzling smile upon the room in general, entirely oblivious to the brain-melting effect it had on him, and apparently everyone else, as they all appeared to be in her thrall. "Now Mr Smith here saw my wicked Sultan leave via the Ipswich road last night. Is that correct, Mr Smith?"

Mr Smith, a farmer with a suntanned face and a pervasive odour of cows, nodded encouragingly. "S'right," he said. "There's a dog in the crate on the back of that cart, see. A bitch in heat, if I guess right. That dog o' yours will follow till he gets to John O' Groats, I reckon."

"Slow you down, Burt," interrupted a stout lady with a basket on her arm. "That dog won't be going that far. For I saw the markings on that crate."

"Oh, aye?" Burt replied sceptically.

"Aye. Fancy, it was, but I seen it before now. You remember, Mrs Munson, the day that la-di-da carriage pulled up outside?"

Mrs Munson, a tiny elderly lady who appeared to have mummified herself with about three dozen shawls, nodded eagerly. "I remember. A big mean fellow 'twas. A duke, they told me. I was afeard, for he was scowling and barking at everyone, but he didn't stay, and we were all glad o' it. But we saw the fancy gold paint on the door, didn't we, Bertha?"

Bertha, for apparently that was she with the basket, nodded. "We did, and 'twas the self-same design."

"Load of ole squit!" Mr Smith said with a snort.

Bertha and Mrs Munson bristled, whilst another lady bustled forward and shoved Mr Smith aside. "Don't you be puttin' on your parts, jus' cause the ladies know summat you don't," she scolded him.

"Now, Martha, love," Mr Smith said, his ruddy face getting redder as his wife silenced him with a look. Mr Smith harrumphed, but turned back to Mrs Munson. "You reckon it's the same, then?" he asked politely.

"I don't reckon. I *know,*" Mrs Munson said, putting her chin up.

"Aye," Bertha replied, nodding her head. "That crate was stamped with a brand, and it's the coat of arms of the Duke of Sefton, so that cart's on its way to Buxton Hall."

Chapter 11

Dearest Torie,

After everything Evie put Papa through with Louis César, he has become ridiculously overprotective. I shall be lucky to be allowed out of the house during the season, let alone to 'come out' properly. It's not as though I've ever given him cause for concern either, so it's a bit galling. Though I suppose Evie didn't until she fell in love with Louis, so perhaps that doesn't prove much?

What gentleman have you made a fool of yourself with? What happened? And why am I only hearing this now? You are a rotten friend! You're supposed to tell me the moment you fall in love with someone. I tell you all the time! And yes, I admit I fall in love rather often but it's only ever from afar, for now anyway. The least you could do was share <u>one</u> with me! You must make up for it by telling me everything, no matter how mortifying.

Of course I'm not jealous of Evie, and not because I'm too nice. It's simply impossible to fancy a fellow who is quite disgustingly in love with one's sister, no matter how beautiful he is.

I can't wait for Christmas. What fun we shall have, though I warn you now, Flo and Henry's brood are the noisiest children that ever lived. Oscar is three now, and a little devil and the baby, Mabel, is a sweet creature but she makes her feelings known in no uncertain terms. Don't say I didn't warn you.

—Excerpt of a letter from Miss Emmeline Knight (youngest daughter of Lady Helena and Mr Gabriel Knight) to Lady Victoria Adolphus (daughter of Robert and Prunella Adolphus, Their Graces, The Duke and Duchess of Bedwin)

20th October 1844, Diss, Norfolk.

"Drat and bother," Cara complained as Wolf guided her out of the inn. Her ankle was much better this morning, but she was still grateful to lean upon his arm. "Why him? I ask you, of all the people that wretched hound could have got us mixed up with, why must it be him?"

Wolf nodded, looking equally grim at the discovery. He would worry for her now, for anyone who could recognise Cara was best avoided, but a man who had recently scolded her in public would not shy away from bringing her and her family further embarrassment. They must try to catch up with Sultan before he reached Buxton Hall. Wolf could very well claim the dog was his and Cara could keep out of sight, but if Sultan did not play along—which, judging by their first meeting, seemed unlikely—then he was sunk. He could not prove ownership, though Cara could if it came to it. The trouble was, Sultan was a valuable animal, and no one would give him up without a fight if they were interested in dogs.

"If we don't get him back before he reaches the hall, I will say your father sent me to fetch him back. I'm certain the earl would back me up in the circumstances," Wolf suggested.

"Well, of course he would," Cara began, because it was a good idea, and then stopped with a tut of annoyance. "Oh, for goodness' sake, I left my gloves inside. The mention of that dreadful man has me all in a fluster."

"I'll go," Wolf said at once. "Stay here."

Cara sent him a grateful smile as he hurried back inside. With a despondent sigh, she wished that the duke would suffer a painful attack of piles, proving she really was as wicked as she'd told Wolf. Pleased with this diabolical if unlikely form of revenge, an increasing commotion took her attention.

Hurrying around the corner to see what was happening, she saw a slender young man of perhaps twenty, trying to stop another, much bigger and older man in his tracks. The blacksmith, she guessed, noting his hands like anvils and muscular arms. A dog of indeterminate breed danced around them, barking and barking.

"No, Da!" the man said, trying to wrest free a sack that the man held in his meaty fist. "Please, I'll take care of them. They won't be no bother."

"I said no! Now clear off." He gave his son a hard shove, making him fall on his backside. The dog rushed up in front of him, barking furiously, and Cara gasped in shock as the man kicked it, hard, making it yelp and scurry away, but both the dog and the young man sprang back up again, determined to stop him.

"No, I won't let you!" the son said, tears streaming down his face now.

"I said, get out of my way!" the fellow shouted, backhanding his son, who gasped, clutching his cheek. The man strode determinedly towards a deep water trough.

"Oh, no," Cara said, realising what was happening. Without another thought, she rushed forward. "Sir! Sir, please, let me take the puppies. I'll see they get good homes."

She gave the fellow her most winning smile and held out her hand to take the sack.

"They're too young," the son said, his voice thick. "They're not weaned yet. They need their mother."

Cara glanced at the dog, the poor creature beside herself at the loss of her babies. "Well, I'll take the dog too, if you'll allow me," she said at once. "How much do you want for it?"

The father sneered. "Oh, will you, Miss Hoity Toity? Reckon you'll take my dog from me, do you, you snooty bitch?"

Cara coloured, having never been spoken to so rudely in her life before. "Not take. I will pay you for the dog, sir," she said coldly. "Or if you wish to keep her, allow her to keep the puppies until they are weened, then I'll send someone to fetch them. I'll buy them from you."

"Go fuck yourself," the fellow said with a nasty sneer.

"But, Da, you don't even like Bessie. If the lady will pay to take the pups that's fair," the man said desperately.

"You get yourself gone before I drown you too, you prancing little sod," the man said, looking at his son with such hatred Cara gasped with shock.

Worse was the lack of reaction on his son's face, and Cara realised he had heard it all before, so many times the words were no longer shocking to him.

"A guinea," Cara said, knowing it was an outrageous amount of money for an assortment of puppies, and not caring a jot. Anything to get them away from this brute.

"Da, a guinea," the young man said, hope shining in his eyes, but it faded quickly as he saw what Cara saw. This was the kind of man who would cut off his nose to spite his face, or refuse a small fortune for the chance to inflict a bit more misery on the world.

His hard little piggy eyes glinted with malice. "What's mine is mine, you interfering whore, and no one—"

He made a strangled choking sound as Wolf appeared from nowhere and grasped the fellow about the neck, lifting him so he was barely on tiptoes.

"What did you say to the lady?" he asked, his voice so low Cara barely heard the words, and yet they sent shivers racing down her spine.

The man made gurgling sounds but seemed incapable of more, his eyes bulging. He dropped the sack. Cara gasped, but Wolf caught it before it hit the floor, frowning down as something in it moved.

"Wolf, there are puppies in the sack," Cara said desperately.

Wolf's face, already set with fury, seemed to grow colder.

"This young man was trying to stop his father from drowning them," Cara said. "I offered to buy them if he would let them stay with their mother, for they are too young to leave her yet."

"And he refused," Wolf said, never taking his eyes from the fellow who was clawing at his hand to no avail.

"I offered him a guinea," Cara said, watching with increasing awe as Wolf held the man as though he weighed nothing at all.

Wolf turned, eyeing the slender young man who had so bravely stood up to his father, and seeing the red handprint on his fair skin and the bloody lip.

"This your pa?" he asked.

The young man nodded.

"Is he always like this, or is it a special occasion?"

The man's mouth twisted. "Not always like this, sometimes he's worse," he said with such weary resignation to his voice Cara's heart went out to him.

Wolf studied him for a long moment, apparently unconcerned by the man dangling from his iron grip. "Want to get away from him?"

For a moment, the son's eyes lit but once again, the light quickly died. "Can't. Got no money, no prospects. Not trained for anything. Da says I'm too weak to work with him."

Wolf looked him over, still holding the gurgling blacksmith. He was neatly turned out for one of his station, his cravat immaculately tied, if worn, and his coat well-fitted. Apart from the dust on his behind where his father had knocked him down, he looked almost elegant.

"You do that?" Wolf gestured to his outfit.

The boy coloured and stood a bit taller, a defensive glint in his eyes. "Yes. I made the coat myself from a cast off. It was much bigger before," he added.

Wolf nodded. "I need a valet. Can you iron, clean clothes, that sort of thing?"

Cara had never seen anyone's eyes grow so round, so fast.

"Can I?" the man said. "I can do all that and more. I'll polish your boots so you can see your face in them. You won't be sorry. I'm a hard worker. I'll be the best valet you ever had!" he said, breathless with excitement.

"That won't be hard, I never had one before," Wolf said dryly, before handing him the squirming sack of puppies. "Get a crate and some straw and make a bed for them and their mother in the back of the pony cart in the stables next door. Take the young lady with you. I'm going to have a little talk to your father about the sale of his dog."

"But, sir… my brothers, sir…." the man said, but Wolf had already turned his attention back to the blacksmith.

The son looked at Cara expectantly. She shook her head and waved him away.

"You go. I'll be there in a bit," she whispered, not wanting to distract Wolf, who had dropped the blacksmith as if he was contaminated. The man gasped, clutching at his throat and staring at Wolf with undisguised loathing.

"Warn him about my brothers, miss. They're just as bad as he is," the young man said, before running around to the stables as though he feared Wolf would change his mind.

"Wolf!" Cara called, gaining herself a frustrated glare from the man.

"Go to the stables," he commanded, and turned back to the blacksmith.

"You'll regret that," the fellow said to Wolf, sounding as if he'd swallowed glass.

"No," Wolf replied serenely. "Don't reckon I will."

The blacksmith stuck two fingers in his mouth and gave an ear-splitting whistle. A moment later, the brothers the young man had warned her about came lumbering out. Good grief. These men were built like their father, but how they were all related to the one with the puppies, Cara could not fathom.

"Wolf!" Cara shouted with alarm, but Wolf was grinning, a feral look in his eyes that Cara could hardly credit belonged to the same man in whose arms she had slept, the man who had treated her so carefully, so gently.

There was nothing gentle about him now, nothing visible of the man she loved every trace of him hidden behind this hard exterior. She had glimpsed it before, the night he had swept into his grandmother's house like the devil himself. This was the person he was in Paris, in that other life where he lived as *Le Loup Noir*.

One of the younger men, cockier and surer of himself than the others, charged at Wolf like a raging bull. Given he was a shorter but wider version of his father, it was a tactic that would likely flatten most men. Wolf casually tossed his hat to one side, stepped out of the way of the oncoming brute, and shoved him hard in the direction he'd already been running. The extra impetus had the fellow crashing into a wall, knocking himself out cold. His brother and father moved together then, clearly deciding there was strength in numbers.

Cara squealed, wincing as the men exchanged blows, but Wolf knocked the son out with a right hook that had him windmilling backwards and sitting with a splash in a water trough. The fellow just sat there, legs dangling, looking dazed. The father, however, was older, more belligerent, and determined to do some damage. He walked back to the shop and picked up an iron bar left leaning against the wall of the smithy. He smacked it into his free hand, giving Wolf a nasty smile.

"Still want to impress your pretty bit of muslin, do you? She looks expensive. Still, if I knock you out, I reckon she can make up for the trouble you've caused me, eh?"

Cara knew the fellow was goading Wolf into losing his temper and only prayed...

Oh, dear.

Wolf flew at him, and the fellow raised the iron bar, but Wolf was too quick, shoving the arm holding the bar with his shoulder and pushing the man's face with his arm. The fellow went down with a crash. Wolf followed him, smashing the hand holding the iron bar against the ground until he let it go.

"Had enough?" he growled.

The man gave a bellow of rage and went for Wolf's throat with both hands. Wolf punched him in the guts and the man

169

subsided with a choked moan. Getting to his feet, Wolf brushed the dust from his clothes and smoothed off his lapels before reaching for his money. Tossing a generous number of coins to the man sprawled on the floor, he gave him a contemptuous look.

"For the dog," he said in disgust, and turned to walk away.

He froze as he saw Cara watching him.

For a moment, he looked horrified that she had seen what he'd done, and Cara could not have that. She flew into his arms, holding him tightly.

"Thank you!" she said, kissing his cheek. "Oh, darling, you were magnificent. I was never so proud of anyone in my life."

He looked at once mortified and pleased, colour rising on his cheeks at her words, and Cara hugged him again, utterly besotted with this wonderful man.

"Oh, you are so lovely, my Wolf, and I do love you so."

"Cara," he whispered, gazing down at her with such a soft look in his eyes, Cara's insides melted along with her brain.

She sighed happily.

Remembering where he was, Wolf cleared his throat. "We'd best get out of here before someone calls a constable."

Cara nodded and watched as Wolf went to retrieve his hat. He was bending down when she saw the man rise, dripping from the water trough, and go after him. Before she could think too much about it, Cara ran after him, ignoring the twinge in her ankle. She picked up the iron bar the man's father had dropped and clouted him around the back of the legs. The fellow dropped like a stone, clutching at his leg and cursing.

"That will teach you to attack from behind," she said in disgust. "A cowardly thing to do, is it not? And do stop making such a fuss. I didn't hit you hard, you'll have a little bruise, that's all, so stop being such a baby about it. You, sir, are a bully, which is hardly surprising with such a father, but need you be so very unimaginative as to behave just as badly as he does? You don't have to, you know. You're a grown man. You could go away from him and begin again, you could—"

"All right, love, that will do," Wolf said gently, taking her arm and guiding her away.

"But I hadn't done talking to him!" she protested with a huff.

"I know," he said. "But it's not for you to scold him, the poor devil doesn't know any better. What chance has he had with a father like that?"

Cara frowned. "You had a father like that, and you're not a bully."

"I had a mother that taught me differently, and then I had Louis, showing me what it was to be a good man, how to be strong without being a tyrant. Perhaps they weren't so lucky."

"He was going to attack you from behind!" she exclaimed, bewildered that he should defend them so.

"Yes, he's a dishonourable cur, but your life and his are worlds apart, love. Don't judge what you don't understand. You've not the right." His eyes were kind, but she did not underestimate the tone of his voice.

Cara flushed, mortified. "I'm sorry," she said, chastised. "I did not know."

"Of course not," he said gently, smiling at her. "And I'm glad that you don't, but sometimes people do bad things for the right reasons. You would not like much of the life I've lived either, Cara, the things I have done. Have you ever really thought about that?"

"Yes," she admitted. "But I believe in you. I believe that you did what you thought you must."

He smiled and touched her cheek, stroking it. "I hope that's true. And now you did what you thought you must to keep me safe."

"I did," she said, understanding in that moment how someone might do something bad to save a loved one, like the blacksmith's sons defending their father. She still thought they were horrid, but she also understood that she did not have the right to pass judgement on them.

"I know," he said, giving her a look that made her feel hot all over. "You saved me."

She put up her chin. "Yes. I did."

"Thank you, love." He smiled.

She grinned at him, relieved he wasn't angry with her for being a spoiled brat. After all, she was as much a product of her background as the blacksmith's sons.

His expression grew serious then, and he wagged a finger at her. "And if you ever do such a hare-brained thing again, I will—"

"What?" she said indignantly.

He sighed. "I haven't the faintest idea."

Chapter 12

My Lord,

I am returning something that belongs to you, as I do not believe you intended for it to be left unattended in Piccadilly.

You may consider it my good deed for the century.

Please do not count upon me being so full of Christian charity in the future, for the next time I shall ignore it and go about my business.

—Excerpt of a letter from The Most Hon'ble Ciarán St Just, Marquess of Kilbane to The Most Hon'ble Lucian Barrington, Marquess of Montagu.

20th October 1844, on the road to Norwich, Norfolk.

The young man was called Jo Taylor and was one and twenty years of age. He told them he had long held the ambition to be a tailor or a valet, but his father had put paid to any thoughts of that nature. His mother had died the year previous. Whilst she'd lived, she had held their father's worst behaviour in check. Since she had gone, the man had taken to drink and using his fists more often than not.

"Poor Bessie will be pleased to be away from the brute," Jo said, stroking the dog's head as the pups suckled greedily, unperturbed by the rattle and jolt of the carriage.

Cara, who was sitting sideways on the seat so she could look at Jo and the pups, nodded.

"The poor thing took a terrible kick, is she unharmed?"

Jo nodded. "Just bruised, I think."

"And you?" Cara asked, her voice gentle.

"I'm well, miss, thank you for asking," he replied, eyes shining with admiration as he looked back at her.

Wolf joined the conversation, glancing over his shoulder at Jo. "Can you be trusted to hold your tongue? For if you're to valet for me, I need someone with discretion. I warn you now, the first sign that you've been gossiping—"

"No, sir!" Jo said, paling with worry. "I never would. I'll keep your secrets. I'll take them to my grave, sir. I never thought I'd have such a chance as this. I won't lose it. I won't let you down, as God is my witness."

Wolf swivelled in his seat and studied the fellow for a long moment. Jo looked to be sweating under the force of his scrutiny, but eventually Wolf nodded.

"All right, then. In that case, you ought to know that this is Lady Cara Baxter."

Jo's eyes grew wider as he darted a look at Cara.

"A real lady," he said, sounding rather winded.

"The daughter of the Earl of Trevick," Wolf added, turning his attention back to the pony. "And if anyone discovers who she is and, worse, who she is with, there will be the most almighty scandal. Do you understand?"

"I do, sir," Jo said at once. "So, you… are travelling as husband and wife?"

Wolf shifted uneasily in his seat.

"Yes," Cara said. "We are Mr and Mrs Jenkins for the time being, and it's because of my dog that we're in this fix. He ran away—took the train if you can believe that. Now he is following a crate, which we believe contains a female in heat. The poor fellow believes himself in love," she said with a wry smile.

Jo gave a startled laugh. "And you've come all this way to rescue him?"

"Of course," Cara said, a little indignantly. "Sultan is my dearest friend and companion. Well, apart from Wolf," she added, tucking her hand into Wolf's arm.

He smiled down at her and Cara sighed.

"Wolf?" Jo queried.

"Wulfric De Vere, Viscount Latimer," Cara said.

Jo looked as if he was about to burst. "A viscount! I'm going to be valeting a viscount?"

"Don't get too excited," Wolf said with a snort. "I'm a very poorly behaved viscount, and society is none too pleased with my arrival in their midst. Don't go expecting me to be giving balls, or even attending them anytime soon."

"Wolf has lived his whole life in France, because his father was a scandal and was forced to stay away."

"Oh, my," Jo said, looking like all his Christmases had come at once. "This is the best day of my life. I'm going to like working for you, my lord."

Wolf snorted with amusement.

Once they got to Norwich, Wolf booked their accommodation in a charming pub called the Brick Kiln. The exterior walls of the pub were pink, a colour traditional to the area and made by adding pig's blood or elderberries to the lime wash. The thick thatched roof gave the place a friendly appearance. It seemed ideal, too, as the back of the pub was busy with animals, with everything from the expected chickens and geese to pigs, goats, and donkeys, and even a tiny Shetland pony. The landlady immediately accommodated their needs for Bessie and her pups with such enthusiasm that they all knew this was the perfect place to stay. Cara adored it and was only sorry that they could not stay longer. They were only an hour and a half from Buxton Hall, though, and they could not turn up looking for Sultan with another dog and pups in tow.

"Now, you're not to worry," Wolf said to Jo, pressing a money purse into his hands. "The rooms are paid for tonight, and your dinner, too. We ought to be back well before then, but just in case you've any trouble, keep that on you."

Jo shook his head, trying to hand the purse back. "Oh, no, my lord, I—"

"Stow it," Wolf said amicably. "See what you can do with the shirt in my suitcase because it needs a wash and I've not another spare, other than that, do as you please. We'll see you later."

Once they were back on the cart, Cara snuggled up to Wolf.

"Alone at last," she said, grinning at him.

Wolf sighed. "Was I that obvious?"

"Only to me."

He leaned down and kissed her and Cara slid a hand behind his neck, holding him in place.

"Stop it," he growled, straightening. "You make me think wicked things."

"What kind of wicked things?" she asked at once.

He snorted. "Dreadful creature, you sound so delighted."

"I am! You must know by now I adore you when you're wicked, and even more when you're very, very good," she added in a low whisper.

Wolf groaned. "Stop it. You're making this unbearable."

"Sorry," she said, sitting back, entirely unrepentant.

She behaved herself for the next hour, chatting about her family, her friends, and peppering Wolf with questions about his life in Paris.

"I don't like the look of that," she said a little later, eyeing a thick, angry tumble of clouds that were moving swiftly towards them. As she spoke, the wind picked up, the mild autumnal day becoming chilly and blustery.

"Me either. Where the devil did it come from? We'd best find shelter fast. That looks like it will be unpleasant."

Wolf urged the pony to a trot and, about half a mile down the lane, Cara pointed.

"Over there!" she shouted, having to raise her voice over the howling wind which was buffeting them with concerning force.

Wolf nodded, directing the pony towards a collection of dilapidated red brick farm buildings. From a distance they could see the roofs had collapsed on two of them, but the third looked sound. The previously bright afternoon had the glowering aspect of impending nightfall now, smothering the daylight, a sickly colour staining the sky as the storm took hold.

"Oh!" Cara shrieked in dismay as the heavens opened and rain fell in an unholy torrent.

Lightning crazed the skies ahead of them, followed not long after by a resounding crash of thunder. The pony, who until this point had been bombproof, tossed its head and danced on the spot.

Wolf jumped down and took the creature by the bridle, hurrying it towards the barns. He opened the big barn doors as

Cara urged the pony inside, all three of them eager to escape the appalling weather.

Another flash of light lit the skies. Wolf fought to shut the doors as the wind howled through the opening. Cara jumped down from the cart and ran to help, securing the doors just as an explosion of thunder erupted overhead.

Cara jumped in shock and Wolf reached for her, pulling her close.

"Are you all right?"

She laughed, hugging him tightly. "I am now. It just startled me, that's all. What foul weather, and so unlucky when we were so close. I felt certain we would catch up to Sultan."

"Well, remember the cart and driver are probably caught in this too, and doing much the same thing. Besides, I think I've had my quota of luck for one lifetime," he added with a crooked smile, gazing at her with such fondness Cara experienced a sensation of giddy happiness the like of which she'd never known. She burrowed closer into his embrace.

"You're shivering," he observed with a frown. "Lord, you're soaked through."

"S-So are you," she replied as her teeth chattered. "Though it's only my cape that's wet, I think."

Wolf rubbed her arms, grimacing at the sodden material of her cape. "Take it off and we'll hang it up, though I don't see it drying anytime soon without a fire."

"Never mind me," Cara said, gesturing at him. "The cape saved me from the worst of it, but you're dripping. You'd best get those wet things off."

Wolf stared down at himself, regarding his sodden clothes with a frown. He glanced back up at her, quirking an eyebrow.

"You've been dying to get me out of my clothes, haven't you?" he said, amusement glinting in his eyes.

"Well, obviously," she said, exasperated. "You didn't expect me to deny it?"

He laughed and shook his head. "No. No, I did not."

She grinned and hurried to help him with his buttons.

Once his waistcoat was hanging on a handy peg, Cara stepped back to watch as he stripped off his shirt. Her breath caught at the sight of him, and Wolf paused, his damp shirt held in one hand.

"Don't look at me like that," he groaned, turning away from her to hang his wet things up.

"Can't help it," she managed, impressed she'd remembered how to use words, because... because.... "You are quite simply magnificent."

"Don't be daft," he said at once, glancing at her over his shoulder.

"Not daft in the least," she whispered, moving towards him as if he were the magnet she'd once compared him to. "What's this?"

Wolf jolted as her icy hand touched his shoulder, her fingers delicately tracing what looked like a severe burn.

"I shan't tell you," he said, chuckling.

She narrowed her eyes. "Yes, you will."

"No. I better not, you'll not be able to keep your hands off me if I do," he warned her.

She snorted at that. "No different to now, then," she said, attempting to put her freezing hands on his taut abdomen.

Wolf danced away. "No, you don't, not with cold hands."

She pouted and made a show of warming her fingers by cupping them around her mouth and blowing. "Tell me."

"No. You'll only swoon at my heroics," he said with a sigh, his dark eyes glinting.

Cara snorted and made a show of folding her arms and stamping her foot, trying her best not to laugh as she attempted to look cross. "Tell me at once, you beastly creature!"

"Did you just stamp your foot?" he demanded with delighted outrage.

"Yes, and I shall do it again if you don't tell me everything."

Wolf laughed and shook his head at her antics. "Very well, but let's get this poor pony settled. By the sound of that storm, we'll be here for a bit."

The barn was obviously still in use and well stocked with straw and hay, so Wolf unhitched and rubbed down the pony whilst Cara watched his muscles bunch and shift with increasing agitation. Once the pony had been settled with a supply of hay, Wolf made them a place to sit by making a comfortable bed of straw. Then he went to the cart and opened the basket, and they were relieved to discover both the picnic blanket and the food had escaped the worst of the wet.

"There," he said, collapsing on the impromptu bed with a sigh and patting the space beside him.

Cara went willingly, surprised he was not trying to fend her off after his words last night.

He yelped as she burrowed into him, her chilled hands against his chest.

"How are you this hot when it's freezing?" she demanded, pressing her cold cheek against his skin.

"I've no idea, considering I'm hugging a little icicle. Lord, Cara, you're freezing."

He rubbed his big hands over her arms, up and down her back. "There's a swifter way to warm me," she said, giving him a hopeful glance.

His gaze darkened, and he bent his head to kiss her. Cara turned onto her back, taking him with her, exploring the delicious landscape of silky skin over hard muscle. She broke the kiss, too tempted to nuzzle into the hair on his chest, provoking a laugh from him until she touched her mouth to his skin. He stilled then, and she kissed him again and again, until her mouth reached the darker skin of his nipple. She kissed that too and then closed her mouth over it and sucked.

He made a pleased sound that rumbled through him, and Cara's hand slid down his belly, diverting to circle his belly button, which made him shiver, and then over the fall on his trousers. She heard his breath catch as her hand settled over the hard shape beneath the fabric.

"I'm not seducing you," she said, and then laughed. "At least, not more than I did before. I'll still be a virgin, so… that's acceptable?"

He nodded, his dark eyes riveted upon her.

"Tell me about the scar," she said, caressing him through the material, her hand sliding up and down.

"My God, you expect me to think?" he asked in astonishment, and then groaned as she squeezed his erection.

Cara stopped, staring at his face expectantly. He glared at her.

"Oh, I see. Cruel, Cara, very cruel."

She grinned at him, pleased.

He sighed. "Louis was kidnapped, taken by… well, that's a long story and not mine to share. But he was kidnapped, and the fellow who had him was barking mad. He stabbed Louis and then set fire to the building they were in, intending that they both die inside."

Cara stared at him in horror, too appalled to keep touching him now. Instead, she laid her hand to his cheek, stroking gently. "Oh, Wolf. How terrifying."

Wolf nodded. "He really was insane, and Louis was badly hurt. I discovered them, fought the madman, who might have succeeded in killing me had Louis not shot him. But by then, the fire was raging out of control. Louis told me to leave him there, but... that was impossible. So I carried him out. A burning timber fell as we went, and that's the result," he said, gesturing to the scar.

Cara's eyes prickled with tears, her throat growing tight. "You saved his life. You really are a hero."

Wolf shrugged, his expression wry now. "Well, on that occasion, I like to think so, though mostly I do it to embarrass him. But, honestly, Louis was all I had then. I rather worshipped him. I don't know what would have become of me if he'd died. I had to get him out, as much for my sake as his. Louis' brother Nic is a good man, a good friend, and he was kind too, but... it wasn't the same."

"You're close," she said.

He turned onto his side, staring into her eyes. His gaze was soft, hiding nothing. Cara stared back in wonder. He was so different to any other man she'd met, so open and ready to share himself.

"We are close, though we are very different. But I don't want to talk about him or my heroic nature right now."

Cara's lips quirked. "No?" she said, feigning innocence.

"No," he said firmly, and kissed her.

With fingers that were not entirely steady, she unbuttoned his trousers and small clothes, seeking skin as he deepened the kiss. He gasped against her mouth as her hand closed around him and, if she'd thought him hot elsewhere, here he was burning. Cara's insides squirmed with longing, wanting to draw that heat inside her with an intensity that shocked her.

"Like this." He guided her, his big hand engulfing hers as he showed her how to stroke him.

"Wolf," she said, feeling as if she'd run mad if he didn't make love to her, yet she knew what he wanted and why, and did not want to spoil his plans.

Her body did not understand this need to wait, though, and the clamouring desire for his touch made her restless with impatience.

"Easy, love," he said, and she sighed with relief as he tugged her skirts up and slid his hand between her legs. "Better?" he asked with a chuckle as he sifted teasing fingers through her curls to her clitoris and caressed her.

"A bit," she ground out. "But I can't wait to be yours, Wolf. This... This is intolerable! I need you. I need you inside me."

He made a choked sound and his body shuddered as he spent. Cara watched, her own need subsumed by her desire to watch him, entranced by the sight of his powerful body entirely at the mercy of her touch in this moment. Wolf collapsed with a gasp and then gave a strangled laugh.

"You will kill me," he observed, shaking his head. He lay still for a while, catching his breath and then fished in his pocket for a handkerchief and cleaned himself up.

Cara got to her knees, aware she was behaving most inappropriately, but at this point in the proceedings it seemed too late to worry about such things.

"Wolf," she said, her voice determined. "I know I ought not ask, but really, I need to be certain you feel the same way I do. I need to know exactly where we stand. I know you care for me and I... well, I am ridiculously, hopelessly in love with you so... will you marry me? *Please?*" she added as an afterthought.

He gazed up at her in stunned silence. She suspected he was still a bit dazed from his climax, but he looked shocked and bewildered, and she wondered if she had gone too far, been too outrageously forward. Then he smiled.

"You didn't need to wait until I was too addled to think straight, you know."

"I know, but—"

She gasped as he rolled her onto her back.

"Foolish girl. Of course I'll marry you," he said, stroking her hair from her face. "Did you think I wouldn't ask? That I wasn't making plans? I'd marry you now, this minute if I could, but I-I don't want your family to hate me, Cara. I've been alone for a long time now and I don't want you to ever experience that, to be cut off from the people you love. And, selfishly, I would like them to like me too, despite... well, *everything.*"

She smiled up at him. "My family would never do that to me, my love, and they will adore you, too. Once they get over the initial shock, at least," she said with a shrug, knowing it would not be quite that easy. "You don't mind that I asked you? I know it's not my place to, but—"

He kissed her, silencing her concerns in the best way possible, and Cara melted against him, sighing with pleasure as he recommenced his explorations under her skirts. All the while he kissed her, slow, drugging kisses that threatened her sanity as his rough hands touched her so carefully, teasing and gentle until she felt the inexorable rush of pleasure steal over her in a wave of heat and rising joy. She laughed, dizzy with it as she clutched at his shoulders, holding on as the world fell away beneath her. He held her steady, held her tight. When she came back to herself, it was to find his dark gaze warm upon her, and everything she saw in his eyes made her heart soar.

Once they had tidied themselves up, they demolished the bread and butter and ham that the cook at The Ram had supplied them with, Cara giving a little yip of delight at the discovery the cook had also packed a wrapped packet of shortbread.

"Oh, if only I had a cup of tea," she said, giving a little moan of enjoyment as she bit into the crumbly, buttery biscuit.

Wolf felt the sound travel straight to his groin and made himself get up before he could get any more ideas. The storm had abated, and they needed to get back on the road.

Dressing again was unpleasant, as his clothes were damp and chilly still. Praying that they caught up with Sultan quickly, Wolf hitched the pony and they set off once again.

Chapter 13

Dear Lydia,

I have been extolling your grandson's virtues and tugging on every heartstring I could find with tales of his father's cruelty to his son. I think many of the ladies I spoke to have softened towards him. No doubt the glimpse they got of his magnificent shoulders at your party had more to do with that than any tender feelings I roused, but if it yields the correct results, it does not signify.

I have discovered the Duke and Duchess of Bedwin will also support him. The duke grumbled somewhat, but what with Mr Demarteau married to their daughter, and our new Comtesse de Villen agitating on Latimer's behalf, there was nothing else to be done. Of course, it is in the Knights' interests that they help Latimer succeed also, as he is so closely associated with their new son-in-law. So, your grandson has some powerful friends, which is an excellent start. Unfortunately, all our good work will come to nothing if the news I am about to impart gets out.

When I called upon Lady Trevick this morning, it was obvious she was in a fluster. After a little persuasion, I coaxed the story from her. Happily, she knows I am to be trusted and am an intimate friend of the Bedwins, so she shared her concerns. It appears Lady Cara has a rather ill-behaved dog which has a habit of running away. She failed to return home after her walk yesterday – the footman she took with her was elsewhere, it appears – and the girl was still missing the following morning. Their fears were confirmed on receipt of a letter from their daughter which arrived whilst I was there. The gist of the thing implied the dog was indeed at fault, but that she was quite safe and having 'a marvellous time' and would be back soon.

After this, I returned home to discover none other than the Duke of Axton awaiting me. His grace told me in confidence that he'd seen Latimer in company with Lady Cara at London Bridge train station yesterday. His daughter-in-law, upon whom he dotes, is a friend of the lady and seeing her with your grandson alarmed him considerably. Thankfully, he had the good sense to come to me with the information – there is a first time for everything.

I was so anxious about this turn of events that I took the first train I could to visit my grandson, Barnaby, who is a guest of the Comte and Comtesse de Villen. I hoped the comte might have information about where

Latimer was going. He was expected here, Lydia, but he never arrived.

I leave you to draw your own conclusions.

—Excerpt of a letter from The Right Hon'ble Hester Henley, Lady Balderston to Lydia De Vere, The Right Hon'ble, The Dowager Viscountess Latimer.

20ᵗʰ October 1844, Aylsham, Norfolk.

By the time they reached Aylsham, they were both chilled to the bone, but a recent sighting of Sultan suggested they were less than half an hour behind their quarry. Wolf cast a longing glance at the Black Boy Inn as they drove past, which promised a cosy parlour and a hot meal. Perhaps once they had the wretched dog back, they could take the time to warm up. For now, they had to press on, hoping to get hold of the troublesome hound before they reached Buxton Hall. Wolf hoped to goodness it was soon, for though Cara had not been as thoroughly drenched as he had, she was still cold, and he could feel the fine tremors run through her as she shivered beside him.

"There!" she cried, startling him so much he jumped in alarm, but then he saw what she was pointing at.

They had finally caught up with the cart. There it was, just ahead of them, turning in behind the inn, and there was Sultan, tongue lolling, loping along behind it. Wolf turned the pony and followed the cart into the yard. It was a bustling place, with grooms and footmen rushing around an elegant carriage and four glossy black horses. Wolf took one look at the gold insignia on the door of the carriage and his heart sank.

"Sultan!" Cara exclaimed, scrambling down from the cart before Wolf could stop her.

At the sound of his mistress's voice, Sultan erupted, giving a joyful woof that made everyone in the yard jump as he bounded towards Cara like a spring lamb.

"Oh, you naughty, naughty boy!" she said, running to him with as much enthusiasm and a laugh that made every head turn in her direction. Wolf threw the reins of the pony cart to a nearby groom and hurried after her, grasping her arm to steady her as Sultan almost knocked her flat in his eagerness to greet her.

"That your dog, then?" asked the driver of the cart they had been pursuing. He had been feeding a carrot to the sturdy grey pony that drew his cart and now gestured to Sultan with the long handle of his pipe.

"He is, yes," Cara said, curling her slim fingers around Sultan's collar. "We've been following him since Colchester."

"Aye, reckon you have. He appeared off the train when we unloaded Miss Lucy." The fellow now gestured to the large crate on the back of the cart. "What are the odds of two great big dogs like that finding each other, eh? True love, I reckon," the fellow said, chuckling.

A deep woof came from the cart, and through the wooden slats, Wolf could see a fawn-coloured dog, her nose pressed to the gap in the wood. Sultan strained forward and Cara struggled to hold him.

"Here," Wolf said, taking hold of the dog's collar. "Would you have any rope?" he asked the driver, who nodded and turned back to the cart.

"What's all this?" boomed an imperious voice, making everyone turn in the carriage's direction. "Slater? Why am I being kept waiting? You ought to have been here this morning, and now I discover you stopping off at the damned pub instead of delivering my dog as you were paid to do."

With dismay, Wolf regarded the man that stepped down from the carriage. He was perhaps close to sixty years of age, of average height but grossly overweight, with a short neck, a shock of white hair, and a florid complexion that suggested a life of overindulgence. The way he carried himself, though, the extravagant manner of his dress and that imperious, cut-glass accent only confirmed Wolf's suspicion.

"I'm sorry, your grace," the driver said, swiping his hat from his head and bowing low. "We got caught in a terrible storm which delayed us some, and then 'bout half a mile away, poor Snowdrop here picked up a stone. I thought I'd best sort her out afore we went too much farther."

The duke harrumphed. "Excuses!" he said in disgust before catching sight of Sultan and frowning. "And why is my dog running about free in the yard?"

"He's not your dog!" Cara said at once, glaring at the man.

The duke's gaze swivelled towards her, and Wolf stifled a groan.

"You!" he said contemptuously. "The ill-mannered chit who threw soup at Mr Handley! What the devil are *you* doing here?"

Wolf's temper sparked but Cara tugged surreptitiously at his sleeve, glaring at him. He held his tongue, simmering inwardly and praying the fellow did not insult her any further, for he could not afford to upset a bloody duke.

"I came to retrieve my dog, your grace," Cara said, clearly struggling as fiercely as Wolf was to treat the man with the respect his title was due. "He has taken a fancy to your Miss Lucy and took it into his head to follow."

The duke stepped closer, regarding Sultan with a keen eye that made Wolf uneasy.

"A very fine specimen," the duke admitted. "Very fine. I've a male myself, Tiberius. Miss Lucy here was for him, though I must admit, this fellow has him beat to flinders. Very fine indeed. How much do you want for him?"

Cara's chin went up, her eyes flashing. "He is *not* for sale."

"Everything is for sale at the right price," the duke said, waving this away as so much nonsense.

"Not Sultan!" Cara insisted, and Wolf could sense the tension singing through her, the desire to tear the wretched man off a strip and give him the set down he so richly deserved, but she could not do that, and she knew it. They both knew it, and it vexed Wolf to the point of fury as she became increasingly agitated. "He was a gift from my father," she added from between her teeth.

The duke scowled, increasingly impatient. "Pfft, so you can get another with the money from the sale. I'll pay you double what your father bought him for."

"No! Never! Sultan is my friend and companion. You do not sell your friends," Cara said, and her face was flushed, her voice strained with the effort of keeping her temper in check.

Wolf gritted his teeth, his hand tightening on Sultan's collar, the desire to give the old duke a piece of his mind making his skin prickle.

"Sentimental claptrap," Sefton said derisively. "I want the dog. How much?"

"He. Is. Not. For sale," Cara gritted out.

The duke narrowed his eyes and Wolf, whose instinct for trouble was finely honed, knew that things were about to take a turn for the worse.

"Really," Sefton said, his voice cool now. "I was prepared to be reasonable, but as you are proving yourself to be every bit the hoyden I knew you were, I see we shall have to speak plain. Where is your father, Lady Cara, and who is this man in whose company you seem to be alone?"

"I am Latimer," Wolf said coldly, giving the duke the benefit of an equally contemptuous look down his nose. "Lady Cara has been visiting the area with her brother, Viscount Harleston, who owns property near here. The dog got loose, and we set out after him. We were all travelling in Harleston's carriage but the storm which Mr Slater referred to caused damage to one of the wheels. Rather than lose Sultan, to whom his sister is so very attached, we hired the dog cart in order to retrieve him. I would have come alone but Sultan has no love for men and only Cara could have coaxed him back. We are meeting up with the viscount now that Sultan is back where he belongs. There is no scandal here, your grace. Though I must point out the viscount and his father would be dismayed to discover you tried to uncover one."

It was a long shot, for it would be easy enough to determine if her brother was close by or not, but the Earl of Trevick was a powerful man too, and not one the duke would wish to insult if he could help it.

"Poppycock! I'd wager fifty pounds Harleston isn't within a hundred miles of here."

"Much as it pains me to disagree with you, your grace," came a drawling voice from inside the carriage. "But it just so happens that Harleston *is* here."

"What!" the duke roared, turning towards the carriage with fury. "And just how do you know that? Did you *see* him?" he demanded with a sneer.

An elegant long-fingered white hand appeared in the carriage's doorway and a footman hastened forward, taking it in his. The young man that stepped gracefully out of the carriage was perhaps six and twenty, and had both Cara and Wolf staring. His hair was guinea gold, a rich colour that caught the light and seemed shocking in the dingy surroundings of the yard on an overcast afternoon. He was tall and lithe and dressed exquisitely. Wolf would have labelled him a dandy, except there was such precision and restraint in his attire that the word did not quite fit, suggesting as it did excess and fussiness. There was nothing fussy about his man, he was starkly handsome, and aware of both his power and the effect he had on people. In one hand, he carried a walking stick, and it was this, together with the strange dark glass spectacles he wore—a glaring contrast to his pale skin—that made Wolf realise, rather belatedly, he was blind.

The duke's comment took on a new, cruel meaning.

The young man's mouth curved into a smile. "I did not *see* him, your grace, but then I cannot see the shit in this yard, yet I am well aware that it is there all the same."

"Mind your tongue, Wrexham," the duke snarled.

"Oh, do excuse me, Lady Cara," the young man said at once. "I am not much in society, and I have forgotten my manners. Ah, but I have done it again, for we have not been introduced. I am Wrexham, but I suppose you gathered that much."

Cara curtsied. "It is a very great pleasure to make your acquaintance, my lord," she said, the sincerity in her voice obvious, for Wrexham knew as well as they did her brother was *not* in the area. Why he had decided to help them, Wolf could not fathom, but he knew little of the English aristocracy and their ways, having never been a part of society himself.

"Never mind doing the pretty. The lady can admire your finery at another time, coxcomb. Where is Harleston?" the duke demanded irritably.

"Why, don't you remember when you stopped at Taverham to berate that farmer for spilling the contents of his cart across the road? Though, of course, you were quite correct to do so. How selfish of him to have broken an axle when you wished to continue your journey unhindered." Wrexham spoke with such utter seriousness Wolf was uncertain if he was mocking the duke or truly agreed with such an outrageous statement. Looking at him, either could be true.

"What the devil has that to do with Harleston?" the duke thundered.

"Why, only that he was there," Wrexham said placidly. "Whilst the road was being cleared, and you went inside the hostelry to refresh yourself, I stayed in the carriage as you bid me. For we do not wish to alarm the populace, do we, your grace?"

"Get on with it!"

Wrexham gave an elegant shrug. "Well, Harleston was there. His carriage was being repaired in the village, but I knew him when I was a boy, and he is such a charming fellow. Never holds a grudge," he said smoothly. "We spoke briefly, and he went about his way. So, there you are. Oh, and Lord Thomas was with him, now I think of it. They are close, I believe, but then Trevick and Montagu are friends, are they not?"

Wrexham dropped the name casually, but Wolf guessed he had nicely calculated the effect it would have on the duke. Cara, never slow on the uptake, leapt in.

"Oh, yes. Montagu is such a dear. I've always regarded him as an uncle, and he dotes on darling Sultan. He's quite the animal lover."

"Yes, I heard that myself," Wrexham said, his lips twitching just a little. "But why the interest in Harleston and this dog?"

"Because your father has been trying to force me to sell him my dog, my lord. I have tried to explain that Sultan is not only an animal but part of the family. We love him far too dearly to let him go, but then your father insinuated he would ruin me if I did not do as he bid."

"Oh, but surely not!" Wrexham replied, his hand pressed to his heart in a theatrical gesture of dismay. "Your grace? I am certain Lady Cara misunderstood, for you would never ride roughshod over a young lady in such a brutish manner. Not when she has such powerful friends, at least," he added, and this time the animosity in his voice was audible.

"Of course she misunderstood, the foolish chit," the duke growled, glaring at his son with undisguised loathing. "Get in the carriage, damn you. I'll not waste another minute on this tarradiddle."

The duke brushed past his son, pushing him off balance. Wrexham stumbled on the uneven cobbles and Wolf stepped forward, steadying him.

"Thank you," Wolf said in a low voice. "If ever you have need of anything, you may depend upon me."

"Ah. You're Latimer, the one who has everyone in such an uproar," Wrexham said, a smile in his voice.

"I am."

"You may depend on me remembering that." Wrexham nodded. "Lady Cara?"

Cara stepped closer to stand beside Wolf. "Yes, my lord?"

"Take care of that dog of yours. They are loyal companions and deserve our protection, even if they cause a frightful lot of bother."

"I will, my lord," Cara said, impulsively reaching out to take his hand and squeeze it. "Thank you so much."

Wrexham sketched an elegant bow before calling for a footman, who guided him back into the carriage.

Wolf and Cara watched as it drove away.

Chapter 14

Dear Hester,

The best thing Latimer could do would be to marry the girl. I admit I hope he does ruin her. A tie with the Earl of Trevick would be just the thing. A fine family, despite that flighty wife of his, though I admit I like the countess, she's an entertaining creature. She's quite a beauty too, does her daughter favour her?

If she's anything like her mama, Latimer will have quite an adventure, I dare say. I hope he's not quite as honourable as I suspect he is, though I hope he's adept at getting himself out of trouble. Don't fret yourself about Lady Cara's safety, and tell Axton I said so. I know Latimer looks a devil and his reputation's as black as Satan's heart, but I'd lay every penny I own that he's not a bit like his swine of a father, despite the resemblance. She's in good hands.

I shall write to Bedwin and request he invite Latimer to a formal dinner. You will get Axton to attend also, seeing as you two are thick as thieves. Are you planning on setting

your cap at him after all these years, Hester?
Or just on rubbing his nose in the past? If we
can get Sefton there too, between us we can
harass the old bully into acknowledging
Latimer in public. If he has Bedwin,
Montagu, Axton, and Sefton on his side, no
one will dare cut him even if he's got cloven
feet and horns.

—Excerpt of a letter from Lydia De Vere,
The Right Hon'ble, The Dowager
Viscountess Latimer to The Right Hon'ble
Hester Henley, Lady Balderston.

20th October 1844, The Brick Kiln, Norwich, Norfolk.

They arrived back at the inn, cold and weary, but in excellent spirits. Introductions were made between Sultan and Bessie, which went better than they had hoped, though Bessie growled and bared her teeth to begin with. Sultan, who was uncomprehending of why the lady was so unimpressed with him, simply sat down and watched her with a placid expression. Puzzled by this, Bessie dared to get close enough to give him an experimental sniff. There was a bit more grumbling and fussing but eventually she settled down quietly guarding her pups, content to glare at Sultan in wary silence.

"Now, you be a good boy and mind your manners," Cara told him sternly, once the dogs had been fed and settled down in adjoining but separate stalls. "And *do not* try to escape. We'll be going home first thing."

Sultan yawned and gave a huff before settling down to sleep.

"I don't reckon he'll be thinking of escaping for a while," Wolf said wryly, before ensuring the door was properly secured and leading Cara inside the inn.

Scents of dinner assailed them as they went up the stairs to their room, and Wolf's belly gave an audible growl as the delectable odour of something rich and meaty filled his nostrils.

They entered their room and Cara gave a little cry of delight at seeing a steaming bath set before a blazing fire.

"A bath!" she said, with such longing Wolf laughed.

He nodded a greeting to Jo, who hurried forward.

"I ordered it earlier, and when I saw the cart come in, I got it prepared for you," Jo said, staring between them and looking a little wary. "I've washed and ironed your shirt, my lord, and ordered dinner to be brought up as soon as you are ready for it. The parlour is being used for a private party and I thought it was more discreet here than the dining room. I hope that suits you?"

"That suits admirably, Jo. I thank you," Wolf said, patting the young man on the shoulder. "Do you reckon you could rustle up a bit of bread and cheese to keep body and soul together before dinner, though? My stomach is making a racket fit to wake the dead."

"Of course, my lord, at once," Jo said, beaming at them both before he dashed out.

"Reckon he'll do fine," Wolf said, watching him go.

"So do I." Cara cast her bonnet aside and began fumbling with the fastenings on her cloak. Wolf brushed her hands away and did it for her, laying the cloak over the back of a chair near the fire to dry.

"I'd best go down," he said, wishing he didn't have to, but the idea of watching Cara bathe was already getting him in a lather, and he knew his limits.

"You don't have to, if you don't want to," she said, sliding her arms around his waist.

"Of course I don't want to!" he exclaimed. How could she even consider it, the daft creature? "But…."

"You want to do things properly."

She gazed up at him and, for a moment, he considered not doing things as he ought and simply taking what he wanted, but no. He knew how to wait, knew too that he wanted to give her the respect she deserved, to do things as the world said they ought to be done. Marrying him would bring her trouble enough, he'd give her no more reasons to feel shame, or let anyone else try to shame her with her actions.

"I do. I want to make you happy. I don't want you to have a single regret."

"I could never regret you," she said with a laugh.

He sighed, settling his head atop hers. "I pray that remains true when you see what we are up against."

"Foolish man," she said fondly. "I would tell the entire *ton* to go to the devil if it were a choice between them and you. Have you not learned anything about me over the years?"

"I've learned a good deal, and not nearly enough." He leaned down and kissed her nose. "Take your bath, love. I'll be back for dinner."

"Wolf."

He turned as she called after him.

"You will stay with me tonight, though. Please?"

Wolf snorted and shook his head. "As if I could stay away. What a henwit you are," he said affectionately, grinning at her as he closed the door.

Cara woke, blinking in the darkness. Judging by the pitch black, it was still far from dawn, so she snuggled back into the delicious warmth of the bed and then came abruptly awake. A heavy, muscular arm was slung over her waist, her bottom tucked against Wolf's big body, his thighs pressed against hers. How strange and wonderful it was to share her bed with him. Would she really get used to such a thing when they married? *When they married.* Cara hugged the knowledge to her. Papa would be concerned, naturally, and he would wish to find out more about Wolf before he allowed them to wed, but mama would understand. Mama was a wonderful judge of character, and she knew the importance of adventures and of fate.

Cara could not help but give a triumphant smile in the darkness. This marvellous man was hers. Her smile faltered as she considered what he faced among the *ton.* At his grandmother's party, everyone had turned up because they were dying of curiosity, and because the old woman wielded enough power and respect to make people think twice about cutting her. But she was still only one old lady, and Wolf was a notorious figure. What if they could not get society to accept him? What if he would always remain an outcast? Whilst Cara knew she would choose Wolf, no matter the circumstances, that did not mean being a social outcast was something she could look forward to. For one thing, it would distress her family, for another, for all she did not enjoy being paraded about like a prize heifer for some man to select as a wife, she would miss being able to socialise with her friends. Navigating the *ton* as an unmarried lady was a bear bait, but with the freedom given to a wife, with a husband at her side… it would be different.

Nonetheless, if she must turn her back on all of that to choose Wolf, she would. The trouble was, would he let her do it? He was a good man, a kind one with a generous heart, and he would never ask her to give up her life as she knew it. If they did not accept him into society, if he remained an outcast… would he still marry her then?

The question sat uneasily in her heart, making her heart tremble with anxiety. She could seduce him, she supposed. It would be easy to do. It was easy enough to see the desire for her in his eyes, and she had seen the effect she'd had on him when they were intimate. No, it would not be difficult to seduce him, but that would mean breaking her word, it would mean forcing him to do something that in his heart he did not want, no matter how he desired her. It would damage the trust they had in each other, and it would hurt him. No. She could no more hurt him in such a way than she could have sold Sultan to the vile Duke of Sefton.

Cara covered the hand that rested on her belly with her own, feeling a swell of protectiveness towards the man curled so lovingly around her. She knew what people thought when they saw him: a villain, a man used to dealing in violence, and perhaps he *was* those things. She knew now that he would not shrink from a fight if he felt it was required. The vision of him fighting the three men at The Ram was indelibly printed upon her mind, but that was not who he was. That was not who he wanted to be. If he failed here, she did not doubt he would return to Paris, to a dangerous world where he was all alone. She could not let that happen.

So, there was nothing else for it. Wolf must find his place in society as Viscount Latimer. The *ton must* accept him. No matter what she had to do to make it happen.

Chapter 15

Axton,

In short order, you shall receive a letter of invitation to a formal dinner at Beverwyck. You will oblige me by attending.

—Excerpt of a letter from The Right Hon'ble Hester Henley, Lady Balderston to Alfred Grenville, His Grace, The Duke of Axton.

21st October 1844, The return to London.

The journey back to London was a good deal less eventful than the one leaving it. Much to everyone's relief, Bessie and her pups, and Sultan seemed to have accepted each other's company. Wolf had made strides with Sultan too, befriending him with cheese and lots of lavish praise until the big dog gazed up at him with almost as much adoration as he did Cara.

They rose early, setting out long before dawn.

Hoping to guard Cara's reputation, Wolf took them first to Norwich, where they hired her a chaperone, paying the woman generously to keep her mouth shut. Then he bought a thick black veil to cover Cara's face and hair and hide her identity. Mourning dress had some advantages, after all.

Without the need to chase Sultan and stop and make inquiries every few miles, they made good time, reaching Colchester station by the middle of the afternoon, in plenty of time to catch the last train to London. After settling Cara in the first-class carriage and Jo and the dogs with the luggage, Wolf settled himself on a hard wooden seat in one of the second-class carriages. After spending so long on the bench of the dogcart riding over rough roads, his backside would have welcomed the well-upholstered seats in first class, but he would have ridden on the roof rather than risk Cara's reputation further than they already had.

As arranged, at London Bridge, Cara and her chaperone summoned a hackney to take her home, with Wolf, Jo, and the dogs following on at a discreet interval.

When Wolf pulled up outside of Cara's home on Cavendish Square, his stomach immediately tied itself into a knot as he peered up at the grand house.

Jo whistled. "That's her home? No wonder you look a bit green about the gills. I never saw such a place in all my days. Is it a palace?"

Wolf snorted. "No, this is just the town house. If you wish to be truly awed, you'd best take a look at Trevick Castle. A great leviathan, it is."

"You've seen it?" Jo asked eagerly.

"No, only sketches of it, but it looks monstrous big." Wolf contemplated the elegant edifice a bit longer.

"You going in, then?" Jo asked.

"I'm working up to it," Wolf grumbled.

Jo shrugged. "All right then. But faint heart and all that…."

"I know, I know," Wolf retorted, stung. "I'm going. In a minute."

He groaned and rubbed a hand over his face.

"Lady Cara loves you, I reckon."

Wolf looked up and nodded. "Yes, though heaven alone knows why. The foolish creature is addled, I'm sure."

"I reckon not. She seems to have her wits about her, and I'd say she knows her own mind. Still, she's in there, having to explain herself to her family... all by herself and...."

"Well, why didn't you say that in the first place?" Wolf exclaimed, flinging the door open and climbing out. He heard an amused snort from inside the carriage and turned back. "Well, don't dither. Quick smart."

Jo paled. "What?"

"Oh ho, not so sanguine now, my young friend, eh? Well, you must look after Sultan, and I'd as soon have someone at my back, just in case."

Jo pulled a face. "It's not a nest of vipers inside, surely? They won't stab you in the back."

"Easy to see you've never been inside a society ballroom," Wolf said darkly. "Come on."

"But what about Bessie and the pups?" Jo protested.

Wolf tossed the driver a glinting silver coin. "Another when we're done, if you stay put and keep an eye on the puppies."

"Yes, sir," the driver said at once, and tipped his hat.

"No excuses now, Jo," Wolf said with a grin, a little happier knowing he wasn't the only one feeling as if he was walking the Tyburn steps.

"I'll kill the bastard!"

"Language, Conor!" Mama exclaimed, glowering at her son with exasperation.

"If there is any killing to be done, I shall take care of it," Papa said, giving Conor a quelling look. "But I wish to hear the rest of this tale. Start at the very beginning, if you would, Cara."

Cara swallowed. Where the devil was Wolf? Not that she thought his presence would help matters at all. Indeed, it was probably best if she got her family on their side first. Well, her parents, at least. Conor looked as if he wanted to murder someone with his bare hands. Mind you, he'd not seen Wolf yet, which might make him think twice. Her big brother was tall and well built, but he was not of the mountainous proportions of her beloved.

"W-Well, it began with a letter," she said, accepting the cup of tea Mama gave her. She took a sip and then set it down as Mama passed her a large slice of cake.

"A letter?" her brother said, scowling at her.

"Cake solves everything," her mother whispered, winking at her.

Cara felt her spirits lift, knowing that Mama was not upset or disappointed in her. She took a large bite of the cake whilst her brother and father waited impatiently. Fortified with cream and sponge, she licked her lips and started again.

"Yes, a letter. You see, Wolf… Viscount Latimer… is very close friends with Louis César, and he happened to be with them when Evie got one of my letters. She told him about me, and about Sultan and… and he was intrigued so—"

"You cannot tell me Evie gave him your direction, for I shan't believe you," Conor said, narrowing his eyes.

"N-No, not exactly." Cara cleared her throat. "Er… Wolf t-took the letter and began writing to me."

A stunned silence filled the room.

Her father cleared his throat. "Lord Latimer stole Evie's letter and wrote to you?"

Cara took another large bite of cake, chewing furiously. "Mm-hmm," she said, watching anxiously as her father's jaw tightened.

"Darling, when *exactly* did Lord Latimer begin writing to you?" Mama asked, her dark eyes twinkling.

"Um," Cara swallowed the cake with difficulty and picked up her teacup. "Two years ago," she said in a rush, avoiding looking at anyone and taking a large gulp of tea.

Another silence.

"You have been writing to this man, to whom you have never been introduced, for two years?"

A muscle in Papa's cheek twitched. Never a good sign. Her father was the sweetest, dearest man in the world, but he had his moments. If his family were put at risk in any way, he could be an absolute bear.

"How?" Conor demanded. "How is it possible? Surely Mama sees all the correspondence?"

Mama had always taken care of the post, handing what she deemed important to each family member and things she felt Papa need not be bothered with directly to his secretary. But she never looked *inside* personal letters.

"Oh! Miss Pinkington," Mama exclaimed, and then gave a bark of laughter. "Oh, how delicious."

Papa and Conor looked at her in confusion.

"Oh, dear," Mama said, trying not to laugh. "The naughty man. I always knew there was something about her, but I just could not put my finger on it."

"I'm sorry, Mama," Cara said sheepishly before turning to face her father and brother, who were staring at her. "I didn't mean to keep writing to him, only... only he was so funny, and rather dear, and... and he became my friend and confidant. I have told him so many things I would never have told another living soul, and he was always so kind and gave the best advice."

"But the night of the party," Mama said in confusion. "You didn't know—"

"No!" Cara exclaimed. "He only ever signed himself W. From the start he told me we could be nothing more than correspondents, for his family was ostracised from society and he was rather notorious in his own right. But that night, I just... I felt a connection to him and later, when I considered the things he'd said I realised. I realised it was him, *my* W."

"Oh, how romantic," Mama said, pressing her hand to her heart.

"Kitty!"

"Mother!"

Mama looked at her husband and son with wide eyes. "Well, it is!" she retorted.

"It is not romantic, it's... deranged and preposterous. This... This villain has been writing to my sister under the guise of being a female friend? And this is the man she's been alone with since she disappeared? By God, Cara, if he's taken advantage of you...."

Cara stood abruptly, completely forgetting the plate of cake in her lap. Happily, Mama's reactions were swift, and she caught it before it smashed to the floor.

"He has done nothing of the sort!" she said furiously. "Lord Latimer is the kindest, most honourable gentleman I have ever known, and I'm going to marry him!"

"What?" her father and brother said at once, and even Mama looked a little startled.

"Over my dead body!" Conor retorted.

"Cara, you are overwrought," her father said.

Mama only looked at her with a considering expression, though there was concern in her eyes.

A knock at the door preceded their butler.

"Viscount Latimer to see you, my lord," he said, seeing Wolf in before leaving the room. The door closed upon stunned silence.

Cara had never been so happy to see anyone in her life. With a muffled sob, she ran towards Wolf and threw her arms about him, holding on tight.

"Cara?" Wolf said at once, and as she looked up, she saw the fury in his expression, the way he glared at everyone in the room, ready to tear someone's head off for upsetting her. His arms closed protectively around her. "What is going on here?" he demanded.

"You son of a—" Conor began, striding forward, but their father caught hold of his arm, checking his motion.

"I had thought you would be beside yourself with joy to have your daughter back home safely," Wolf said, the words so gruff they were almost growled. "But she's here barely half an hour and I find her in tears. What is the meaning of this?"

"You dare!" Conor said in outrage. "Father!" he protested, turning to their papa, but Father did not let go of his arm.

Much to Cara's relief, Mama got to her feet. "Lord Latimer. We were just speaking of you, as I am certain you have gathered. Cara is a little upset, yes, but so are her father and brother at the thought of her being in your company, alone, for two nights. I am quite certain you understand."

Wolf's eyes lost a little of the murderous glint that promised retribution and he gave a taut nod. "Of course I understand. If I could have avoided it, I would have."

Conor snorted with disgust and Wolf shot him a glare.

"And now she announces her intention to marry you," Mama said placidly. "So, you can understand us being a little... surprised."

"I can," Wolf admitted. He tilted Cara's chin, looking down at her. "You knew they'd not like it, my lady. We can neither of us blame them for that."

"I can blame them!" Cara said hotly. "I am not an idiot. I know you. I have known you for two years through hundreds of letters, and nothing I have seen of you since contradicts everything I have learned. You are a good man, an honourable one, and I *will* marry you."

"That's for your father to decide," Wolf said, though the words were filled with regret as he looked towards Papa. He took a breath and let Cara go.

Mama smiled and slid an arm about her waist, pressing a handkerchief into Cara's hand.

"Lord Trevick, Lord Harleston," Wolf said, sounding stiff and brittle and not at all like himself. "I know well that I am the last man in the country you would wish for a son-in-law. I can only promise that I will do all I can to change your minds. My conduct to this point has not been such to endear me to you, or to give a good opinion of my character, and for that, I apologise. But I do not apologise for loving Lady Cara. Indeed, I don't think there was ever any choice in the matter."

He turned back to Cara with such a tender look in his eyes that her heart ached.

"Oh," Mama said, sighing.

Papa shot her a warning look.

Conor appeared disgusted.

An impatient woof accompanied scratching at the door.

"Sultan!" Cara said, hurrying to let him in.

The dog charged inside, pulling out of Jo's hold with ease. Barking joyfully, Sultan greeted every member of the family in turn, his whip of a tail narrowly missing sending the entire tea tray crashing to the floor.

"Oh, that dog!" Mama exclaimed, snatching up her precious Sèvres teapot.

"Get down, you oaf!" Conor protested as Sultan leapt up at him, paws planted firmly on his chest, swiping his chin with an enthusiastic lick. "Eugh!"

Grasping the dog's paws, he got the gigantic animal to stand down, exclaiming with frustration at the dirty marks on his waistcoat.

Undaunted, Sultan headed for Mama, who was still clutching the teapot. She gave a panicked little shriek.

"Sultan!" Wolf's voice silenced the room and Sultan skidded to a halt on the polished wood floor, sitting in an ungainly heap as his enormous paws struggled to find purchase. Wolf gave the dog a fierce look before snapping his fingers. "Here," he said, pointing at the spot beside him.

Sultan got to his feet. Tail wagging sheepishly, he walked to Wolf and sat down beside him, swiping his hand with his tongue.

"Good boy." Wolf's voice was gentler now, and he put his hand on the dog's head, stroking, before slipping him a small piece of cheese.

"Well," Mama said, looking impressed. "It's about time."

Wolf nodded. "He only needs a bit more training. Sultan is a good dog, he's just not been taught how to behave. Once he knows the rules, he'll be fine. He just needs a chance to learn them is all." He quirked his lips, giving Cara a rueful glance. "We have a lot in common."

Conor snorted. "You mean to say you didn't know it was bad form to be alone with an unmarried female?"

"I knew," Wolf said, meeting her brother's eyes. "But I could not in all conscience leave her to fend for herself, and she was determined to get Sultan back. Perhaps I could have done things differently, but... I would not have missed the past days for the world."

"A charming sentiment," her father said, his expression unreadable. "But it remains to be seen if anyone is aware of Cara's absence. Her reputation hangs in the balance after your little adventure, for you may have been seen together."

"I wish to marry your daughter, my lord. That manner of scandal will not ruin her once we are wed."

"No, but she might be ruined by marrying you," Papa said bluntly. "I have heard a good deal about you since your appearance in society. None of it good. Your father... well, the less said about him, the better, and in truth I do not see why you ought to bear his shame. But as for you... a criminal, a smuggler, and heaven alone knows what else, if rumour is to be believed. I shall say no more in front of Cara, for I do not wish to frighten her."

"Wolf would hurt no one who did not deserve it, Papa!" Cara said, alarmed by the turn the conversation had taken. "I know the world he has lived in has been dangerous and violent, but he lives to protect, not to do harm. I know he has broken the law and profited from it, but how else was he to survive? I—"

"That's enough," her father said, giving her a look that brooked no argument. "I have a great deal to consider, and I wish to speak to Gabriel Knight, who has had dealings with both Latimer here and the Comte de Villen of late."

"Papa, please! I love him," Cara said, her throat tightening as emotion threatened to overwhelm her.

Her father frowned, his expression pained. "Cara, I only want your happiness. For all I know, this is an infatuation that will pass in a short time and, if I agree, you could find yourself married to a man who has ostracised you from your friends, from the world you were born to."

"But he's going to change that," Cara said desperately. "His grandmother is going to help him, and if we help him too, then society will accept him."

Her father sighed, a sympathetic look in his eyes. "That's by no means certain, my dear, as I think you know at heart."

"Come, darling," Mama said, hugging Cara to her. "We are not saying you won't marry your young man."

Conor and Papa sent her an exasperated glare, but Mama put up her chin. "Well, we are not. There is much work to be done and we must get to know him better, but it is not hopeless. Have courage, darling. Things looked hopeless for Papa and me once upon a time, remember?"

"Kitty, do not go giving her ideas!" her father said, raising his hand. "Do not even think of eloping, Cara. I mean it."

"Oh, she's not thinking of it, Luke," Mama said with a tsk of impatience. "But you might consider how we felt when we took such drastic action. Take heart, love," Mama said soothingly.

Cara nodded, her lip trembling with the effort of not crying, but Wolf looked so stricken she did not want to make him feel worse by turning into a watering pot. She went to him and took his hand, squeezing it, wishing she could hug him but not daring to in front of everyone when they were all so cross with him.

"Go to your grandmother. Beg her to help us," she said, her voice thick.

Wolf stared at the floor, his dark brows tugged into a frown, his expression bleak.

"Perhaps—" he began, and Cara shook her head, glaring at him and wagging her finger.

"No!" she said furiously. "No! Stop it. Don't you dare. Please. *Please,* my darling lunatic."

He smiled at that and nodded. "Yes, love. Anything for you."

With that, he bowed and bid them a good day, and walked from the room. Sultan gave a piteous whine and lay down, resting his head on his paws with a discontented huff. Cara was less restrained and burst into tears, running into her mother's arms.

Chapter 16

My Lady,

I perceive that nothing has changed. You are still the most managing female that ever drew breath.

Why the devil should I go to this blasted dinner? Give me a good reason, and I shall consider it. It had better be a <u>good</u> reason, though.

—Excerpt of a letter from Alfred Grenville, His Grace, The Duke of Axton to The Right Hon'ble Hester Henley, Lady Balderston to Alfred

20th October 1844, Queen Anne's Gate, Queen's Square, Westminster, London.

"Here he is then, cap in hand," his grandmother said with evident satisfaction as Wolf strode into the inferno that was her private sitting room later than day.

"Oh, and looking ferocious. What has he been up to?" Lady Beauchamp said, sitting up straighter in her chair.

His grandmother snorted. "No good, I don't doubt."

"How lovely," Mrs Dankworth said, settling herself more comfortably to observe what happened next.

Wolf sighed as his diminutive grandmother raised her lorgnettes to her eyes and looked him up and down.

"Well?" she demanded, imperious as ever. "Out with it."

"I wish to marry Lady Cara Baxter," he said, alarmed by the explosion of exclamations that followed.

"You owe me five pounds, Dorcas," his grandmother crowed, clapping her hands together with such glee that Regina the cat shot from the chair beside her and ran straight out the door.

Wolf rather wished he could follow.

"Wait," Mrs Beauchamp said, holding up her hand. "You were away two nights. I take it you ruined the gel?"

"No!" Wolf retorted indignantly.

"Ha!" his grandmother said. "Make that ten."

Mrs Beauchamp huffed and sent Wolf a reproachful look. "You let me down. How can you look so deliciously wicked and behave like a gentleman? I was never more deceived."

"There, there, Dorcas," Mrs Dankworth said, patting her hand. "We still have plenty of fun to come yet."

Mrs Beauchamp gave a disappointed little sniff. "I suppose," she said grudgingly. "But really, Cora, what is wrong with the gel? I really don't know what young women these days are thinking. I mean, *look* at him." She waved a lace edged hanky at Wolf, her expression bewildered.

Mrs Dankworth sighed. "Oh, I am, Dorcas, *I am.*"

Wolf shook his head, still unused to being ogled so by the wicked old women who had bet *ten pounds* on his ruining Cara! There was a more important concern, however. "How the devil did you know we were together? Is there gossip? Who saw us?"

"Oh, don't fly up into the boughs. We have it all in hand. And sit down, will you? You're giving me a crick in the neck," Lydia grumbled.

Wolf sat, staring at his grandmother, who rolled her eyes at him.

"The Duke of Axton saw you. Lucky for you, Cara is a favourite of his daughter-in-law. He went straight to Lady Balderston, who told me the news. I do not know what the devil you thought you were up to running off with the chit, because you could easily have ruined all my lovely plans, but as it is, I'm pleased with you. Lady Cara is an excellent catch. Trevick's daughter, no less. I can't imagine he's pleased, mind. His eldest has already married beneath her. Who was the fellow, Dorcas?"

"Sylvester Cootes, De Ligne's younger brother. A handsome fellow, charming too, but no title nor fortune."

"That's him." His grandmother nodded. "So, in the ordinary run of things, a wealthy viscount would not be something to turn his nose up at, but it's *you*," she said with a sigh.

Wolf sat back in his chair, not about to take offense at this point. It wasn't like he didn't know it would be an uphill battle.

His grandmother made an impatient sound, apparently irritated that he hadn't defended himself. "I've spoken to Bedwin. His lady has agreed to host a formal dinner to introduce you to some of the most influential people of the *ton*. The duke has agreed to support you."

Wolf felt his eyebrows go up in astonishment. "He has? Why?"

His grandmother sent him a look of exasperation. "Don't be a dolt. His daughter married Mr Demarteau. The whole world knows you, Demarteau, and that beautiful brother of his are as thick as thieves." She gave a bark of laughter at the unintended but accurate description. "He's worked hard to make his son-in-law something like respectable. The high sticklers will never accept a bastard, but he's done well, and Bedwin don't want you undoing all his hard work."

"Right, of course," Wolf said, frowning.

"Lady Balderston is going to get Axton to support you, too," she added, looking appallingly smug.

Wolf widened his eyes in shock. "How the devil does she intend to do that?"

"Oh, Hester has her ways," Dorcas said, winking at her companion, Mrs Dankworth, who chuckled.

"Never you mind," his grandmother said. "The lady has influence with Axton, is all you need to know."

Wolf shrugged. "Fair enough."

The door opened, and the butler came in, followed by a footman and two maids who set up a lavish tea before them. Conversation paused whilst Lady Beauchamp poured the tea and handed out tiny sandwiches and slices of cake on delicate fine china. Once the ladies had been served, she looked at Wolf and, after a moment's hesitation, simply handed him the plate they had brought the sandwiches in on. Wolf grinned and popped two in his mouth in one go.

"The challenge will be Sefton," his grandmother said a little later, chasing cake crumbs around her plate with an arthritic finger.

"Sefton?" Wolf said, almost choking on the sandwich he was chewing. "Why would you invite him?"

"Are you questioning my judgement?" Lydia said, narrowing her eyes at him.

There was a steely glint in them that Wolf did not underestimate. For all she was an old lady, this woman had birthed his devil of a father. She was a De Vere. A man would be an idiot to underestimate her.

"No, my lady," Wolf said, aware of how badly he needed her help. "I apologise. However, you are not in possession of certain facts. We had a run in with the duke. It did not end well."

Briefly, he explained about Cara and Sultan, and how Wrexham had stepped in to help them.

"Interesting," Mrs Beauchamp said when he had finished. "Poor Wrexham. Now, there was a wicked boy. Handsome as sin, too. I rather adored him. Such a shame what happened there."

"Well, it's no mystery why Wrexham stepped in," his grandmother said. "That young man would take any opportunity to vex his father, and I don't blame him. How Sefton has treated him since he lost his sight, shutting him up in that great mausoleum, as though it were something to be ashamed of! Now, that's wickedness if you ask me, and not the good sort. Still, I have no influence there. You, I can deal with," she said as she turned back to Wolf.

"You terrify me," Wolf said with a sigh.

The three ladies chuckled.

"I still do not understand why Sefton would come to the dinner at all, let alone support me in my bid to return to society," he repeated.

"And you don't need to. Not yet, at least," Lydia said, a glint in her eyes that was most unsettling. "I thought I would be the last of the true De Veres. I thought our name would die tarnished and unredeemed, but you, my boy, you have given me hope, and a means to see us rise again, back where we belong. If you do as I say, you'll have your lady, and more besides."

There was such determination, such fierce pride and resilience in the old woman that Wolf could only admire her. Whatever happened, she would fight for him, for their name, and that meant something.

"I am yours to command, grandmother," he said, meaning it.

To his surprise, the old lady's eyes grew misty, and she reached out to him. Wolf took her hand, startled by how frail and insubstantial it felt in his much larger one, the skin fine and papery.

"You're a good boy," she said thickly, before taking her hand back and putting up her chin. "Now, that's enough of that sentimental nonsense, and I'm sick of tea. I want a proper drink. Dorcas, ring the bell and order some brandy. I think we all shall need it."

Prunella Adolphus, the Duchess of Bedwin, sat in her private parlour, staring down at the most vexing letter with consternation.

On the other side of the fireplace came a constant snoring that was grating on her nerves and not helping her think of a solution. Looking about her, she picked up a heavy velvet cushion and lanced it at her eldest son.

Jules, Marquess of Blackstone, whose long legs were sprawled out in front of him, head tipped back and snoring doggedly, jolted awake, fighting off his tasselled attacker with a yelp. Bleary-eyed, he stared at the cushion, and then at his mother with reproach.

"Well, that was uncalled for."

"You were snoring," Prue said impatiently. "And really, I need help, so wake up and pay attention."

Jules groaned and shook his head, settling back against the well-padded wingback chair with a groan.

"Headache," he muttered. "Ask me later."

"That is your own fault, and I need an answer now. Honestly, Jules, I know young men are supposed to sow wild oats, but this is the fourth night this week you've come home at dawn, and it's Friday! Your father will have something to say about it."

"Father has plenty to say about most things I do," Jules grumbled.

"Well, and can you wonder at it? You're five and twenty. If you keep this up, you'll have no oats with which to furnish us with grandchildren."

"Ugh, Mother!" Jules protested. "Please! Delicate constitutions over here, not aided by hearing you speak of such things."

"Well, someone must, but never mind that now. I shall not tell your father that story circulating about you and the ballet dancers—note the plural, please—if you wake up and help me out of this fix."

Jules flushed. "Oh," he said, mortification writ large across his handsome face. "You, er... heard about...?"

Prue snorted. "Yes, I did, and frankly, I wish I had not. There are some things a mother does not wish to know. Your reputation is, quite frankly, appalling. How any reputable young woman could consider marrying you now is beyond me."

"I'm in line for a dukedom, Mama," Jules said, his tone sour. "I could turn green and croak like a frog and they'd still hound me, batting their eyelashes."

And that was the problem in a nutshell. Prue sighed and shook her head. Jules needed sorting out, but she had a more immediate problem at present. She glared at him, giving him the look all her children knew better than to ignore.

Jules sat up straighter and rubbed at his face with his hands before smacking himself on both cheeks so hard that Prue winced.

"Right, I'm awake. Tell me," he said, blinking at her owlishly.

"It's this wretched dinner party," she lamented.

"The one to make that devil Latimer respectable?"

"Yes, that one," she said darkly. "I have to invite Sefton, the brute, on the dowager Lady Latimer's orders."

Jules shuddered. "She scares me."

"She scares everyone," Prue said tartly. "Which is why I must invite Sefton, damn his eyes, but that's not the problem."

"Well, cut to it," Jules said impatiently. "Some of us have sleeping to do."

Prue sighed. "Sefton has accepted the invitation, drat him, but worse than that, he demands I invite Wrexham, and in such a manner I simply cannot refuse him."

"That's outrageous!" Jules objected. "It's not for him to dictate who you invite. You're the Duchess of Bedwin."

"Yes, yes, as well he knows," Prue said with a huff. "Which is why he's playing the sympathy card. 'Poor Wrexham doesn't get out, and he's an invalid etc.,' which is utter tosh because it's Sefton's fault the poor boy is hidden away from the world. Since he lost his sight, Wrexham must have to depend on his father far more than is comfortable for him. Everyone knows they despise each other, and I don't doubt Sefton only wants me to invite his son with the sole purpose of mortifying him in public."

Jules frowned. "I don't understand. Surely, Wrexham would be glad of an invitation to get out for once? He was always the life and soul."

"Darling," Prue said, holding onto her patience by a thread. "It is a formal dinner. At least seven courses."

Jules shook his head. "No, you've lost me."

"He's blind, Jules!" she exclaimed. "How is he to manage eating in front of everyone? How will he know which knife and fork to use, where his wine glass is?"

"Oh." Jules sat up straighter. "Hell. Why the diabolical old bastard."

"Quite," Prue said with feeling. "I can't refuse to invite his son, not when it risks him declining the invitation after all, *and* taking offense, because Lady Latimer insists he must be there."

"Well, that is a thorny one." Jules frowned and sat back, mulling the problem over. "Well, we must make things easier for him, then."

"Yes, exactly, but how? I thought if we dined *à la russe* that would help. At least then each course is placed directly onto his plate."

Jules nodded. "We can make certain to have a footman attend him who is aware of the difficulty, too. One who ensure they serve him things that will be easy to deal with."

"Yes," Prue said, chewing her lip anxiously. "I won't serve a fish course, for any stray bones would be a nightmare for him, but we can't avoid a soup course. And he can't possibly decline, for he always had impeccable manners. Such a silly rule. He need not eat it, though."

"Of course, and if the Knights are coming, you can sit Emmeline Knight next to him," Jules said, his tone considering. "She's the sweetest creature, but not one to shy away from a difficult situation. A bit too honest for her own good, but that might suit Wrexham rather than someone who dances about and pretends he isn't blind at all, which must be worse. She's very good at putting people at ease, too."

Prue sighed with relief. "Oh, that is an excellent suggestion. I needed another unmarried lady to make the numbers up. Oh, but poor Wrexham," she said with a frustrated sigh. "He was always such a dashing figure, and so independent even when he was a little boy. He'll be so mortified. How can his father be so cruel? Just you wait, when Lady Latimer has achieved whatever it is she is up to, I shall have a few words to say to that devil, you mark my words."

Jules' mouth kicked up at the sides. "You are quite splendid, Mama. Truly."

Prue laughed and wagged a finger at him. "You are still in the doghouse," she retorted.

"I never doubted it," Jules said with a yawn, and settled himself back to sleep.

Chapter 17

Dear Lady Trevick,

I beg you will forgive me for writing to you concerning such a delicate subject, however I believe you know that my husband and Lord Latimer are close. Indeed, it would not be stretching the point to say they are as brothers to each other. Though I can perfectly understand why you would hesitate to accept Lord Latimer as a suitor for Lady Cara's hand, I would beg you to permit me to offer a word or two in support.

I have known his lordship for more than two years now, and whilst his reputation in France is one which would make most right-thinking parents run away screaming, I wish for you to consider what I know to be true. Like my husband, Lord Latimer was raised by a father who was not only negligent, but abusive. His father dragged him into the world into which he has lived his life and Latimer was forced to survive. The man his reputation speaks of is not the man I know.

In short, Lord Latimer is the kindest and gentlest soul, unless someone seeks to harm those he cares for, or those he feels have no one else to stand up for them. He would be a steadfast and attentive husband, and one upon whom Cara could always depend. Over the past years, he has become a dear friend, and I am very fond of him. I would hate to see him disappointed in this matter, for I believe his feelings are engaged and it will hurt him more deeply than you can realise to lose the woman he loves.

—Excerpt of a letter from Evie de Montluc, Madame la Comtesse de Villen (daughter of Lady Helena and Mr Gabriel Knight) to The Right Hon'ble Kitty Baxter, Countess of Trevick.

24th October 1844, en route to Beverwyck, London.

"Arrêtez ça!" Louis exclaimed, smacking Wolf's hand away from his cravat.

"It's too tight," Wolf grumbled, sitting back against the plush seats of the carriage. They would be at Beverwyck soon enough and his stomach had tied itself into a Gordian knot. He folded his arms, glaring at Louis. "I can't breathe."

"I don't care," Louis retorted. "It took Elton forever to get that cravat right, what with your fidgeting and grumbling. If you mess it up, I shall wring your neck with it."

Wolf subsided with a huff. Whilst Jo was doing sterling work alongside the dozens of staff Wolf had hired to get his crumbling home back in some semblance of order, tonight was too important to rely on his untried valet. As they had not yet had time to find themselves a house in London, Evie and Louis had moved into Louis' old apartment whilst they were in town. Understanding at once how important the occasion was to him, Louis had insisted that Wolf take Nic's old room in their apartment, and that Elton dress him for the occasion.

"You look very handsome," Evie assured him with a warm smile. "And if it makes you feel better, this gown is pinching me, but it's my favourite, so I insisted on wearing it. By the time I've had dinner I shall be in agonies," she added with a laugh.

Louis sent her a sharp look. "But why did you not say so? We could have had it altered."

"We did have it altered," she said sheepishly.

"So, we could have altered...." Louis broke off, frowning and giving her a look of such intensity, Wolf wondered what the trouble was. "Evie?" he said, a note to his voice Wolf could not read.

Evie was studiously staring out of the carriage window, but her cheeks were very pink.

"Evie, look at me," Louis demanded.

"Oh, Louis, really!" Evie said, sounding exasperated, but she did as he asked, and for some inexplicable reason, her eyes were shining far too brightly.

Louis gasped. "Evie!"

"Oh, drat you, you wretched man, I ought never to have spoken so unthinkingly. I should know better by now. I'm only astonished you didn't already guess, but I was going to tell you when we were alone!" Evie protested, laughing and crying at once.

"Tell him what?" Wolf demanded, worried now. If there was something wrong with Evie, Louis would be devastated. "What's the matter? Are you ill—"

He broke off abruptly as Louis placed a reverent hand on Evie's stomach and gave a choked laugh. *"Mon Dieu."*

"Oh," Wolf said with a sigh of relief as things became clear. "Congratulations."

Evie sent him a warm smile before turning to look at Louis. The poor fellow looked as if he'd been hit in the head with a cricket bat.

"You're pleased?" she asked, which was a daft question, but Wolf couldn't blame her for asking it as Louis appeared more stunned that overjoyed.

"Pleased?" he repeated, sounding dazed. He laughed and pulled Evie to him, kissing her hard before letting her go with an exclamation of concern. *"Amour de ma vie,* I could not be any happier. But, Evie, are you well? Have you seen a doctor? You're not wearing a corset, are you? How long? When did you find out?"

"Good God, man, give her time to answer before you ask another question, and obviously she's well. Glowing with good health, I should say," Wolf replied, amused by how thoroughly overset his usually unflappable friend was.

Evie shot him a grateful smile and turned back to her anxious husband. "I haven't seen a doctor, but I will tomorrow. I have spoken to Florence, though, and she says there's nothing to worry about. As Wolf says, I'm in excellent health, and yes, I am wearing a corset, but it's loosely tied, and I've hardly a bump at all yet, darling. And as for how long, I think perhaps two months. I was only certain this past week, though, after I had spoken to Flo."

Louis had gone very quiet, his hand resting protectively on Evie's stomach. His throat worked and Wolf realised how much his friend had wanted this, how much it meant. He suspected this was why they had returned to England, so that Evie could be close to her family before they began trying for one of their own. Louis would never have rushed the wife he adored into giving him a child at once, but now the timing was perfect.

"What is it?" Evie asked him quietly, covering his hand with her own.

Wolf tried to make himself invisible, which was patently impossible, but the knowledge that he was intruding on such a private moment made him feel exceedingly awkward. He rather wished he could jump from the moving carriage.

Louis cleared his throat, clearly struggling to compose himself. "I want this child very much, Evie, you know that, but… but what if…?" He took a breath. "I don't know how to be a father, what if I—"

"Oh, don't be so bloody idiotic," Wolf butted in, entirely forgetting the fact he was trying to fade into the corner of the carriage. "You'll be a marvellous father. You were the nearest thing I ever had to one which, considering you're not much older than me, is something."

"Really?" Evie asked with interest.

"Really," Wolf said gruffly. "My father was a vile human being. Anything I have learned about being a man, a *good* man, I learned from him. From manners to the facts of life, which fork to use, how to dress, how to talk to women and what not to say to their fathers… well, all of it was him. He looked after me, looked out for me, and gave a damn, which was a novelty in itself. Louis was the first role model I ever had, the first person I ever respected and looked up to. I'm not sure I ever thanked you enough for that," he added, amused by how emotional Louis looked now.

"Damn you, Wolf," Louis said, his voice thick. "We'll be at Beverwyck any moment and now I…." He threw up his hands and gave a choked laugh.

Wolf snorted and handed Louis a clean handkerchief. "For heaven's sake, wipe your eyes. What a watering pot you are."

Louis snatched it from him and made use of it before taking a deep breath and composing himself. *"Je t'aime,"* he said softly to Evie. "You too," he added, smoothing a gentle hand over her stomach.

"What about me?" Wolf demanded, affecting a hurt expression.

Louis huffed out a laugh, but his expression was fond. *"Oui,* you too, my friend, which is why we shall do all in our power to see you happy. I will move heaven and earth, if necessary, but we shall see you wed your lady. For I want you to be as happy as we are. You deserve it."

Wolf stared at him for a long moment.

"Give me that damned handkerchief back," he grumbled as the pair of them burst out laughing.

Wolf sat down at the vast and elegantly arranged dining table and tried to force his face to appear amiable and pleased to be there. That this was his idea of hell on earth was not something he could share with the other guests. Especially as most of them had bestirred themselves on his behalf, either through kindness or to evade his wicked grandmother's threats of blackmail and retribution.

Much to his relief, he discovered Louis sitting opposite him, Evie to his left, and his grandmother to his right. The duchess had flanked him on all sides with people ready to leap to his defence, which was reassuring. Less fortunate for her, that august lady had the Duke of Axton on one side, looking exceedingly impressive and ducal in his black eveningwear, and the Duke of Sefton on the other. Wolf glanced at his grandmother, who sat between him and Sefton and looked mightily pleased with herself. He wished he knew what she was up to, though it might be better for his nerves if he remained in ignorance. He heartily wished that Cara were here, but she was in mourning and unable to socialise. The family had decided they could bend the rules enough that her older brother might attend and report back, which Wolf was less sanguine about. Harleston had also escorted a distant cousin of theirs, a delicate looking blonde by the name of Lady Violetta.

There were two and twenty sitting down this evening, including the Bedwins' two sons, the Marquess of Blackstone and Lord Frederick, and their eldest daughter, Lady Eliza, with her husband, Nic—also reassuring—as well as the younger daughter, Lady Victoria, who was sitting next to Louis. His grandmother's dreadful friends, Lady Beauchamp, Mrs Dankworth and Lady Balderston, were also present, along with Gabriel and Lady Helena Knight, the Marquess of Wrexham, and Miss Emmeline Knight.

Wolf glanced at Wrexham, wondering why on earth he had agreed to attend this evening. The man looked pale and, though his posture was relaxed, Wolf suspected the truth was rather different.

"Latimer, did the young lady get her dog home in one piece?"

The Duke of Sefton spoke over the low murmur of conversation as people settled and arranged napkins. Footmen passed seamlessly between them, filling water and wine glasses as others placed a neatly arranged plate of elegant *hors d'oeuvres* before each guest.

"She did, your grace," Wolf replied politely, not missing the calculating glint in the duke's eyes.

"And you, Harleston? You got your carriage mended, did you?" the duke bellowed down the length of the table, stopping all other conversation in its tracks.

Harleston, sitting on the same side as the duke, was forced to lean back in his chair to avoid doing the same. Naturally, he knew all about the lies they'd told, and was not about to contradict them and plunge his sister into scandal.

"Indeed, your grace. An irritating business, but that's the way of it. I was grateful to Latimer here for stepping in. My sister is desperately fond of that wretched dog and would be beside herself to lose him."

"Hmph," the duke said, and returned his attention to his food.

Wolf did likewise, though his appetite had fled before he'd even sat down. Louis sent him an encouraging smile before falling into conversation with Lady Balderston, who sat between him and the Duke of Axton. Axton kept glowering at the lady, who looked most elegant tonight in a vivid emerald green, with a matching tiara of emeralds and diamonds that looked well against her glossy white hair.

"Still pining, Axton," Sefton said with a snort of amusement. "I thought you'd have got over that little infatuation years past. Your mama put a stop to that one, did she not? Though I reckon your father would have shot you rather than see that mesalliance come to fruition."

Both Axton and Lady Balderston stiffened, and Axton turned an arctic stare upon Sefton that Wolf could not have bettered.

"I do not know to what you are referring, Sefton," the duke growled. "But if you slight the lady again, I shall make you sorry for it."

"Oh, I'm not in the least slighted, Axton," Lady Balderston interrupted blandly before things could escalate. "As a mere baronet's daughter, I had no expectations of reaching the heady heights of duchess. Axton and I were mere acquaintances, but the scandal sheets will make something out of nothing. I married well enough to please my family and, more importantly, to please myself. Balderston was the best of men, but you met him once yourself, did you not, your grace? When was that again?" she asked, nonchalantly lifting her wineglass and taking a sip, her keen gaze never leaving Sefton's face.

"Damned if I know," Sefton growled, and gestured for a footman to fill his glass before turning to speak to the Duchess of Bedwin.

Wolf bit back a smile, suspecting that the lady had just successfully routed the duke.

"Round one, my dear," Axton murmured in Lady Balderston's ear with a low chuckle.

Lady Balderston sniffed and turned her attention back to Louis.

Axton caught Wolf watching the exchange and flashed a toothy grin, which put him in mind of satisfied crocodiles.

"How's that daughter-in-law of yours, Axton?" Wolf's grandmother demanded of the duke.

"A dreadful, managing creature. Never gives me a moment's peace," Axton replied, though the fond glitter in his eyes was obvious. "Breeding again," he added proudly.

His grandmother gave a bark of laughter. "Good heavens! Again? Will that be her fifth?"

Axton nodded. "Can't fault Bainbridge. Chip off the old block," he said, looking dreadfully smug.

The duchess gave a wistful sigh. "How lovely."

"Eight is a sufficiency for any woman," his grandmother said to the duchess, wagging a finger at her. "I had as many, though only three of them lived through infancy. Then my eldest boy had to go and break his neck in a riding accident. Always horse mad, he was. My daughter did well enough until the last brat took her, and as for Charles, well, the less said about him, the better. Always knew he'd come to no good. Happily, I have another chance. Wulfric here might look like the devil, but he's got a good heart and knows what is due the family name, too. Now he's claimed it, at least. Better late than never, eh?" she said, sending him a challenging look.

Wolf raised his glass to the old lady. "I will do all in my power to live up to your expectations, grandmother."

She laid her gnarled hand on his sleeve for a moment before returning her attention to Axton, who was speaking again, but the brief gesture of solidarity touched Wolf profoundly. It had been so long since he'd belonged somewhere. That the old lady wanted him, meant more than he'd realised until that moment. He looked up, finding Louis watching him. His friend smiled before turning back to Lady Balderston.

"How's your brood, Sefton? Got yourself an heir yet?" Axton's far too glib comment had Lady Balderston sucking in a breath.

To Wolf's astonishment, she elbowed the duke, who muttered an oath and glared at her.

"Not as yet," Sefton replied, regarding Axton with undisguised loathing.

Wolf felt for the duchess, who was going to end up refereeing a boxing match or a duel if she wasn't careful. Still, as the highest-ranking men, their places were closest to the hostess and slighting either of them by sitting them further away would have caused a riot.

"No wonder, if you will keep the poor boy a prisoner," his grandmother snapped. "What are you thinking, Sefton? He's blind, not crippled. I assume his manhood is still in working order, so what are you doing hiding him away? He's a handsome young man. Any gel in her right mind ought to be proud to wed him."

"I quite agree, Lady De Vere," the duchess said, her voice firm. "Wrexham is a fine young man with his whole life ahead of him. He has a challenge to meet is all, and I am certain he will rise to it admirably. He was always such a determined boy, and so wickedly charming. We miss seeing him out in society."

Sefton snorted. "He can't ride, can't set a foot outside his rooms on his own, let alone out of the house. He can't read nor write. What a fine prospect for a new bride, to end up a nursemaid, forever at his beck and call. His fiancée refused to go through with the wedding, and I don't blame her, why should anyone else be any different?" the duke said, with such callousness Wolf could only empathise with Wrexham.

He knew what it was like to be despised by your own father, to be seen as weak or defective, and it cut deep. He hoped Wrexham had been luckier in his mother. Without his own mother's love and guidance, Wolf did not know what kind of man he might have become.

His grandmother sent the man a look of disgust. "So what? You've not got an alternative if you want an heir."

"I have Lord Cecil."

"That creature." Wolf's grandmother spoke with such contempt, he shot a look at her and then at Sefton, whose expression was pure murder. "He won't inherit while Wrexham lives and the fellow looks to be in excellent health to me, if a bit pale. The result of being shut indoors for weeks on end, I don't doubt."

"I'll thank you to look after your own misbegotten family, Lydia. At least mine are neither traitors nor criminals," Sefton snarled.

"Ha! So you say," his grandmother said with a bark of laughter.

Wolf prayed to God that the old woman knew what she was about because Sefton would be a powerful enemy. Surely, they were supposed to be getting into the man's good books, not aggravating him.

"Grandmother," he said, his voice low. "Are you quite sure…?"

"Shhh," the wicked woman said, waving a hand at him. "I know what I'm about, and I'm enjoying myself too, don't spoil it."

Wolf sighed and held his tongue whilst the footmen cleared the plates and brought in the next course.

"Who is Lord Cecil?" Wolf demanded, too curious to let it drop once a plate of mulligatawny soup had been set before him.

His grandmother leaned towards him, speaking in a whisper. "Sefton was married three times. His first wife gave him four boys. Scarlet fever got three of them and they lost the youngest to cot death. Poor little creatures. The rest were girls, so he was pleased enough when she died in childbed. Wrexham is the only child of the second wife. The third gave him a son and a daughter. The daughter is a sweet creature, but the son...." She pulled a face. "A spiteful fop who would stab you in the back without a second thought. His father's creature. He despises Wrexham, and the feeling is mutual. I suspect that poor young man is living in a vipers' nest, and a dangerous one at that. I only hope he has friends to look out for him."

"Does he?" Wolf asked, glancing down the table to the elegant nobleman, who was ignoring the soup in front of him and nursing a glass of wine, his expression impassive.

His grandmother shrugged. "I couldn't say. He was a wild one before he lost his sight, made as many enemies as friends, I'd reckon. He was never one to hold his tongue when it might avoid a scene or a fight. Yet for all that, I liked him. There was something of the charming rogue about him, for all his airs and graces. A troublesome boy rather than a bad one, I suppose."

Wolf nodded at the information and decided he'd best try to befriend Wrexham. The fellow had done Cara no small kindness, and he wished to return the favour. For now, he had his own vipers' nest to attend to, so he applied himself to his soup and kept his attention on the conversation.

At the other end of the table, Emmeline Knight was having no easier time of it than either her hostess or the guest of honour. Opposite her, Lady Beauchamp was flirting wildly with Jules, who was enjoying the old woman's banter immensely, judging by the amount of laughter coming from that side of the table. To her left, Monsieur Demarteau was involved in a lively discussion with Lord Frederick, Evie, and Lady Victoria. Which left her dining companion on her right, the Marquess of Wrexham. He had barely eaten a bite all evening, but was drinking steadily, much to her disquiet. She had tried to draw him into conversation several times, only to receive stony answers. Her mama had explained that Aunt Prue had sat her next to the man on purpose, hoping that Emmeline might put him at ease, but she was at a complete loss.

As the soup course was removed and a small dish of smoked haddock en cocotte put in its place, she tried again. Checking to ensure no one was looking, she reached over and took the appropriate spoon from his table setting and rested it in her lap for a moment.

"My lord," she said, waiting until Wrexham turned slightly towards her. Reaching over, she touched the back of the spoon to the hand that rested on his thigh. He jolted at the touch of the cold silver.

"For the cocotte," she said, wondering if he would skewer her with some cutting remark for her temerity in trying to aid him. "It's haddock."

For an endless moment he did not move or speak, but then he turned his hand palm up and she watched as his elegant, long fingers curled about the spoon. He inclined his head in thanks, transferred the spoon to his right hand, and used the left to find the bowl before him. Emmeline turned her attention back to her own meal, certain that he would not wish to be observed.

"That was delicious," she ventured a little while later, when her dish was empty. She noticed he had only eaten a little of his, but it was better than nothing.

"Miss Emmeline Knight," he said, and Emmeline suppressed a shiver at the way her name sounded when he spoke it. His voice was deep, the words announced with a precision she suspected he gave to every aspect of his life, judging by his attire alone.

"That's me," she replied, dismayed to hear herself sound rather breathless.

He was a rather daunting figure, though. Impeccably turned out, he was somehow far more flamboyant than anyone else at the table, yet with exquisite taste. Whilst all the other men wore simple black evening attire with a white waistcoat, Wrexham's waistcoat was white with intricate black and gold embroidery. Ashton Anson would have coveted it, she thought with a smile. Then there was a large cravat pin, onyx and diamond, and on his long fingers several rings glittered in the candlelight. This was a man who loved beautiful things. Her heart ached for him and all he must have lost with his sight.

"You are the poor sweet creature the duchess has given the unenviable task of babysitting me," he said, the mockery in his words perfectly audible.

Emmeline swallowed, determined not to be discomposed. She was used to dealing with forceful men, and one had to stand up to them or step aside. Emmeline did not like stepping aside. She was far too stubborn for that.

"I'm afraid you're wrong on that count," she said, her voice tart. "I'm not the least bit sweet."

She glanced at him out of the corner of her eye when he did not reply and was far more pleased than she ought to be to discover a slight curve to his mouth at the fact she had not denied the part about babysitting him. He really was very handsome.

"Very good, Miss Milly."

"Emmeline," she corrected sternly.

"No," he cocked his head a little. "You're a Milly. I had a governess once called Millicent. A dreadful tartar. You sound just like her."

He was goading her, she knew. She had a brother, after all, and legions of cousins, too.

"I'm certain she needed to be to keep you in line. You must have been the bane of her life, the poor creature."

"Oh, that I was," he said, and then gave a bitter huff of laughter.

The dishes were removed, and the next course was set in its place, forestalling any reply. Roast beef and roast potatoes followed with various vegetable accompaniments. Wrexham waved the footman away, refusing anything, but Emmeline stopped him.

"His lordship will have some roast potatoes, please," she said to the footman before whispering to Wrexham. "If you don't soak up some of that wine, you'll be crawling out of here."

"If I trip over the furniture as I am wont to do, the result is the same. It makes little odds, so I may as well enjoy the wine. Besides, it would be such a shame to disappoint his grace."

Emmeline did not understand the comment about his father, the duke, but pressed the point. "Please, eat something. The meat is very tender. I… I could cut it for you if you wish me to?" she added, wondering if he would hate her for the suggestion.

"Perhaps you should feed me," he said, the words at once savage and suggestive, as he bared his teeth in a feral smile. She had a sudden vision of placing a delicate morsel between his strong white teeth, of brushing those sensuous lips as she did so. It would be rather like feeding a beautiful, sleek leopard with no bars between you and danger. Losing her fingers would be the least of her worries.

A wash of heat rolled down Emmeline's spine. "Well, if you're going to act like a baby, perhaps I will," she retorted, relieved that her voice gave away no trace of her inner turmoil.

"Ah, Miss Milly, how fierce you are. Are you pretty?"

"W-What?"

"It's a simple question. Are you pretty?"

"It is not in the least a simple question," Emmeline said impatiently. "It is a most improper question, and one I cannot possibly answer."

"Oh, come, come, Miss Milly, improper questions are the most interesting kind. Don't be coy. You could tell me you are a great beauty and I'd be none the wiser."

"Oh, a fine opinion you have formed of my character, my lord, I thank you. Keep that up and I shall pour the gravy boat over that splendid waistcoat. I've heard such acts of self-defence are *de rigueur* at the best dinner parties these days."

He gave a low chuckle and Emmeline preened a little at having made him laugh, despite being cross with him.

"You still did not answer my question," he pointed out.

"No. I did not," she replied. "And I shall not, though why it should matter to you, I cannot imagine."

"Can you not?" There was a silken tone to the question that made her heart skip about in the most unlikely manner.

"Well, if you are so very curious, you shall have to discover it for yourself," she snapped.

He replied without missing a beat. "Ah, but surely you know how blind people discover the world, Miss Milly?"

There was a taut silence as Emmeline digested that. "I have a fork," she said darkly. "And I know how to use it."

Much to her discomfort, Wrexham roared with laughter, and everyone turned in their direction to look. Blushing furiously, Emmeline bent her head and concentrated on her dinner.

By the time they got to the dessert course, Wolf's nerves were jangling. He thought he'd acquitted himself well enough, but was still uncertain what his grandmother hoped to achieve with this dinner. Having Axton and Bedwin support him was obvious enough, and that they had invited him to dine among such illustrious company sent a clear message to the rest of the *ton* that he was to be accepted within their ranks. Perhaps not all would follow suit, but most would heed the word of the Duke of Bedwin; and Axton, though mostly retired from society, was not a name to trifle with. Yet he could not shake the unsettling suspicion there was more going on here than he was aware of, and that the diminutive woman beside him was pulling all their strings like a master puppeteer.

Distracted by his own thoughts, Wolf forced himself back to the conversation just in time to hear his name mentioned.

"Yes, Wrexham favours his mother in looks, which is a blessing," his grandmother cackled, ignoring a furious glint from Sefton. "A pity my Wulfric takes after his father. The spit of him he is, the poor devil, though handsome for all that. Yet his eyes are his mother's. That's the real difference. Now, she was the dearest, sweetest creature you could ever wish to meet. I was never sorrier for anyone than I was for her when Charles married her. Not that he intended to do that much. You'd have been a bastard had I not forced his hand," she told Wolf, shocking him so deeply he could do nothing but stare as the room fell silent. That she had told him something he had never known was one thing, but to do it here, in front of everyone...!

"Grandmother!" he said sharply, but she returned a fierce look that told him she was playing a deeper game than he knew, and he forced himself to hold his tongue.

"The poor girl never had a chance, though. Her father despised her and refused to give her the same advantages as her sisters. Well, he knew she was a cuckoo in the nest. I confess, I am uncertain whether you knew it too, your grace. Did you?"

The already silent room crackled with tension as his grandmother studied the Duke of Sefton with sharp eyes.

"What the devil do you mean by that?" the duke growled, the fury in his voice enough to make Wolf tense, ready to leap to his feet if the need arose.

"I mean that my grandson's mother was Miss Lillian Plover, your illegitimate daughter, and Wolf here, is your grandson too."

All the colour drained from the duke's face, and he stared at Wolf as if he'd never seen him before. Wolf stared back, too stunned to know what to think, let alone what to say.

"You didn't know," his grandmother said to Sefton with satisfaction. "I reckoned Rachel wouldn't tell you she was carrying your bastard, but her husband knew. He made her pay for that, and the daughter she carried, too. So much that poor Lilly thought catching Wulfric's father was her best option to escape that unhappy household. The poor child," she said sadly. "From one desperate situation to another. I always thought you cared for Rachel, though. Perhaps more than you ever did for anyone."

The duke's jaw tightened, but this time Wolf thought it was emotion that hardened his features, not rage. Slowly, he turned to Wolf, searching his face, his expression pained now.

"I see it," he said roughly, his voice thick. "I see her in his eyes."

His grandmother nodded, watching Sefton avidly. "Yes, I thought you would. Mother and daughter were two peas in a pod. A pity you never knew the child. I almost interfered there when she was a little girl, but I was afraid of making things worse. I regret it now. Such a sweet girl. She was a good mama to you, I think?" she said to Wolf.

Wolf cleared his throat, overwhelmed by what he had just learned, but determined that his mother be acknowledged for the wonderful woman she had been. "She was the kindest and most devoted parent I could have wished for. For every terrible thing my father did and said, my mother made up for tenfold. I am certain there are rules that say I ought not to speak with such sentiment, but I miss her still, even after so many years. You could not possibly be in possession of a heart and not love her."

Wolf let out a breath, relieved he had spoken without making a fool of himself. Darting a quick glance at his grandmother, he saw her eyes were shining with emotion and pride.

"Oh."

His gaze went to the duchess, who had made the choked exclamation and was weeping openly now. She accepted a handkerchief from Axton so she might wipe her eyes.

"She would be proud of you," Louis said, his voice firm and loud enough to be certain to carry the length of the table.

"She would indeed," Nic seconded, raising his glass.

"To Lord Latimer," Evie said, following suit.

Wolf stared in astonishment as the rest of the table followed, everyone raising their glasses. He turned his head, heart thudding very hard, to look towards the Duke of Sefton — his *grandfather* — and though the man's expression remained taut, he too raised his glass.

"To Lord Latimer."

The toast rang out and Wolf gave a startled laugh, quite at a loss for what to say or do. His grandmother's hand reached out and settled on his and he swallowed hard, very afraid he would follow the duchess' example and weep in front of everyone. To his great relief, the duchess came to his rescue instead.

"Champagne!" she declared, sending footmen scurrying to do her bidding.

Wolf took a deep breath, steadying himself, and gave an incredulous laugh as he caught his grandmother's eye. She was looking exceptionally smug, the wicked old woman.

"I'll drink to that," she said, winking at Wolf.

"Yes, well, we must have champagne to end such a successful evening," the duchess insisted, smiling warmly at both Wolf and his grandmother, and still sounding a little emotional.

"As usual, duchess, you have the right of it," Axton said, nodding his approval.

The room gradually relaxed after the scandalous revelations. Wolf wondered if the story about his mother and grandmother would become the stuff of gossip by morning, but looking at the guests gathered here, he suspected not. Wrexham was an unknown quantity, but he had been kind before, so Wolf hoped he might hold his tongue. After all, somehow the young man was Wolf's uncle! That thought was an amusing one, for he suspected he was older than Wrexham by a few years. He wondered if the marquess would acknowledge the connection or not.

Wolf wondered too if Axton might flap his gums about the night's events, but suspected Lady Balderston might put a stop to that. Axton was staring at the lady now, waiting for a lull in her conversation with Louis before asking, "Will you be returning to Scotland for Christmas, my lady?" sounding a little too nonchalant to be truly disinterested in the answer.

"No, I have been invited to Heart's Folly. The Comte and Comtesse are celebrating their first Christmas in England and have asked me to join them. I'm so looking forward to it," she said to both Evie and Louis with a smile.

Axton frowned. "Oh, very nice, yes. You'll have a splendid time, no doubt."

Louis, who had been paying close attention to the exchange, leaned forward. "I am certain you will wish to spend Christmas with your ever-expanding family, your grace, but if you could spare a few days in the week before, you would be most welcome to join us."

Lady Balderston shot Louis a glare of pure outrage. He met it with one of utter guilelessness, which Wolf didn't buy for an instant. The devil was matchmaking.

"Well, that's very civil of you, Villen. I don't mind if I do," Axton said, obviously delighted by the invitation.

"Won't you miss your dogs?" Lady Balderston demanded, sounding a little desperate. "And what about the new grandchild? When is that due? You won't want to miss that."

"Oh, no. Bella won't drop the brat before the spring, I reckon, and Bainbridge will see to the dogs. They pay him more heed than they do me these days, in any case," he said with a chuckle. "No, no, Hester, I shall see you for the festive season, so you'd best get used to the idea." He grinned, mightily pleased with himself, and accepted a glass of champagne.

The guests relocated to one of Beverwyck's opulent parlours and the evening carried on until the early hours of the morning, by which time his grandmother was nodding off in her seat. Wolf wrapped her up in her heavy fur-lined cloak and guided her out to her carriage. On his way outside, he saw Louis and Nic each take Harleston by the elbow and draw him aside.

"Lord Harleston," Louis said smoothly. "We've not had a chance to speak properly this evening. I should like to remedy that. Might you spare us a few moments?"

Harleston looked from Louis to Nic and sighed. "Do I have a choice?"

"Probably not," Nic replied with a grin, and the two of them led him away.

Wolf snorted as his grandmother gave a low chuckle. "Now those boys are what I call good friends," she said with satisfaction. Wolf nodded and lifted her carefully into the carriage, so she didn't have to manage the steps.

"That they are. I am lucky to have them. And you are a very wicked old lady, and I find I am exceptionally glad of that, too." He leaned down and kissed her cheek. "Thank you for everything," he said softly.

"Ah," she said, reaching up to pat his face. "You're welcome. I did it for my own sake as much as yours. But if you wish to repay me, you just make sure you marry that young woman and start giving me grandbabies. I don't have time to wait around."

"Nonsense, you're too wicked to die for a long while yet, but I'll see what I can do. Goodnight, grandmother."

Wolf closed the door, gave the footmen strict instructions that she be carefully helped out again once they were home, and watched the carriage disappear down the drive. Louis' carriage rolled up to take its place, but Wolf made no move to get in. Instead, he stared up at the night sky. Stars pierced the velvet darkness and a waning moon cast the magnificent, landscaped gardens around Beverwyck with an ethereal, silver light.

He gazed up at the moon, remembering his beautiful mother and all she had taught him. "I think I can put the cloak aside now, Mama," he whispered and, smiling still, went back inside to rescue Harleston from his friends.

Chapter 18

Dearest Rex,

(And greetings, Humboldt, who I know will be reading this to you)

I will be back with you by the week's end. I do hope you have got along in my absence and our father has not made things too horribly difficult in my absence. Aunt Lucy was sorry not to see you this time but sends her best love and is glad you are feeling better.

Is it true you are attending a dinner at Beverwyck tonight? Father's manipulation, I do not doubt. What did he threaten you with that made you capitulate? I shall be thinking of you and praying it is not too very dreadful.

Though I know father means the outing to punish you, perhaps it might be a good thing. Now, hear me out before you get on your high horse. It is time you returned to society and Father cannot keep you a prisoner always. If people see you and see how well you are, they will visit and ask father why you do not appear more often. It might force his hand into giving you more freedom.

Have courage, my favourite brother. When I get home, you can complain all you wish and I shall give you all the latest gossip, though perhaps this time you shall have some of your own to share? I am dying to hear about Lord Latimer. What is he like? And I hope you remember to give my regards to Lady Beauchamp, such a dreadful creature she is but I rather adore her.

Is there still no news of Genevieve? I do worry about her.

—Excerpt of a letter from The Right Hon'ble Lady Cordelia Steyning to her older brother, The Most Hon'ble Leander Steyning, Marquess of Wrexham.

28th October 1844, Cavendish Square, Marylebone, London

Wolf stayed away from Cara and her family for the next few days on his grandmother's advice. He almost refused to do as she asked, too desperate to see Cara and tell her everything that had happened on that extraordinary night. However, his grandmother promised she would call on the family to put in a good word for him, and sneak a letter to Cara herself when she did so. Wolf negotiated she must also bring him any reply if she wanted him to do as she asked. The old lady agreed, and he could hardly refuse such an offer. He had duly explained all to Cara as briefly as he could, and her excitable reply, littered with capital letters, underlined words, and many, many exclamations, was everything he could have hoped for.

Cara wrote that her mama was on their side, and even Harleston had suggested they might wish to give him a chance. Wolf suspected Louis and Nic's little talk was responsible for this. So, now only her father needed persuading. Which explained why, today, Wolf was en route for a meeting with the man, in the company of the Duke of Bedwin.

The duke had sat contemplating him silently for much of the journey, which was enough to make Wolf want to fidget like a schoolboy. There was something about the duke's assessing gaze that made you feel like your shirt was untucked and you had a gravy stain on your cravat. It was most disconcerting.

"What will you do?"

"Do?" Wolf repeated, uncertain what it was the duke was asking.

Bedwin waved his gloved hand. "Your entrée into society is assured, thanks to my duchess. Your grandmother has welcomed you back into the fold and, if you don't mess things up with Trevick, I believe you will be given permission to court his daughter. But what then? Won't you be bored? Will you not long for the excitement and danger of your old life in Paris?"

Wolf stared at the man in disbelief. "Will I miss constantly looking over my shoulder to see if I'm being followed, or if someone among my ranks thinks they'd do a better job than I would, and slits my throat so they can find out? Will I miss sorting out fights, dodging the law, greasing palms, and trying to stay one step ahead of every petty criminal who thinks to steal what is mine?" He gave a derisive snort. "No, your grace. I will not. It was never the life I wanted. I did it because I didn't think I had another choice, and I was damned good at it. But I reckon if I can do all that, then I can bring the ruins of my father's estates back to something the family can be proud of, something my children can inherit without beggaring them."

The duke nodded, his gaze still troubled. "But what will happen to your empire?"

"I've handed it all to Jacques Toussaint. I'll sell much of it, but Jacques can keep what he wishes to handle himself. Louis and I owe him for his loyalty, and he's got a good head on his shoulders. He's more than capable of carrying on or getting out and getting the best profit for what remains. That will be his choice to make."

"You wouldn't care? To see your empire crumble?" Bedwin asked, watching him curiously.

Wolf snorted. "An empire is worthless if you have no one to share it with, no family to hand it to when your time is done, and all I achieved in Paris, that is not the kind of legacy I wish to leave behind me. I want a chance to make something good, something honest and decent. Something I can be proud of."

Bedwin smiled, and there was warmth in his expression now, rather to Wolf's surprise.

"I think you'll do well enough, young man," he said with approval. "Yes, indeed. I think you will."

"Cara, do stop fretting, love," her cousin, Violetta said gently, laying her embroidery hoop to one side.

"But what is taking so long?" Cara cried in frustration. "They've been in there for hours, Letty!"

"I know, but wearing a hole in the carpet won't make them come out any quicker," Letty replied, holding out a hand to her.

Cara sighed and took it, sitting down beside Letty with a flounce that made her skirts seethe and rustle, as if they too were impatient. "Sorry," she said with a sigh. "I just don't know what I shall do if Papa is stubborn about things."

Violette squeezed her hand. "Your father dotes on you, he just wants to satisfy himself that you're making the right choice. You must admit Lord Latimer is rather intimidating."

"Oh, but he isn't, that's the thing," Cara said, throwing up her hands. "People look at him and make assumptions which are all wrong."

"That's human nature," Violetta said with a shrug.

Cara snorted. "True. Most men look at you and think you need protecting and cosseting. If only they knew what a sharp-tongued harridan you are."

Violetta pulled a face and stuck her tongue out, making them both laugh.

The sound of a door opening, and male voices had Cara leaping to her feet with a squeal and running for the door. She skidded into the grand entrance hall, almost crashing into Wolf as her shoes slid on the marble floor.

"Steady there!" he said, grabbing her by the elbows.

"Wolf!" she said, breathless, staring up and him and darting glances at her father and Bedwin. "Well?"

"Well," Wolf said slowly, "Your father thinks—and I must agree—that you're a dreadful girl, a terrible hoyden likely to cause a great deal of trouble if you're not married quickly. So, even though you're officially still in mourning, providing it is a quiet affair—"

Cara did not let him finish, instead throwing herself into his arms with a delighted laugh. Wolf hugged her tightly and then let her go, sending her father a rueful glance. Her Papa just snorted and shook his head.

"Good luck, Latimer. I think your experiences in Paris may stand you in good stead in the years to come. She'll lead you a merry dance, if I know anything."

"I hope so," Wolf said, gazing at her with such a look in his eyes that Cara blushed.

They all jumped in alarm, the tender scene shattering as Sultan came bounding into the entrance hall, barking joyfully. At the sight of Wolf, he gave a happy yip and threw himself at him.

Taken unawares, Wolf went down, crashing to the floor with Sultan licking his face and slobbering over him enthusiastically.

"Ugh! Sultan! Get... bfff," he spluttered as the dog made his approval of the marriage plans evident. "Cara!" Wolf protested, but Cara just stood laughing, delighted to see that Sultan had got over his distrust and clearly adored Wolf as much as she did.

"Well, you did promise to train him," she snorted, only laughing harder as Wolf sent her a look of outrage, before laughing himself as Sultan lay down across his chest and gave a satisfied bark.

Chapter 19

Dearest Delia,

No news of Genevieve as far as I know, not that the old bastard would confide any information to me if there were. She's a resourceful young woman though, I have confidence she is thriving wherever she is.

I await your return with impatience. Humboldt does not appreciate my wit nor my humour and is a terrible companion. He refuses to read me the books I want because they're too scandalous and make him blush. How dreary he is, I bet he is even writing this missive faithfully word for word without changing it a bit, the wretch. How dull to be so honourable. Hurry back and bring salacious gossip, I beg you. The latest on dits, crim cons and fashions to nurture my thirst for anything approaching entertainment. I am so bored I am like to cause a dreadful scene just for an end to the tedium.

The one bright spot on the horizon was the dinner at Beverwyck, strange as that may seem. I fully expected father to revel in the sight of me making a fool of myself as I fell at one of the many pitfalls that litter the way for me these days. However, the duchess contrived to make things bearable. I always did like her, a warm and compassionate woman. No doubt I have awakened her pity and her maternal nature. How revolting, but it saved me from too much difficulty, as did her choice of dining companion. A Miss Emmeline Knight. She is a curious young woman, two parts sweet and one part sharp as a lemon. Still, she was an entertaining neighbour and I flatter myself that she will not forget me in a hurry. Yes, I was my usual delightful self, sister dear. No doubt she despises me.

As for Latimer, brace yourself dearest, as it appears our doting Papa has been busier than we knew. We have another branch to this encroaching family tree. Latimer's mother was our father's natural child. Can you believe it? So the devil is our nephew. I am uncle to a man older than I am! Just when you think the wicked old bastard can't possibly surprise you, his grace pulls the rug from under our feet. Still, I confess I liked Latimer. He's a bit rough around the edges, the kind who speaks the truth with no bark on, methinks, and thank God for that. A bit like Miss Emmeline. Have you ever met her? What does she look like?

—Excerpt of a letter from The Most Hon'ble Leander Steyning, Marquess of Wrexham to his sister, The Right Hon'ble Lady Cordelia Steyning.

12th November 1844, Trevick Castle, Warwickshire.

They were married quietly at Trevick Castle two weeks later., though *quietly* was a relative term in Wolf's opinion.

Cara's family, including her heavily pregnant older sister, Aisling, her husband, and their young daughter, Tryphena, were in attendance. Louis and Evie came at Wolf's request. Lady Balderston came too, as she had played an active part in helping them avoid a scandal, and she brought her nephew, Barnaby, whom Wolf was warming to now he'd got to know him better. Wolf's grandmother was also there, of course, which meant she brought with her the other two Viragoes, Lady Beauchamp and Mrs Dankworth, and—for some reason Wolf did not bother to discover—a foul-mouthed parrot.

A rather harried clergyman performed the ceremony whilst casting anxious glances at Sultan. The dog had been bathed and brushed to a shine for the big day, and Cara had insisted on tying a large blue silk ribbon about his neck. Wolf wasn't certain Sultan appreciated that addition, but had the good sense to hold his tongue. Still, he spent the first few minutes of the service with one eye on the dog as his instincts prickled. Sultan sat looking very solemn as proceedings took the usual route, however, and so by degrees, Wolf relaxed—as far as a fellow getting married could do—and concentrated on his vows.

That was harder than he might have expected. Not because he wasn't paying them proper mind, or because he did not place enough value on the sanctity of the promises he was making. It was simply that Cara looked absolutely radiant, and his poor brain only had to glimpse her beautiful face to come to a standstill. How had he managed this? The question had been circling his mind for the past two weeks and still he had not discovered an answer that did not rely heavily on the fact he was the luckiest man alive. What had seemed simply impossible such a short time ago was now to be his life. He could marry Cara without bringing her shame, and she would be his for all time. Perhaps his name was still one that caused people to whisper and speculate, but he had time to show people what he was made of. There was time enough for people to forget the rumours of the person he had been, and cast himself anew, in the shape of a man he could be proud of.

Suddenly the vows were done, and Cara was staring at him expectantly, her beautiful eyes shining with happiness. Wolf's throat felt dreadfully tight, and he let out a breath, half laughter, half emotion. Cara laughed too and reached out, taking his hand. Wolf bent his head and kissed her, closing his eyes and allowing the magnitude of the moment, of the vows they had just spoken, to settle over him. Slowly, he broke the kiss, seeing the same sincerity and wonder in his wife's gaze as she stared up at him.

"Husband," she whispered, and squeezed his hand. "There's no escaping me now."

Wolf laughed, shaking his head. "None at all."

Cara looked up as a shadow glided silently overhead. "Oh dear," she murmured.

Alarmed, Wolf followed her gaze to where the parrot had settled itself on the plumed helmet of an ancient suit of armour. Sadly, they were not the only ones to notice.

"Sultan!" Harleston made a grab for the dog just a second too late as Sultan gave a bark of outrage on seeing the parrot enter what he considered his private territory without a by your leave.

"Who's a pretty boy, then," the parrot taunted, bobbing up and down on the suit of armour.

Still somewhat discombobulated by the emotional ceremony, Wolf took a second too long to react, opening his mouth to tell Sultan to heel as the dog sailed into the air. Canine hit armour, and the two crashed to the floor with a sound loud enough to have the wedding guests covering their ears. The parrot, unimpressed by noise and the loss of his perch, took flight again.

"Bad boy! Naughty, naughty, Bainbridge," scolded the parrot, searching for a new place to settle.

Mrs Dankworth gave a muffled snort. "Oh, Dorcas, that's a new one. Whatever has that wicked man been up to?"

"I don't know," Lady Beauchamp mused, watching the parrot with interest and making no move to capture the dreadful bird. "Perhaps that's why he insisted we take him away for the weekend. He did threaten to roast the poor dear otherwise, but really Mac is a wonderfully apt pupil. He picks things up so quickly. I mean, I only once said that the vicar's wife was an interfering old fussock, and he repeated it *almost* exactly."

Cora cackled with delight. "Yes, and to her face, the old sourpuss. Has she been back to the house since?"

"Not once," Lady Beauchamp said with a smirk.

Sultan bounded past them as the parrot circled overhead and Lady Trevick gave a little gasp of horror as the bird settled upon the rim of an enormous vase.

"Sultan! *Sit!*" Wolf bellowed, startling the dog so that his back end met the floor before he'd finished running. He slid the rest of the way across the room, directly into the leg of the elegant table supporting the vase.

"Hell!" Wolf muttered, and lunged, catching the vase just before it smashed into a million pieces. He hit the floor instead and lay on his back clutching the vase, winded and staring at the ceiling, until Cara peered down at him and quirked one delicate eyebrow. "If you've finished playing with the animals, I'd rather like my honeymoon now, please," she said, with apparent sincerity.

A single red feather drifted down and landed on his forehead. Wolf picked it up and regarded it solemnly. "Will it always be like this?"

"Oh, no," Cara replied, her lips only twitching a little. "Sometimes it will be much, much worse."

Wolf shot her a grin. "How wonderful," he said, and got to his feet, setting the vase carefully back in its place. He turned to her, his expression grave. "Let's get on with it, then."

Cara kissed him and caught hold of his hand and, with a shriek of laughter, ran out of the door, pulling her new husband behind her.

Mackintosh, the parrot, screeched with excitement as they left the bemused wedding party behind, his lewd cry following them as they went.

"Ooooh, what a big one!"

On Cara's insistence, they were to honeymoon in France the following summer, but for now she was on fire to see the home that Wolf had inherited in Hampshire, close to Southampton. Wolf had warned her the place was probably little more than a pile of bricks, but she was undaunted. Wolf, however, determined that their wedding night and any nights that followed be spent in comfort, had booked them a room at a coaching inn in Burford to break their journey and insisted they would *not* be spending a night in their new home until it was ready to receive them. Jo and a veritable army of staff had gone ahead two weeks ago, but Cara was realising that Wolf liked his home comforts and was not about to rough it. Not that she minded in the least. She was eager to see the place they would call home, and to make it their own, but she was eager for other things too. For those, access to a warm room and a comfortable bed were not only preferable but essential.

The coaching inn was a pretty stone building with low beams, upon which Wolf narrowly missed knocking himself out. Cosy fires blazed in all the rooms.

"Oh, it's charming," Cara said, staring around at the well-polished furniture, including an impressive four poster, made up with bright white linen and warm blankets. She moved to the window and peered out. It looked out over a small private garden, rather bare now but still neat and well kept. Beyond, she could glimpse the rolling hills of the Cotswolds, but it was scenery rather closer to hand that was of interest now. She turned back to the room, feeling suddenly shy as Wolf closed the door behind them and locked it.

"I've told them we'll dine in our room tonight," he said, smiling at her. "But that's hours off yet," he added with a glint in his eyes.

"Oh, yes. Yes, of course," Cara said, returning his smile and deciding she needed to look out of the window again. Her cheeks were blazing and suddenly her stomach was alive with fluttering wings.

"So, we've ages yet..." Wolf added, and Cara wrapped her arms about her waist as she heard him moved closer.

"Mm-hmm," she agreed. "Ages."

She jumped as his big hands settled on her waist. "Cara," he said, his deep voice a caress against her skin as he pulled her closer. "Don't tell me you're shy *now?*"

"Of c-course not. How silly. I practically seduced you when we were looking for Sultan. It would be ridiculous for me to feel sh-shy now."

Wolf turned her around, tipping her head up to face him. "No, love. Not the least bit ridiculous, so don't worry. I would never hurt you, never do anything you didn't want."

"I know that!" she exclaimed, more impatient with her own foolishness than with him. "Only—"

He pressed his mouth to hers before she could say another word, brushing his lips back and forth until she sighed and opened to him. Wolf gathered her close, holding her carefully as he deepened the kiss, slowly and tenderly. Cara melted into him, her sudden explosion of nerves soothed away as he reminded her how it was between them, how very much she wanted this, wanted him, and how worthy he was of her trust.

He pulled back, his eyes glinting with satisfaction as he regarded her, pink cheeked and flustered. "Better?" he asked, lips quirking.

Cara shrugged, attempting to look nonchalant. "A little, but I think you ought to do it again, just to be certain."

Wolf chuckled, but obliged her before letting her go again. He kissed her nose, and then went to the window and pulled the curtains across, shutting the cold outside before lighting the lamp. It flooded the room with a welcoming glow, even though the cold November day still lit the room from behind the curtains.

"It's the middle of the day," Cara said uncertainly, aware she sounded a little scandalised.

"That didn't bother you during our picnic," he replied, unbuttoning his coat and hanging it up. "And that was out of doors, if you remember."

Cara felt her already pink cheeks blaze hotter as she remembered that. A smile tugged at the corner of her mouth and her insides turned hot and liquid when she remembered the pleasure he'd given her.

"Ah, you do remember," he said, his voice low as his hands fell to his waistcoat buttons.

"Hardly something I would forget," she exclaimed, laughing.

"Are you quite certain? Perhaps you need a little reminder?" he suggested, never taking his eyes off her.

He slid his waistcoat off and threw it on the nearest chair before untucking his shirt and tugging it over his head. He cast that aside too and Cara could only stare. Though she had seen his broad chest up close before, the sight had lost none of its impact. How magnificent he was, his body a rugged landscape of muscle and dark wiry hair, a vision of an ancient warrior come to life, flesh and blood, and all hers.

Cara swallowed, her heartbeat becoming fast and erratic with anticipation. "Perhaps I do need reminding," she said, uncaring that she sounded breathless. He knew how much she wanted him. It was hardly a secret.

Instead of going to her, he went to the fire, which was blazing merrily enough already, and built it higher. "Is the room warm enough for you, love?" he asked, glancing back at her.

Cara, who had been studying his powerful shoulders move with fascination, nodded.

"And getting hotter by the moment," she admitted.

"Don't you think you should at least take your cloak off then?" he asked, lips quirking.

"Oh." Cara looked down at herself and all the many layers she wore with dismay. It would take an age to get that lot off. Suddenly gripped with urgency and all traces of shyness abandoned, she tugged off her gloves and dropped them on the nearest surface before scrabbling at the fastenings on her cloak.

A moment later, her hands were gently batted away.

"Let me," he said, his voice low and soothing and doing peculiar things to her insides, which seemed to melt whenever he spoke.

She let out an uneven breath and allowed him to do as he wished. He removed her cloak and set about unbuttoning and unhooking with sure, patient fingers. Cara was not feeling patient in the least, now that her shyness had evaporated as quickly as it had arrived.

"Stop fidgeting," he said with a huff of laughter as he wrestled with the ties on her quilted petticoat. Finally undone, he pushed it down her hips, and she stepped out of it.

"It's like unwrapping a Christmas present," he said, sounding so delighted that she looked over her shoulder to find him smiling at her. Cara turned in his arms and, unable to wait a moment longer to touch him, smoothed her hands over his broad chest, tangling her fingers in the coarse hair there. He sucked in a quick breath.

"Devil take it, your hands are freezing!" he said, goosebumps cascading over his body. Cara gave a wicked laugh, and he snorted. "Pleased with yourself, are you? I see how it's going to be. Our married life for years to come is suddenly very clear. You love to torment me."

"And you love it when I do," she countered. "Only it's you doing the tormenting now. Do hurry up and get the rest off!"

"Stop distracting me, then!" he exclaimed and returned to the business of divesting her of her petticoats.

Finally, he had her down to her chemise and stockings. Before he could move or she could lose her nerve and become anxious all over again, she grasped hold of the fine fabric and tugged it over her head. Cheeks hot, she reached up and began ruthlessly tugging pins from her hair, all the while aware of the still figure standing close behind her. She could feel the heat blazing from his body as tangibly as she could feel the heat of the fire on her other side, but she did not turn and look at him. Finally, all the pins were gone, her hair cascading down her back to her bottom. Behind her, she heard his breathing hitch and, slowly, she turned to face him.

He stared at her as though he could not quite believe she was real, the wonder and appreciation in his eyes so ardent that her heart skipped.

"Cara," he said, his voice rough. "My God. I've never in my life seen anything so lovely as you."

She let out a soft laugh, love for her new husband and relief at knowing she pleased him making her giddy with happiness. Wolf closed the distance between them, pulling her into his arms and claiming her mouth in a kiss that was as overwhelming as the feel of her breasts against his chest. The contradiction of his smooth, hot skin and coarse, wiry chest hair tantalised her sensitive flesh. She pressed closer, eager for more, wanting to touch him everywhere, needing to finish what they had begun that day by the river, and during the violent storm that had forced them to find shelter.

"Take them off," she insisted, tugging at the waistband of his trousers.

"As impatient as ever." Laughing, Wolf obliged her, unbuttoning them and pushing them down, kicking them heedlessly aside.

Cara stepped back to stare at him, to admire his long, strong legs, the powerful thighs, and that potent, masculine part of him that made her heart skitter about with combined lust and anxiety. Before she could touch him, he tugged her to the bed, lifting her up onto the mattress with ease and following her down. After the things they had done before, Cara thought she knew what to expect, but the feel of his naked body pressed to hers was a decadent pleasure beyond anything she had ever known. Her hands explored him as he kissed her, stroking down his powerful back to grasp his backside.

He made a pleased sound and slid his body against hers, provoking a gasp of shock as his arousal slid over her in just the right place. He grinned wickedly and nipped at her mouth before doing it again and again until she was breathless and clutching at his shoulders, raising her hips to seek more and more as he moved against her.

"Wolf," she said, too breathless to say anything coherent. "Now... please."

He shook his head, kissing a path down her neck to her breasts. "So lovely," he murmured, suckling her until she cried out.

"Wolf, *please!*" she demanded, but still he shook his head, laughing softly as he nuzzled against her stomach, moving lower.

"Not yet. Don't be in such a rush. We have all the time in the world."

"I don't," she insisted, certain she would spontaneously combust if he didn't do *something*, and soon.

He lifted his head, his dark eyes warm and gently amused. "Don't trust me?"

Cara huffed, sitting up on her elbows to frown down at him. "Of course I do."

"Then stop grumbling and let me love you."

"Oh," she said with a heavy sigh. "If you put it like that. I'll try to be patient."

She flopped back on the bed with an expression of stoic endurance, which fled a second later as he settled between her legs and applied his mouth with obvious relish. Cara snatched at the bedclothes, writhing beneath his questing tongue and wondering why she'd been in such a rush. For this... *this* was every bit as wickedly divine as she remembered.

Wolf's big hands held her immobile, holding her open to him as he lavished her with every attention until she was wound tight as a bowstring. The feel of his hot mouth against her, the slick caress of his tongue, was sinful and delicious and she dissolved, reduced to incoherent whimpering. Finally, she reached the crescendo and snatched a pillow from the bed, covering her face with it to muffle the wild cries she could not hold back, afraid she would scandalise the entire village if she did not smother the sounds of her pleasure.

Once she had subsided into a quivering heap, she felt Wolf climb back up the bed and relinquished the pillow as he tugged it away from her.

"There you are," he said with amusement. "You're not hiding under there, are you?"

"No," she said with a choked laugh, sliding her arms around his neck. "Why would I hide from you when I've wanted you for so long, my amiable lunatic?"

"Have you?" he asked, his voice quiet as he stared down at her.

"For the longest time," she admitted.

"How long?" he pressed, his handsome face full of warmth.

"I think...." Cara considered for a moment and then laughed. "Since the first moment you created Lavinia Pinkington. I decided there and then that any man who could do such a ridiculous thing simply to keep writing to me, must be worth loving, and so I did, and I shan't stop now I've begun. I'm stubborn that way."

"I'm glad to hear it, and I shan't stop either, Cara. When I began all this, I think I was chasing a dream, something frail and insubstantial. I'm not sure I ever believed I could really have such a life, but... I hoped. You've made it all real. You are my every dream, and I shall never take that for granted. I love you."

"You are just the sweetest man," she said with a sigh, tears blurring his wonderful face. "I love you too, my adorable madman."

He laughed then and stole what remained of her wits by pressing his mouth to hers, and there was no more talking, no need to say anything else as their bodies spoke for them, a language of caresses and kisses and sighs. Cara lost herself in sensation, in the absolute trust she had put in him, assured of his tenderness and his desire to please her. He did please her, rousing her passion with mouth and hands until she was wild with wanting him, so desperate she almost sobbed with the need for him.

"Easy, love," he whispered, settling between her thighs and easing gently inside her.

Cara gasped and tilted her hips, trying to take more, to take all of him. He made a choked sound, stilling her hips.

"Slowly, I don't want to hu—"

But she was too impatient, too greedy, and she hooked her legs about him, tilting her hips just so and pulling him inside. He slid home with a muffled cry, her body offering no resistance, though she gasped at the feel of him inside her, so hot and heavy, filling her so intimately.

He lay still, breathing hard, his hard chest warm against her breasts as she felt his heart thunder.

"So impatient," he said with a strangled laugh.

She pulled him down again, kissing him hard, and then he moved. Cara sucked in a quick breath at the feel of him inside her and tipped her head back with a soft moan as he slid home again.

"Cara?" he said, her name a question as her eyes fluttered open to see him rising above her, moving as he loved her.

"Lovely," she said, holding onto his powerful shoulders. "You're lovely. So good. Don't stop."

He made a choked sound and shook his head. "Wasn't about to," he managed, and then moved harder and faster, and she had the fleeting thought that his endless patience must have been all used up by now. She sensed the urgency in him as he moved with increasing passion, and she clung to him, holding on for dear life to all that restrained power, that physical strength that could easily have overwhelmed her, could have taken instead of giving, but she knew that he never would. Instead, he gave her all of himself, without restraint, never hiding how much he felt, how much he loved her, until his breathing became erratic and his movements jerky as his big body tensed. He slid his hand between them, seeking the tender place between her thighs as he whispered in her ear, his voice harsh.

"Cara. You too… *please*…."

For a moment she did not know what he meant but then it didn't matter as the pleasure swept her up and she cried out, her intimate muscles tightening around him and then he was shattering too. He held her tightly, too tight, not that she cared, content to be crushed in his arms, held securely as she soared somewhere in the glittering darkness, and took a very long time to float back to earth.

Cara lay panting, staring up at the ceiling. Wolf turned on his side, gazing down at her, his big hand reaching out to cup her cheek, turning her to face him.

"Cara, are you…"

"Oh, that… *that* was splendid!" she said breathlessly, gazing at him with wide eyes.

"You're sure I didn't—"

"I've never felt so… and it was simply… and oh, my gosh."

Wolf snorted and shook his head. "So, you—"

"When can we do it again? Can we do it again?"

"Well, of course, just give me a—"

"Oh, darling!" Cara sat up and pushed him onto his back, straddling his hips. "You are so lovely, so good. I am the happiest girl in the world!" she exclaimed, giving a delighted laugh.

Wolf sighed. "Well, that answers the question, not that I actually got to—"

He made a muffled sound as she kissed him, once again interrupting his attempt to speak to her. Wolf rolled her onto her back, staring at her adoringly.

"Ah, well. Conversation is overrated," he said, and kissed her again.

Epilogue

Dearest Cat,

Papa tells me I haven't had a letter from you because you are "in disgrace" and are forbidden to speak to anyone or see anyone or even leave the house! Whatever did you do this time? Was it the Egyptian Museum in Piccadilly? Did you see the talking machine like you said? I don't know whether you are allowed to read this letter, but do write back as soon as you can or at least get a message to me. I am dying to know what you've been up to.

—Excerpt of a letter from Miss Agatha de Montluc (adopted daughter of Louis and Evie de Montluc, Comte et Comtesse de Villen) to The Right Hon'ble Lady Catherine 'Cat' Barrington.

14th November 1844, Micklemersh, Hampshire.

"Oh," Cara said, as they stepped out of the carriage and stared up at the home Wolf had never set eyes on before.

Wolf thought he probably ought to say something too, make some exclamation or say, *well, would you look at that* or *thank goodness, the walls are still upright,* or... or something. He couldn't. All he could do was stare at the building before him with his throat growing tighter by the moment. Cara slid her hand into his and squeezed.

"Welcome home, my love."

Wolf slanted a glance at her and swallowed hard, trying to find something to say, but it was no good.

"I know, darling. It's a lot to take in, but, oh, isn't it beautiful!" she said, and he heard the emotion in her voice.

He nodded, staring at a building that might have been as familiar to him as the fortress had been, if things had been different. But then, he would never have met Louis, would never have saved him from the terrible fire, would never have seen his best friend marry the woman he loved... the woman who just happened to receive a letter from her madcap friend about her adventures with her dog. He might never have met Cara, and that thought was too terrible to contemplate.

"Woof!"

A large, muddy paw raked down Wolf's thigh, and he sighed. "Thank you, Sultan. You are quite right, I was becoming maudlin."

The dog gave a happy *woof* and sat down, tongue lolling, until footsteps sounded from the front of the house. Sultan scrambled to his feet, scattering gravel and barking joyfully as Jo appeared. Sultan charged after him.

"I've really got to take him in hand," Wolf said, shaking his head.

"There's plenty of time," Cara said, leaning into him. "Well, then, what do you think of it?"

Wolf returned his gaze to the building before him, a lovely mishmash of thirteenth century Augustinian priory and eighteenth-century elegance. It looked at once grand and friendly, like a wonderful place for a family.

"It looks like home," he said, turning to look down at her.

Cara stood on tiptoes and tilted her head back, and Wolf obliged her, giving her the kiss she wanted. "Let's go home, then."

Tugging him by the hand, she led him inside, and into their future together.

Next in the Daring Daughter Series just in time for the holidays…

The Dare before Christmas
Daring Daughters Book 15

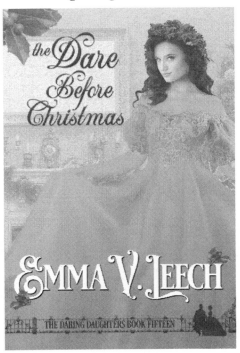

To be revealed …

Pre-Order your copy here:

The Dare Before Christmas

And coming in **2023**, an exciting new series based on the male children of the Girls Who Dare…

Their mothers dared all for love.
Their sisters did the same.
Something wicked this way comes…

The first book in the **Wicked Sons** series….

The Devil to Pay
Wicked Sons, Book One

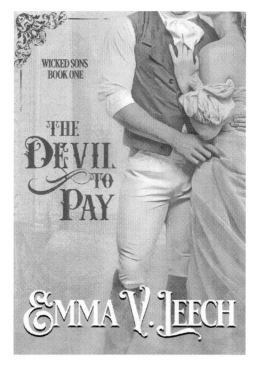

To be revealed

The Peculiar Ladies who started it all...

Girls Who Dare—The exciting series from Emma V Leech, the multi-award-winning, Amazon Top 10 romance writer behind the Rogues & Gentlemen series.

Inside every wallflower is the beating heart of a lioness, a passionate individual willing to risk all for their dream, if only they can find the courage to begin. When these overlooked girls make a pact to change their lives, anything can happen.

Twelve girls—Twelve dares in a hat. Twelves stories of passion. Who will dare to risk it all?

To Dare a Duke
Girls Who Dare Book 1

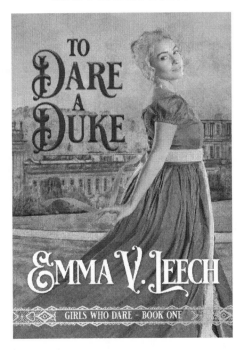

Dreams of true love and happy ever afters

Dreams of love are all well and good, but all Prunella Chuffington-Smythe wants is to publish her novel. Marriage at the price of her independence is something she will not consider. Having tasted success writing under a false name in The Lady's Weekly Review, her alter ego is attaining notoriety and fame and Prue rather likes it.

A Duty that must be endured

Robert Adolphus, The Duke of Bedwin, is in no hurry to marry, he's done it once and repeating that disaster is the last thing he desires. Yet, an heir is a necessary evil for a duke and one he cannot shirk. A dark reputation precedes him though, his first wife may have died young, but the scandals the beautiful, vivacious and spiteful creature supplied the ton have not. A wife must be found. A wife who is neither beautiful nor vivacious but sweet and dull, and certain to stay out of trouble.

Dared to do something drastic

The sudden interest of a certain dastardly duke is as bewildering as it is unwelcome. She'll not throw her ambitions aside to marry a scoundrel just as her plans for self-sufficiency and freedom are coming to fruition. Surely showing the man she's not actually the meek little wallflower he is looking for should be enough to put paid to his intentions? When Prue is dared by her friends to do something drastic, it seems the perfect opportunity to kill two birds.

However, Prue cannot help being intrigued by the rogue who has inspired so many of her romances. Ordinarily, he plays the part of handsome rake, set on destroying her plucky heroine. But is he really the villain of the piece this time, or could he be the hero?

Finding out will be dangerous, but it just might inspire her greatest story yet.

To Dare a Duke

Also check out Emma's regency romance series, Rogues & Gentlemen. Available now!

The Rogue

Rogues & Gentlemen Book 1

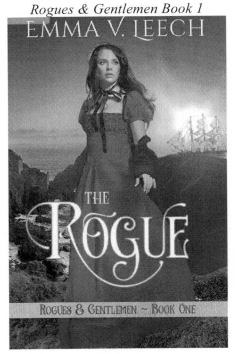

The notorious Rogue that began it all.

Set in Cornwall, 1815. Wild, untamed and isolated.

Lawlessness is the order of the day and smuggling is rife.

Henrietta always felt most at home in the wilds of the outdoors but even she had no idea how the mysterious and untamed would sweep her away in a moment.

Bewitched by his wicked blue eyes

Henrietta Morton knows to look the other way when the free trading 'gentlemen' are at work.

Yet when a notorious pirate bursts into her local village shop, she can avert her eyes no more. Bewitched by his wicked blue eyes, a moment of insanity follows as Henrietta hides the handsome fugitive from the Militia.

Her reward is a kiss, lingering and unforgettable.

In his haste to flee, the handsome pirate drops a letter, a letter that lays bare a tale of betrayal. When Henrietta's father gives her hand in marriage to a wealthy and villainous nobleman in return for the payment of his debts, she becomes desperate.

Blackmailing a pirate may be her only hope for freedom.

**** **Warning**: This book contains the most notorious rogue of all of Cornwall and, on occasion, is highly likely to include some mild sweating or descriptive sex scenes. ****

Free to read on *Kindle Unlimited*: The Rogue

Interested in a Regency Romance with a twist?

A Dog in a Doublet

The Regency Romance Mysteries Book 2

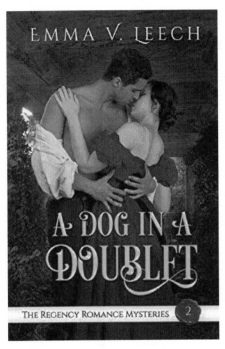

A man with a past

Harry Browning was a motherless guttersnipe, and the morning he came across the elderly Alexander Preston, The Viscount Stamford, clinging to a sheer rock face he didn't believe in fate. But the fates have plans for Harry whether he believes or not, and he's not entirely sure he likes them.

As a reward for his bravery, and in an unusual moment of charity, miserly Lord Stamford takes him on. He is taught to read, to manage the vast and crumbling estate, and to behave like a gentleman, but Harry knows that is something he will never truly be.

Already running from a dark past, his future is becoming increasingly complex as he finds himself caught in a tangled web of jealousy and revenge.

A feisty young maiden

Temptation, in the form of the lovely Miss Clarinda Bow, is a constant threat to his peace of mind, enticing him to be something he isn't. But when the old man dies his will makes a surprising demand, and the fates might just give Harry the chance to have everything he ever desired, including Clara, if only he dares.

And as those close to the Preston family begin to die, Harry may not have any choice.

Order your copy here. *A Dog in a Doublet*

Lose yourself in Emma's paranormal world with The French Vampire Legend series…..

The Key to Erebus
The French Vampire Legend Book 1

The truth can kill you.

Taken away as a small child, from a life where vampires, the Fae, and other mythical creatures are real and treacherous, the beautiful young witch, Jéhenne Corbeaux is totally unprepared when she returns to rural France to live with her eccentric Grandmother.

Thrown headlong into a world she knows nothing about she seeks to learn the truth about herself, uncovering secrets more shocking than anything she could ever have imagined and finding that she is by no means powerless to protect the ones she loves.

Despite her Gran's dire warnings, she is inexorably drawn to the dark and terrifying figure of Corvus, an ancient vampire and master of the vast Albinus family.

Jéhenne is about to find her answers and discover that, not only is Corvus far more dangerous than she could ever imagine, but that he holds much more than the key to her heart...

Now available at your favourite retailer.

The Key to Erebus

Check out Emma's exciting fantasy series with hailed by Kirkus Reviews as "An enchanting fantasy with a likable heroine, romantic intrigue, and clever narrative flourishes."

The Dark Prince
The French Fae Legend Book 1

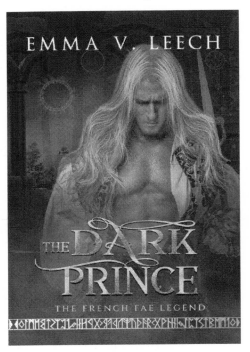

Two Fae Princes
One Human Woman
And a world ready to tear them all apart

Laen Braed is Prince of the Dark fae, with a temper and reputation to match his black eyes, and a heart that despises the human race. When he is sent back through the forbidden gates between realms to retrieve an ancient fae artifact, he returns home with far more than he bargained for.

Corin Albrecht, the most powerful Elven Prince ever born. His golden eyes are rumoured to be a gift from the gods, and destiny is calling him. With a love for the human world that runs deep, his friendship with Laen is being torn apart by his prejudices.

Océane DeBeauvoir is an artist and bookbinder who has always relied on her lively imagination to get her through an unhappy and uneventful life. A jewelled dagger put on display at a nearby museum hits the headlines with speculation of another race, the Fae. But the discovery also inspires Océane to create an extraordinary piece of art that cannot be confined to the pages of a book.

With two powerful men vying for her attention and their friendship stretched to the breaking point, the only question that remains…who is truly The Dark Prince.

The man of your dreams is coming…or is it your nightmares he visits? Find out in Book One of The French Fae Legend.

Available now to read at your favourite retailer

The Dark Prince

Want more Emma?

If you enjoyed this book, please support this indie author and take a moment to leave a few words in a review. *Thank you!*

To be kept informed of special offers and free deals (which I do regularly) follow me on *https://www.bookbub.com/authors/emma-v-leech*

To find out more and to get news and sneak peeks of the first chapter of upcoming works, go to my website and sign up for the newsletter.

http://www.emmavleech.com/

Come and join the fans in my Facebook group for news, info and exciting discussion...

Emma's Book Club

Or Follow me here...

http://viewauthor.at/EmmaVLeechAmazon

Facebook

Instagram

Emma's Twitter page

TikTok

Can't get your fill of Historical Romance? Do you crave stories with passion and red-hot chemistry?

If the answer is yes, have I got the group for you!

Come join myself and other awesome authors in our Facebook group

Historical Harlots

Be the first to know about exclusive giveaways, chat with amazing HistRom authors, lots of raunchy shenanigans and more!

Historical Harlots Facebook Group

Made in the USA
Monee, IL
05 June 2023

35281548R00171